Winter Jacket:
New Beginnings

ELIZA LENTZSKI

Other Works by Eliza Lentzski

CONTENTS

DEDICATION

To Troi and Nik

PROLOGUE

Malibu, California: Winter Break

She was singing in the shower when I walked through the bathroom door. I could just make out her slender silhouette through the flimsy material of the opaque shower curtain. There was no music for her to sing along with, but that didn't seem to bother her.

The air was thick with steam from the heat of the shower. I silently stripped out of my pajamas and carefully folded and placed them on the ample counter space. The rental condo's bathroom was massive. In addition to the double sinks, it had a separate shower and a bathtub so large that it needed a designated deep end. When Troian had first shown me the property online when I was looking for a place to escape to after my tenure review, I'd teased her about paying extra for a full-time lifeguard for the bathroom.

When I pulled back the shower curtain, a noise that I can only describe as a "yelp" echoed against the tiled bathroom walls.

I bit back the snicker that came at her expense. I hadn't meant to scare her; I only wanted to join her. But she'd been singing so loudly and was so much in her own world that I'd gone undetected even though I hadn't been trying to be stealthy.

"Sorry, baby. Did I scare you?" I asked with a smug smile. I stepped in under the warm spray of the shower and let the water hit the tops of my shoulders. There was only a single showerhead, but it was one of those oversized rain showers that allowed both of us underneath the falling water.

1

"No," she snorted stubbornly. "You just surprised me, that's all."

I didn't consider all women in the midst of a shower to be attractive; some women seemed to *glisten* from the spray of an overhead water fall, but some women just got wet. Hunter, however, was stunning. She should have looked comical with her blonde hair thoroughly plastered to her forehead and the flustered look on her face, but beyond that was a banquet of naked flesh. And believe me, I was a glutton when it came to this woman.

I watched the spray of water hit the top of her shoulders to collect in concentrated rivers that traveled down the expanse of her taut, limber figure. Her normally porcelain skin was flushed across her shoulders and breastplate from the exertion of her earlier run on the beach and the heat of the shower. Her more-than-a-handful breasts were pert, supple, and capped with rose petal pink nipples.

I could tell she was internally wrestling with how to respond to my unannounced appearance. She could be angry with me for scaring her or impressed that I'd finally taken her up on her flimsy offer to save water and reduce our carbon footprint. I could also tell she was having a hard time not gawking at my naked body, and it made me smile a little to feel her stare. I wasn't a runner like she was, but a religious routine of other cardio-activities kept my stomach flat and my legs and arms toned.

I stepped behind her and wrapped my arms around her bare waist. I held her close so my hardened nipples pressed against her back. The hot water felt good. *She* felt good. I tilted my head backwards to let the water cascade down on my face. I'd been out on the balcony earlier and the chill from the saltwater-sprayed air had me chilled to the bone.

"I was starting to think maybe you didn't care about the environment," she murmured. She pressed her backside more fully against me.

A low moan fell from my lips at the contact. I ran my hands over her full breasts and down her flat stomach. Her skin was slick from a mixture of soap and water. My hands met at the apex of her sex.

I fully expected us to continue in this way, me gently stroking the length of her body and murmuring intimacies into her ear, until she was panting for me to take her from behind. A graphic image of her bent at the waist, palms flat against the shower tile, and legs spread shoulder-length apart, flashed before my eyes.

Unexpectedly, she spun on her heels and pushed *me* against the cold tile wall. Her hot mouth bit down on the top of my shoulder. My eyes rolled from the multiple sensations – the icy shock of the cold tile against my back, the warmth of her mouth on my shoulder, and the sharpness of her teeth, which threatened to break the skin. "Fuck, Hunter," I gasped.

She looked up at me from beneath thick eyelashes and an army of butterflies assaulted my stomach. "That's kind of the plan, isn't it?" she smiled coyly. Her hand was instantly between my legs.

"God," I panted, trying hard to keep my composure as she started rubbing my clit in a circular motion. I spread my legs just a little wider, letting my body language inform her that I was game for whatever she had in mind. She cupped my naked sex, and I released another guttural moan.

When she pressed against my slit, two fingers just barely inside me, not even to the first knuckle, I bit down on my lower lip. I wanted to lower myself completely onto her slender digits and surrender myself to her. I was rarely a bottom, but I'd let this woman dominate me if she kept making me feel this way.

To my great disappointment, she pulled her hand away from my core. My frustration was short-lived, however, as she began kissing and licking water droplets from my skin like she'd been wandering around a desert all her life. Her tongue worked at my right nipple; she flicked the bud back and forth with just the tip of her tongue and she scraped her teeth across the surface skin. I resisted the urge to hold her head there and enjoy the sensations because I anticipated she had other plans in mind.

As she slid down my body, her tongue continued to capture the random water droplets that stubbornly clung to my skin. I sucked in a breath when she dipped her tongue into the shallow of my belly button. I'd always been sensitive there; it was like she knew my body as well as I did. She continued moving lower and lower, and I couldn't help but hold my breath in anticipation of what was going to happen next.

She was on her knees in front of me, breathing warm air on my shaved pussy, eyeballing it like she was going to devour me whole. And then she did. With no warning, she pushed her long tongue inside and began fucking me with her tongue, clenching onto my thighs with either hand. She held my thighs so tightly, it felt like she

3

was going to brand her fingerprints on my skin, but I would have been an idiot to care.

Every time she bottomed out, her nose bumped deliciously into my throbbing clit, sending waves of pleasure through my body. And the biggest turn on of them all were the little sighs and grunts that told me she was loving this as much as I was.

This had to be Heaven – Hunter on her knees in front of me, and fuck if I didn't want to just grab her by the ears and have my way with her talented little mouth. I wanted to hold her face there and tell her all the dirty thoughts streaming through my mind. I wanted to tell her every single naughty thing I wanted to do to her tight body; but I amazed myself by showing some restraint, and only tugging on her blonde locks a little. She looked up at me with those blue-grey eyes and they perceptively narrowed when I pulled on her hair. I couldn't tell if she was angry or turned on, but suddenly she began pistoning her tongue in and out of me like she was on a mission.

"H-Hunter," I stammered. "You know I can't…st-standing up." I stumbled on my words. My tongue wasn't up to the task. Her tongue, however, was more than adequate.

Her nostrils flared and she licked her lips. "Challenge accepted."

+++++

CHAPTER ONE

"Professor Graft, can you sign this form for me?"

"Professor, can we meet later to discuss this assignment?"

"Dr. Graft, I had a question about the syllabus."

"Professor, when is this due?"

It was a Wednesday, the third day of classes in the new semester, and I'd just finished teaching my first class of the morning. I had another two writing seminars to instruct later and a slew of committee and departmental meetings to round out the day. Students hovered around me, firing off questions. I was bombarded with voices ranging from curious to panicked, but one clear voice rose above them all.

"Professor Graft?"

My eyes snapped up from the crowd and met hers. We had a silent exchange, there in that congested hall, as students scattered from one class to the next. A peculiar smile twitched at the corners of her mouth. When I licked my own, she abruptly cast her eyes away. I thought she might be blushing, but she still had some of that California tan leftover from Winter break so I couldn't be sure.

Hunter was beautiful – hair the color of warm sunshine, piercing blue-grey eyes, high cheekbones, and a wide, expressive mouth that was quick to laugh. She was tall and angular, with unblemished, snow-white skin that wrapped around long, willowy limbs. Those elongated arms and legs could have looked awkward, like a bird preparing for flight, if she didn't possess the natural grace of a dancer. Her fingers were long and slim and they fit perfectly with mine. She always wore a tattered woven friendship bracelet on her right wrist, the bones fine and delicate, and a small silver cross that rested against a defined collarbone. She was a distance runner and years of self-denial and sacrifice had rewarded her with a supple firmness all over. She was slender enough that when reclined I could mark the space between her ribs, but not so skinny that when I grabbed her backside or thighs that I could mistake her femininity.

She was polished and put together in a way unlike other undergraduates I'd taught. When high ponytails and sweatpants with words screen-printed across the backside was standard issue for most female students at my school, Hunter never looked like she'd rolled out of bed just minutes before class. Her hair was always meticulously flat-ironed, even when it was up in a ponytail. She wore light makeup, mostly mascara that gave depth to her blonde eyelashes, and a light blush that colored her otherwise porcelain skin. And while she had never unusually dressed up for class, her jeans were always fitted and the collars of her shirts crispy pressed. I hadn't see much else of her clothes when she was a student of mine because she never took off her winter jacket in class. It was blue, puffy, and reached her knees. It was that jacket that had originally drawn my attention to her; while the rest of the class had melted when the classroom heater refused to shut off, she had never looked more comfortable, even while wearing her coat. I was thankful for that winter jacket.

The students scattered, moving on to their next class of the day, and the hallway emptied, but I remained rooted to the spot. My grin grew as she walked closer, eliminating the distance between us. I self-consciously straightened the hemline of my pencil skirt and adjusted the infinity scarf around my neck.

"I didn't expect to see you on campus today," I said as she stopped close enough to touch me, but not necessarily in my personal bubble.

"I had to pick up some books from Interlibrary Loan," she explained.

"It's the first week of class," I pointed out.

She shrugged. "Maybe I'm feeling pressure to do extra well this semester since I'm dating an Associate Professor."

I loved hearing those words out of her mouth. It was kind of like when I'd first gotten my Ph.D. and had insisted everyone call me Dr. Graft or at least Dr. Elle. Now that I'd recently been awarded tenure, it came with a jump in official title from Assistant Professor to Associate Professor. I'd have to wait another 6 years or so to become a full Professor.

"I was also thinking about sitting in on one of your classes to see if you'd notice me."

I cleared my throat as a mixture of anxiety and arousal washed over me. I generally taught writing seminars no larger than a dozen and a half, but I'd notice Hunter even in a large lecture hall. Her presence made me feel like a magnet, attracted to her opposite charge.

She took a small step closer and her voice dropped an octave lower. "And I'd raise my hand in the middle of your lecture."

"And you'd ask an astute question," I interjected, a willing participant in this fantasy. "And I'd wonder why you were never this bold when you actually took one of my classes."

A sly smile crossed her lips. "Maybe my thoughts were otherwise occupied; it's hard to focus on thesis statements and topic sentences when a gorgeous woman is parading around in a tight skirt."

I had to bite the inside of my cheek to keep from smiling too wide; I knew we probably had an audience. The time slot for the next class of the day had begun, but there were still a few tardy stranglers in the hallway. Even though we'd never dated when I was her professor, plus she was graduating in May, it still felt at little taboo to see and talk to her on campus – like we had a shared secret to which the rest of the world wasn't privy.

Her head cocked to the side and she looked contemplative. "Am I allowed to kiss you good morning?"

My smile broadened despite myself, but who could blame me? I was happier than I'd ever been. Hunter was pure bliss. "Are you really asking permission?"

She lowered her gaze and fiddled with the bottom loop of my scarf. Apparently she really was asking for my consent. I wrapped my fingers around her wrists, stopping her anxious fidgeting. I pulled her hands from the scarf and tugged on her arms until I had them thrown around my neck. I stared into those crisp, cornflower blue irises. They changed colors on any given day, and today they looked a darker blue than her usual grey-blue.

"Don't ask for permission," I said, leaning in so she could feel my warm breath against her ear. I gave her just the tiniest of licks against the shell of her ear, hidden from view. I could practically feel her knees buckle. "If you want something," I husked, "take it."

Her response came in a burr much lower than her usual tenor. "You're making it very hard for me, Professor Graft."

I pulled back just slightly to keep my libido under control. Even if Hunter was comfortable with PDAs, I was still mindful that we were at my place of employment. "I've got to get to a meeting in a few minutes," I said, allowing my voice to return to its regular tone, "but are you free for lunch later?" I might have been able to control my libido, but I was still unable to resist digging my fingers into her hips.

"In the cafeteria or someplace else?"

"I would love to take you someplace off campus, but I don't think I'd have enough time to really enjoy myself. I've got two more classes this afternoon." An additional line about me "taking" her wherever she wanted came to my lips, but I let it die there. I didn't need to be unnecessarily cruel when I knew we both had a full schedule that day, me teaching and she with her internship at the hospital.

"You and your being-late phobia," she smirked. Being late was one of my worst fears. If we went for lunch off-campus, I'd be checking the time the entire meal.

"What about tonight? Are you free?" I asked. Normally with a partner I wouldn't be so obviously desperate for her time. With Hunter, though, I couldn't hold that desire back.

I felt her arms tighten at my pencil-skirted waist. "What did you have in mind?"

"Nothing special," I shrugged. "Maybe get a drink at Peggy's?"

"I could go for Peggy's," she approved with a curt nod. "Will Nikole and Troian be joining us?"

"I should probably extend the invitation," I said, thinking out loud. "If Troi hears we went without her, she'll accuse me of breaking up with her."

"Well, we wouldn't want that to happen," Hunter chuckled.

I hummed a wordless tune on my way over to the campus library where my first meeting of the day was being held. I pulled my scarf higher to block a particularly vicious wind.

Hunter and I had parted with a fleeting kiss – too brief and too chaste for my liking – but I was again mindful of where we were. This wasn't the privacy of my home or Hunter's apartment or even the bathroom at the local lesbian bar. Hunter and I were currently enjoying the honeymoon of a new relationship, but circumstances and our environment forced me to be more tempered.

"Good morning," I greeted as I walked into the library conference room. Most everyone on the Women's and Gender Studies Committee was already there, probably having come straight over from the previous class period. Hunter's appearance had delayed me, but I thankfully wasn't late. I was serious about my being-late phobia, especially when I was the junior faculty member on the committee. I couldn't wait until someone newer joined so I didn't feel like such a child. I was thirty years old, but in academia, age was really irrelevant.

The Women's and Gender Studies Program was an interdisciplinary program with faculty members representing the English, History, Psychology, Sociology, and Theology departments. It had become one of my favorite committees to be a part of because there was no posturing or competition amongst the women in the group like I'd experienced on some other campus committees. We genuinely got along and we wanted to do what was best for the students, not for our own personal careers.

I sat down in the vacant chair next to my friend and mentor, Emily Sullivan, who was from the English department like myself.

"Have a good break?" she asked me as I removed my jacket and winter gear to get settled.

"I did," I confirmed. "And you?"

Emily rolled her eyes. "Henry's parents ended up staying with us from Christmas through New Years. I've never been so happy for school to start up again just so I had an excuse to get away from the house. How about you?" She leaned forward. "Did you and Hunter do anything special?" she asked conspiratorially.

I didn't want to blush, but I could feel the heat on my cheeks from her question. "We had a nice time in Malibu," I dismissed vaguely. I considered Emily a close friend, but not close enough to give her the intimate details of how I'd spent my Winter break. "I even found some time to finish the book proposal for my next manuscript and sent it off to a few trade presses."

"Impressive, Dr. Graft," Emily murmured approvingly. "But you know you're supposed to sit back on your laurels for at least a few semesters, right? You won't be up for another promotion for six years," she pointed out. "Take your time."

I shrugged, nonplussed. My first book – a collection of short stories about individuals with unique abilities and powers – was so new it wasn't even out in print yet. But I'd wanted to keep working while I was motivated to do so. You never knew when one's Muse might stop working. "I was feeling particularly inspired."

Emily smirked knowingly. "I bet you were." She threw in an extra wiggle of her eyebrows for my benefit.

I never took for granted how lucky I was not to have to hide my private life from my co-workers. But before I could pretend to be shocked, Penny, the Chair of the Women's and Gender Studies Program, called our meeting to order.

Now in her early 70s, with no signs of slowing down, Penny was one of the most senior faculty members on campus. She had a weathered face with deep lines, but it was probably one of the kindest faces I'd ever come across. Her grey hair was long and wiry, and she habitually wore it in a thick braid. She reminded me of someone's grandmother and I knew the students loved her for it.

"First order of business," she announced, getting us focused and on track, "welcome back to campus," she smiled. "I trust you all had a relaxing yet productive Winter break."

Obscured by the conference table, I felt Emily nudge my ankle with the toe of her shoe, and I swallowed down a telling laugh.

"Second on our agenda today," Penny continued, "is staff changes. Over break there was some movement among the higher-ups; Dean Krauss, our venerable Dean of the College of Arts & Sciences, has accepted a position as Provost of a school down South."

"Wow. That's unexpected," Suzanne Jay from the History department commented. "I didn't know he was looking for other jobs."

"His family is originally from Virginia, I think, so he wanted to go back," Emily remarked. I could always trust Emily to have her finger on the pulse of campus gossip. She had been the one to "inform me" the previous semester about the rumor that I was dating a student.

"I don't blame him – I've had enough of these winters for a lifetime," Betsy Martinez from the Theology department snorted.

Even though the academic calendar said it was Spring semester, it was mid-January in the Midwest, which meant that Winter would refuse to be disposed of for several months. It was the kind of prolonged freeze where my cat, Sylvia, buried herself under the afghans on my couch and hibernated for hours at a time.

I was getting sick of the season as well, but I couldn't be too mad at the weather. I owed an unseasonably long winter from the previous year to my attraction to Hunter. If she hadn't kept on her puffy winter jacket every day, all class long, even when the in-room heater was broken, I might not have noticed her. It wasn't a large classroom with a lot of students, but she'd been just shy enough in class discussions that she could have flown under my radar.

"What are you smiling about, Elle?" Emily asked, a laugh barely hiding behind the question.

My head snapped up. "Me? Nothing," I squeaked defensively, feeling like I'd been caught. "Aren't I allowed to smile?"

"Oh, leave her alone," Penny gently chastised. "She's young and in love, not jaded by life like the rest of us." The rest of the committee members chuckled at my expense.

I cleared my throat, embarrassed by all the attention. My relationship with Hunter would be at the center of campus gossip until the next new "scandal." I couldn't wait for that day to come. I wanted to be known on campus, but for the right reasons.

The faculty were decidedly split in their support of my decision to date a former student. I hadn't done a formal tally or anything, but that was my sense of the situation. Those in my own discipline, including Bob, the Chair of the English department, had been nothing but supportive. But I could still feel the icy glare of judgment coming from others outside of my department, particularly from those who'd been employees of the university since The Beginning of Time. Emily and I referred to them as Dinosaurs, but they were just of a different generation, I supposed.

It wasn't my job to change their attitude though. I hadn't experienced any over-the-top confrontations, just a few eyeballs when I went to collect my mail at the Campus Mail Center, but then again it could have just been my own paranoia and I could have been imagining it all.

The students themselves didn't treat me any differently, either, for which I was grateful. I didn't know what I'd expected – maybe whispers as I walked into a classroom, or female students throwing themselves at me during my office hours, trying to get an Easy A – but everyone had been very mature about the whole situation.

"So do they know who's taking over for Dean Krauss?" Betsy from Theology asked.

"I can't imagine the Board of Directors would have moved *that* fast," Suzanne from History remarked.

"They'll probably make one of us take over his responsibilities in the interim *plus* keep teaching a full load," Kathy Wagner from the Sociology department huffed. "All without extra compensation." If there was one person on our small committee who I thought abrasive, it was Dr. Wagner. Whenever she talked, I felt like I was being scrubbed with sandpaper.

"Actually," Penny said, raising her voice just slightly to regain control of the conversation, "they've already moved forward and made a hire."

"Really?" Emily looked surprised by the news, which surprised me.

"Yes," Penny continued. "And word on the street is that Dean Krauss' replacement is a savant at fundraising."

"Well, I hope so," Kathy from Sociology snipped. She crossed her arms across her chest. "Our budget has been slashed every fiscal year for the past five years."

The rest of the meeting continued in that fashion, Penny making announcements and then someone on the committee derailing our productiveness with a bit of gossip. I started to take notes on a legal pad just to keep myself focused. Admittedly, I was finding it a little hard to get back into the swing of things of the new academic year. Maybe I was a little burned out from the tenure process. Maybe I should take Emily's advice and slow down on this new book proposal. I tried to focus on Penny, who wanted to discuss things like course selection and budgets for going to conferences, but my thoughts kept drifting back to a Malibu beach and watching a girl defiantly face-off with the ocean.

+++++

"Hey, Doc. How's it going?"

A former student of mine approached me before the start of my 20th Century American Literature class that afternoon. His name was Jeff, and even though he wasn't an English major, he'd been in a few of my classes to satisfy general education credits. He was quirky; he'd probably been an introvert in high school who'd found his voice in college. When I'd first interacted with him outside of class I'd thought him to be a bit of a brown noser, but he was polite and outgoing and affable.

"Not too bad, Jeff. How's your semester?"

He shoved his hands into the pockets of his pants and rocked back on his heels. "It's still too early to tell, but I wish I had you again this semester. I feel like all my professors this term were born in the 1900s."

"I was born in the 1900s, Jeff, and I believe you were, too," I chuckled.

He ducked his head, looking sheepish. "You know what I mean."

I smiled, but kept my personal opinions about the Dinosaurs on the faculty to myself. Being around students who were perpetually 18 through 21 kept me abreast of the latest fads and technologies and hashtag language. At some point though I would become too old and all of that would pass me by and I'd become the professor who told Dad-jokes and tried just a little too hard.

"How's Hunter?"

I nearly swallowed my tongue. This was the first time another student had acknowledged our relationship. It was no secret that Hunter and I were dating – it was a small campus that sometimes felt like the petty gossip of my high school years all over again – but no student had asked me about it, face to face.

"I hope that's not out of line," he said with a smile that showed no trace of cruelty or malice. "She was quiet in class, but I thought she was cool."

I'd completely forgotten that Jeff had been in that class with Hunter.

"She's, ah, she's good," I said, feeling wildly uncomfortable. The hallway had suddenly become very warm. There must have been another broken heater somewhere. I tugged at my scarf.

"Well, time to get to class," he said, redistributing the weight of his backpack from one shoulder to the other. "Nice seeing you, Professor."

"You, too."

I felt self-conscious through the rest of my next class. We were discussing the first few chapters of one of my favorites, Ralph Ellison's *Invisible Man*, which traditionally confuses students because they think it's supposed to be sci-fi, but discussion that day held no joy for me.

I went over my roster sheets afterwards in my office to see if I currently had any students in my other classes who'd been in Hunter's class. In a few semesters everyone from that course would have matriculated, giving me a clean slate. I hoped for no other conversations like the one I had had with Jeff. As innocuous as it had been, it still reminded me of how unorthodox our situation was.

+++++

Peggy's was crowded for a Wednesday night, but the semester had just begun and students were overly eager to exhibit their independence from their parents so close to wrapping up Winter break. I'd finished working before Hunter had gotten off at the hospital. She'd come straight over to my house after work to get ready to go out. We'd met up with Troian and Nikole to have dinner at our favorite burger bar and afterwards we'd all made the trek across town to Peggy's. I usually avoided the lesbian dive during the school year so I wouldn't run into any current students. I had tried to stick to that policy the previous semester, but if I'd stayed away, Hunter and I might not be together.

I maneuvered my way to the front of the bar crowd, catching the eye of Megan, one of the bartenders working tonight. She looked annoyed by a gaggle of barely-legal baby butches all vying for her attention, but when she saw me working my way closer to the bar, her dimpled grin made an appearance.

"Elle!" she greeted, voice carrying over the din of music and conversation. "How are you?"

I allowed myself an inviting smile to match her own. "Thirsty."

"Fair enough," she laughed. "What can I get you?"

"How about a pale ale on draft and a Malibu and pineapple if you've got it."

Megan leaned back and grabbed a pint glass from beneath the bar. "Malibu?" she said, her painted eyebrows rising on her forehead. "When did you join a sorority?"

I smirked at the jab. "My girlfriend's not a beer drinker." Hunter hadn't been 21 for very long and so wine and mixed drinks were her territory. After enough time with me though, I was convinced she'd graduate to hoppy craft beer.

Megan nodded knowingly. "Sounds like you need to convert the girl."

I accepted the drinks and left my credit card to keep an open tab. "I'll see what I can do," I said, saluting her with my pint.

It felt nice that there was no awkwardness between Megan and me. But I shouldn't have been surprised; Megan had never brought drama, not even when I basically kicked her out of my bed after the almost-one-night-stand. It was a lucky thing, too; Troian and Nikole would have never forgiven me if I'd gotten us banished from the only lesbian bar in the area. Community was hard to find in our remote, conservative region.

I maneuvered around the clusters of bar patrons that had seemed to grow more condensed since I'd first gone to the bar. I felt not a few pairs of hands pass along my backside as I tried to make it to the back of the bar, near the dance floor. If my hands hadn't been preoccupied with drinks, I probably would have started a fight.

"Hi," I murmured into Hunter's ear when I finally returned to my spot in the crowd. I brought her drink up to eye level. "I'm glad you didn't die from thirst."

"It was touch and go for a while," Hunter laughed. Her grin spread and she took the proffered glass. She took an experimental sip and her eyes widened. "Oh wow. That's good. And dangerous," she added. "What is it?"

"Malibu and pineapple juice, compliments of Megan," I said. "She knows how to mix a good drink."

"Sure she didn't spit in it?" Hunter asked with a lift of a skeptical brow. She examined the contents of her glass.

"I watched her the entire time," I assured her.

I wrapped my arm around her waist and she seemed to reflexively shift her body so we fit together. I kissed her hair, near her temple. Even in a crowded bar and after a full day of interning at the hospital she smelled clean, like bar soap and fresh laundry.

All my life I'd worked toward some far-off goal; getting tenure at a teaching college had been my goal for such a long time it had been hard to focus on anything else. I was lucky to have friends like Troian and Nikole who forced me to stop and enjoy the journey rather than put on the blinders until I got to the destination. I spotted Nikole at the bar, laughing about something with Megan. The combination of all those white teeth was blinding. I assumed Troian was nearby, glowing green with unwarranted jealousy.

If it hadn't been for their prodding, I might never have pursued Hunter, dismissing it as too professionally risky to date a former student. I would have missed out on getting to know this amazing, gentle-souled, open-hearted individual. She would have forever remained a What If or an If Only – an enigma in a blue winter jacket.

I didn't want us to grow out of this honeymoon phase. I knew it was inevitable that our relationship would evolve at some point, but I wanted to hold onto this feeling for as long as I could. I wasn't unreasonable. I understood that long-term relationships couldn't stay electrically charged forever. One day you're having sex in a public restroom and ten years later it's tight-lipped kisses goodnight because you're exhausted and you have to get up early in the morning. Relationships change. They evolve. But I didn't ever want to evolve. Damn you, Charles Darwin.

I felt the phone in Hunter's back pocket vibrate against me. She fished it out to see who was texting her, but set it down just as quickly on a nearby cocktail table. "God," she fumed. She made a frustrated noise. "Sara has the worst timing ever."

I let my arm lax around her waist, but didn't let go entirely. "What's wrong?"

Hunter's roommate, Sara, made me uncomfortable. She'd been a student of mine in her Freshman year. That in and of itself was unremarkable, but it hadn't been too long after we'd been at Hunter's apartment one night that the rumors about me having a relationship with a student had started to accumulate on campus. I still suspected that it had been Sara who'd told the University about my relationship with Hunter. The timing was too suspect. I'd petitioned Dean Krauss, the then-Dean of the College of Arts & Sciences, and Bob Birken, the Chair of my department, to discover who had been my anonymous confessor, but neither, understandably, would reveal who had informed the school.

Hunter growled again as she typed back a response on her phone. "Our lease isn't up until after graduation, but Sara's just decided she doesn't want to live with me anymore. I've got to either replace her with a new roommate or find a studio or single bedroom apartment I can afford on my own."

"She doesn't want to live with you anymore?" I echoed with a frown. Hunter and Sara had been friends in high school and that friendship had carried over when they'd both attended the same local university. They'd been roommates since Freshman year. "Is it because of me?"

"No. I made it sound overly dramatic, sorry," Hunter said, waving her free hand. "She graduated a semester early and just got a job out of state. I should be happy for her, but now I've got this added stress."

I anticipated it was going to be a tough semester for my girlfriend. Senioritis was a challenge to combat, even for the most dedicated student, plus she had a demanding internship at the local hospital. She'd secured a very competitive position in the Maternity Ward this semester, which included rounds in the neonatal intensive care unit. I was extremely proud of her and not a little in awe.

"You wouldn't want to, I don't know, move in with me?" The words slipped out of my mouth before I could shove them back in. I found myself unable to look her in the eyes, so I averted my gaze. The dark green carpeting looked stained even through the dimmed bar lighting. I shuddered to think about what it looked like when all the lights were turned on.

"That's really sweet of you, but I don't want to U-haul you." Hunter frowned slightly and fine creases formed between her blue eyes. "I hear that's a thing we lesbians do."

"U-haul, eh? Did you finally get around to reading the lesbian handbook?" I shakily teased, hoping I didn't look like I might puke. I couldn't believe I'd asked her to move in with me so casually. That was moving at the speed of light for me.

She nodded, still looking serious. "Troian's been educating me."

I stood up a little straighter. "Oh she has, has she?" I flashed a look in the direction of my best friend. Troian was talking animatedly with one of the other bartenders, Leah. I wondered if Troian had had something alcoholic to drink because her face looked a little pink and she was talking with her hands more than usual. "And what else besides U-hauls has she educated you about?" I was only half kidding.

"I hope you're not mad." Hunter bit down on her lower lip. "I know I practically live with you anyway, but it's nice to have a space that's all my own."

"No. I know we're not there yet," I quickly agreed. "I just got a little carried away."

We'd jumped headfirst into this thing, having sex before we'd even been on our first date. We needed more dates – I was convinced of this. Our schedules had gotten so busy with the ebbs and flows of the academic year, and the drama surrounding my tenure review had probably accelerated the pace of our relationship even more so. Our age difference and the unconventional way in which we'd met had forced us to defend and justify being a couple.

An adorable half-smile curled onto Hunter's mouth. "I'm glad you're thinking about it though. That the idea doesn't completely terrify you."

"Confession." I winced. "It does kind of freak me out."

She cocked her head and looked thoughtful, not offended. "Really?"

"It's my own problem though," I said, shaking my head. "It has nothing to do with you, or me questioning our relationship."

"You know how to make a girl swoon, Professor Graft," she chuckled.

I cleared my throat. *She* was the one who knew how to make me swoon, actually. Whenever she called me by a title, my knees buckled.

I watched as she finished her drink with alacrity. She licked at the corners of her mouth, gathering any remnants of her sweet mixed drink. "I've had enough of Peggy's for tonight. Take me home, will you?"

She never had to ask me twice.

+++++

CHAPTER TWO

I was in my campus office, catching up on emails. Even though the semester was new, that didn't keep the number of emails down. If I didn't check my Inbox every few hours, it would become overwhelming.

There was a hesitant knock on my open office door, and when I looked away from my computer screen, a young woman was sitting in the chair opposite my desk. Her presence momentarily startled me, and that seemed to make her smile. She looked to be in her early twenties, a student perhaps. She was fair skinned with slightly wavy blonde hair. Even sitting down and wearing a modest polo shirt and jeans, I could tell she was attractively proportioned with generous curves.

"Hello," I greeted formally. "Can I help you?"

She scooted forward in her chair, sitting just on the front edge. "I was hoping you'd have time to look over the paper we just got back. I didn't do as well as I thought."

She produced a typewritten essay from her backpack, and I recognized my handwriting in the margins. I frowned because while my own handwriting was familiar, the girl wasn't.

"Sure thing," I said. "Did you have any specific questions?"

"Not really," she said with a small shrug.

I rummaged around in my top desk drawer to get out my reading glasses. "Well, let's take a look at your essay and see where you went wrong."

The name in the top left-hand corner of her essay didn't look familiar. It was early in the semester, but I was normally pretty good at learning students' names right away. I didn't recognize her face, and I couldn't even pin-point which class of mine she was in. But here she was in my office, during office hours, with an essay with my handwriting on it. She had to be one of my students.

"Since I didn't do well on this first essay, do you assign any extra credit so I can make up the points?" she asked.

I leaned back in my chair and adjusted my glasses on my nose. "Not usually. I do allow you to write multiple drafts though, so as long as you're on top of that, you should do well."

The girl frowned, petulant and pouty. "I'm not a very good writer."

"Oh, don't sell yourself short." I silently berated myself. *Why couldn't I remember this girl?* "There's no magic to writing. It's a skill just like everything else. Give it some practice, and you'll be a much stronger writer by the end of the semester."

She sighed and toyed with the collar of her shirt, a button-up light yellow polo. The movement drew my eyes to her hand, which drew me to her breasts. I hastily looked away.

"I might need a tutor or something."

"We do have a Writing Center on campus," I supplied. "Let me just find the contact info for you." I rifled through some papers on my desk. I had the contact information for the writing lab somewhere, but my desk seemed messier than usual.

When I looked back at the student, I swore she'd unbuttoned something on her shirt. I could just make out the scalloped top of her bra. The light pink cotton material contrasted attractively with her alabaster skin. She leaned forward again, and I worried how sturdy her bra was constructed; she was threatening to spill over the cups already even without the extra tilt.

"Actually, I was hoping that maybe *you* could tutor me, Professor."

I cleared my throat and looked anywhere but in the direction of her exposed breasts. "I'm afraid I really don't have the time. That's what the Writing Lab is for."

"That's too bad," she said wistfully. "I was hoping we could help each other out. I know you have particular tastes." The tip of a pink tongue peeked out from between two plump lips and slowly traveled the distance around the perimeter of her wide mouth.

"T-tastes?" I stammered inelegantly.

"Students," the young woman supplied. "Female? Blonde?" A sardonic smile crossed her lips. "And lucky for me, I happen to be all three of those."

Oh shit.

I needed to get out of there. I wasn't normally claustrophobic, but even with my office door open, the walls felt like they were closing in on me, and I began to feel faint.

I launched out of my office chair, nearly stumbling over the student on my way out. I caught the edges of the doorframe before I threw myself completely into the hallway. Outside my office was a line-up of students, snaking down the corridor of the English department. All of them, attractive females, waited, holding typewritten essays in their manicured hands.

"Oh God, no."

I sat up in bed, my eyes flying open. My heart raced in my chest and I gripped the sheets tightly in clenched fists until the beating of my heart slowed to a more measured pace. My cell phone alarm chose that moment to go off, and I hastily reached over to the bedside table and silenced its morning call.

Sylvia, the cat I'd adopted last Spring, gave me an annoyed look. She was currently hogging my side of the bed. I was convinced she was, little by little, creeping up the mattress. In a week's time she would have crawled up to my pillow. She stood up and humped her back in an exaggerated stretch before hopping off the bed and padding out of the bedroom.

"Morning, baby," came a husky voice, lower and thicker than usual due to the early morning hour. Hunter rolled onto her back and brushed her sleep-wild hair out of her eyes. The sheets rearranged as she fought to tame her stubborn hair, revealing more of her slightly tanned skin, a leftover from our trip to California.

"Hey."

She looked over at me with a sweet, sleepy smile. She had lines from her pillow on one cheek and her mascara and eyeliner were smudged. Her hair became impossibly tangled in the night, curling ever so slightly at her temples. She was a hot mess, but she was *my* mess, and I loved it.

I pulled my own brunette tangles into a loose ponytail. "Sleep okay?" I asked, still feeling uneasy from my dream.

Hunter stretched and emitted a sound that resembled a low purr. The sheet traveled further south down her elongated torso. "Mmmhmm. Like a log." She paused and cocked her head to the side. "What does that even mean, anyways? 'Sleep like a log'...I mean, logs don't sleep?"

"Well, if that's not a rhetorical question, the phrase originated in the 1600s and refers to one sleeping immobile –."

"Thanks for the history lesson, Dr. Graft," she teased.

"Well actually, it's not history; it's an idiom," I corrected.

"Uh huh," she said through a yawn. "You're cute."

I anxiously toyed with the top edge of the comforter. "Have any, um...weird dreams?"

She gave me a lopsided grin as she turned on her side and rested her weight on one elbow. "Nothing except the memory of some hot action last night."

I felt my face flush, unable to resist the lascivious grin Hunter was currently giving me. She often looked ready and eager to devour me. It was a part of her personality I hadn't expected when we'd first started dating, but I certainly had no complaints.

"I've got to review some lecture notes," I announced, pushing back the covers. If she kept grinning at me like that, we'd never get out of bed, and I actually had to be productive today. "You getting up soon?"

Hunter buried her face back into the downy goodness of her pillow. She wasn't much of a morning person. Her eyes, like a newborn kitten, didn't quite fully open until she'd had her coffee. She mumbled incoherently and waved a hand at me, shooing me away.

Before crawling out of bed, I turned and kissed her bare shoulder, the soft skin peeking above the top of the comforter. "I'll make coffee," I mumbled into her soft, fragrant skin. "Come down when you're ready, okay?"

Hunter growled into the pillow, but made no motion to get up. Despite the memory of my unsettling dream trampling noisily through my brain, I smiled at the disgruntled woman beside me. Finally, I slid out of bed and redressed in my pajamas, not wanting to disturb Hunter's rest anymore than I already had that morning.

+++++

Chewing on her toothbrush, Hunter bounced downstairs and found me in the kitchen, sitting on a stool at the island counter. I looked up from my lecture notes when I heard the wooden floorboards creak upon her entrance. Today I was teaching my writing seminar students about Quote Sandwiches and lecturing about the Harlem Renaissance in my 20th Century American Literature class.

Hunter helped herself to some coffee and grabbed a box of cereal out of the pantry. I was a fan of the cartoon-on-the-box sugary stuff, but Hunter was more about raisin bran and granola. Sometimes I forgot which one of us was in their thirties.

"What do you want do for Spring Break?" I asked.

"Spring Break?" Hunter looked up from pouring cornflakes into a bowl. "Babe, the semester *just* started...like three days ago."

"I know, but I've been looking online for some travel deals, and I was thinking someplace in the South Caribbean might be nice, or I could ask Troian if she could get us a good price on that Malibu condo again."

Hunter bit her lip and her face visibly crumpled. I could anticipate what she was going to say.

"And don't you dare feel guilty about money," I asserted before she could mount a protest. "I know you don't want me to be your Sugar Mama. But this isn't about me wanting to take care of you. This is about me wanting to see you in a bikini," I said with a cheeky smile.

An elegant eyebrow lifted on her forehead. "I wasn't going to decline because of the money," she admitted. "I just don't know if I can go anywhere because of my internship. The hospital will probably want me there, even over break. If I want to set myself up to get hired when I graduate, I should probably make myself available."

"Oh." I hadn't thought about her internship, but I supposed she was right. Even though she was doing the smart thing, the responsible thing, I couldn't hide my disappointment. We'd had so much fun in Malibu, I wanted another adventure with her.

She stood in front of me and swung a leg over my thighs so she was straddling me like a chair. Her arms draped around my neck and my hands instinctively went to her waist to hold her steady. "Just because I can't go doesn't mean you shouldn't," she said. "You work so hard during the semester; you deserve a *piña colada* on a beach."

"I wouldn't have any fun without you," I insisted with a hard shake of my head.

"Is that so?" she said in a near-mocking tone. She wiggled a little on my lap, getting comfortable or reminding me of where she sat – probably the former because there was no way I could overlook something like that. My hands went to the tops of her thighs, taunt and hard beneath the material of her jeans. "You would have absolutely *no* fun sitting poolside somewhere, drinking alcohol, and looking at girls in their bathing suits?"

My wandering eyes were infamous; I didn't think I could ever be like Troian who seemed to have blinders on when it came to attractive women who weren't Nikole. "It would be a *little* fun," I admitted with a playful grin. "But the entire time I'd be wishing you were there because I know how much *more* fun I'd have with you."

She swung her long legs off of me and stood up from my lap. I wanted to grab onto her hips and pull her back for more.

"You don't need a foreign country to get me into a bikini, you know."

I leered at her as she poured herself a cup of coffee. "I'm filing that away on my list of Things To Do."

She smiled and returned to her bowl of cereal. "What's your plan this morning?"

"I'm supposed to meet Troi for a coffee date," I said, tapping a pen on the countertop. "Nikole might join us since it's her off-season. I don't think she's planting seedlings in her greenhouse yet. Are you free to come with?"

Hunter made a face. "I don't have classes today, but I should probably get back to my apartment and help Sara pack boxes or something. She's moving in a few days, so naturally she's a complete disaster."

"You're a better person than me," I remarked. No amount of karma points or the promise of free pizza and beer could convince me to help someone move on my day off.

She leaned across the counter and kissed me on the tip of my nose. "I know."

+++++

Troian hustled through the front doors of my favorite coffee shop, Del Sol. She looked disheveled from a fierce late winter wind. Her jacket, scarf, and hair were dusted with powdered snow. It was the kind of overcast, stormy winter day where you'd rather be snuggled up at home than be out in it.

She spotted me across the room at our usual bank of chairs. "I'm going to strangle that groundhog," she openly complained. She tossed off her wool overcoat with her usual dramatic flair.

"As if a rodent seeing its shadow or not even matters," I chuckled. "It's not even February, Troi. We're not gonna see green grass until April."

Troian plopped down in her leather easy chair. Usually I sat by myself at a table for two, but when Troian and I hung out at Del Sol we always commandeered a corner location with comfortable chairs and our own coffee table. "All the more reason to move full-time to California."

"Don't even joke about that," I complained with a sour expression.

Troian made a more than comfortable living writing screenplays. She'd recently made the transition into writing for television, but the work was such that she could telecommute or take short trips to California where the studio was, while still keeping her permanent residence in the city of her alma mater, the small liberal arts college where I taught.

Troian ruffled her long, dark hair, knocking the melting snow from her locks. "Why do I even bother fixing my hair?"

"Because you're high maintenance?" I teasingly guessed. She wasn't really – that was more her girlfriend Nikole's *modus operandi*, which I found ironic since she was the one who played in dirt all day as a landscaper. Both of my friends were more concerned with their appearance than me. Unless I was teaching, I had no problem going out in my glasses instead of contacts, my hair in a ponytail, wearing clothes that could pass for pajamas.

Troian grunted, but didn't take the bait. "You need a refill?" She dug around inside her messenger bag for her money.

"I'm good right now. I've gotta pace myself," I said, covering the top of my coffee mug with a cupped hand. I had a long day ahead of me on campus; if I loaded up on caffeine now, I'd crash later.

"You're going first today," Troian said when she returned with her coffee. We always started our coffee dates with a few rounds of a game we'd invented – Top, Bottom, or Switch. We made up stories about people's lives – mostly about their sex lives – while they waited in line for overpriced coffee and cranberry bran muffins. It was fun and I justified it as not being mean or judgmental, but as being creative; fabricating back-stories and plots was part of my professional life.

"Guy third in line," Troian said with a jerk of her head. "Why does he look so pinched?"

I regarded the man who stood in line, three people from the cashier. He was dressed professionally and he fiddled anxiously with his phone. Troian was right. He did look pinched. He looked no older than me, but his eyes were narrowed and his forehead was furrowed. There were two deep-set lines between his eyebrows.

"He fought with his wife all morning," I said. "They've got a pact never to leave for work angry with each other, and he's thinking about calling her right now to apologize, even though he doesn't think the fight was his fault. But he knows from experience that his wife thinks she's always right."

Troian nodded wistfully as she took a drink of her coffee.

"Woman in the yoga capri pants," I assigned next. I had noticed the woman nearly right away. She was wearing a heavy winter jacket, but the bottom half of her legs were bare. "Why isn't she wearing full-length pants? Doesn't she know it's Winter?"

Troian set her mug down on the small end table beside her chair. "They *are* full-length pants," she announced with a grin. "They're just not hers."

"Oh, really?"

Troian nodded. "She stayed over at her girlfriend's house last night and she had nothing to change into this morning. Her girlfriend is only four foot ten."

"Oh, so she took *your* pants?"

"Asshole," Troian scowled. "I'm five foot one. We can't all be Jolly Green Giants like you."

At five foot eight, I hardly considered myself a giant, but adolescents hitting puberty were taller than Troian. I kept that observation to myself. Troian was sensitive about her height, but that didn't stop me entirely from teasing her about it. "Top, Bottom, or Switch?" I posed.

Troian sat forward in her chair to more closely inspect the woman standing in line. "Bottom," she finally decided on.

I arched an eyebrow. "Oh, yeah? She lets her four foot, ten inch girlfriend dominate her?"

Troian settled back in her chair, looking smug. "You'd be surprised what a Napoleon Complex translates into in bed."

I nearly snorted coffee up my nose. "Speaking of which," I said, regaining my composure, "your girlfriend just showed up."

"Very funny." Troian wrinkled her nose, but didn't bother to turn in her chair to look toward the door. Instead, she picked at my blueberry muffin even though I had every intention of eating it myself. "What kind of mutant just walked in?"

"I'm telling Nik you called her a mutant."

"Hey, guys," Nikole announced cheerfully as she walked up to our grouping of chairs. She must have been on her way to work; her dark hair was pulled back in a ponytail, and her company's logo peeked out from the opening of her jacket. "Fancy running into you two here."

Troian jerked her hand away from my breakfast muffin. She flashed a warning look at me. I grinned even wider. "Jackweed," she muttered under her breath for my ears only. "Hey, babe," she said louder, flipping her most genuine smile on. "I didn't expect to see you until later today."

Nikole's head bobbed. "My client this morning had to reschedule, so I had some free time. I figured you guys would still be here pretending to work."

"We work!" I protested valiantly. I kept out the part about how she'd just interrupted a game of Top, Bottom, or Switch.

"I'll be right back." Nikole jerked her thumb in the direction of the coffee bar. "I need to get my morning fix. You two good on coffee?"

Troian nodded. "I'm good, but get more for Elle. She's being a pussy about caffeine today."

"I'm already on my second mocha!" I protested.

Nikole made a clucking noise. "Then I guess you need more."

I had the strangest friends. Instead of encouraging me to drink more beer and make bad life-decisions, they were the breakfast mafia, pushing double caramel macchiatos and lemon poppy-seed muffins on me.

"So it's my turn," I announced as Nikole strolled away to get me a caffeine drip.

"Oh, right." Troian's face became serious. "Ginger with the baby stroller."

I spotted the woman with little trouble. The stroller was too large for the limited space of Del Sol, but she appeared determined to get her hot chai. I watched Nikole motion for her to go ahead of her in line, and the woman looked relieved.

"What about her?" I asked.

"What's her life story?"

"The usual: stay-at-home mom, gave up her career for the promise of emotional fulfillment through children while her husband is out making the money. Now she only leaves the house for coffee or the charade of her book club which is just an excuse to talk to other adults and drink wine."

"Wow. What's eating you?" Troian eyeballed me warily. "Trouble in paradise?"

"No," I insisted. "Everything's fine."

"So you're not projecting yourself onto that chick?"

"Not at all – everything's perfect."

"Things with Hunter still good?"

"Yep." I'd be lying if I wasn't waiting for the other shoe to drop, however. In my experience, good things didn't last long, especially when it came to my relationships. Happiness had an expiration date.

I dipped the tip of my finger into the design on my mocha and swirled it around, destroying the barista's handiwork. "And, I should be hearing back from publishers soon about my next book proposal."

"Oh yeah?"

"Yeah. Since I've already got tenure I don't have to worry about publishing with some stuffy academic press and can go with a trade press instead."

"That's great." Troian sat up a little straighter in her chair and seemed to be straining her neck to see something better.

"If I can get a trade press to agree to publishing in hardcover and paperback simultaneously, I might actually make money on this book."

Troian hummed, but was clearly distracted. Her gaze and her

thoughts were someplace else.

"So I told them I wasn't going to take out the pirates," I said experimentally. "I'm more flexible about the pink elephants, but if I can't have a big sword fight, then I'll walk."

Troian made another noise of agreement and nodded, but failed to comment on the absurdity of what I'd just said. She clearly wasn't listening to me.

"What's so interesting over there?" I asked, finally giving up on the conversation.

"Nik is getting hit on."

I twisted in my seat and spotted Nikole at the front register ordering her drink from our usual barista, Tony. He was your typical hipster coffee shop employee with interesting facial hair and a plunging v-neck. All that body hair must have been a health-code violation, but Del Sol was a little bit of a dive and nobody cared.

"You always think that," I laughed, turning back to my friend.

"Because it's the truth," Troian scowled.

Nikole returned to our seating area and sat at a vacant leather recliner. When she set her paper cup on the coffee table to take off her scarf and jacket, Troian made an unpleasant sound.

"See? What did I tell you?" Troian's eyes narrowed. "I don't think the phone number on the side of her cup leads to a customer service survey."

"Oh, it's just Nik," I dismissed. "She collects crushes like they're Pokémon Cards."

Troian wasn't exactly the jealous type. She trusted her girlfriend explicitly. But I knew she didn't trust the rest of the world to maintain their distance.

"I would like to punch that kid in his giant Adam's apple," she said in a quiet, serious tone that almost had me convinced.

"Simmer down, lady," I cautioned. "Tony's harmless."

"Yeah, he will be when I castrate him."

Nikole made a shushing noise. "Don't mind her; she's all bark, but no bite."

"That's not what you said last night." Troian sat back in her chair with her arms folded across her chest.

"*Anyway*." Nikole raised her voice to change the topic. Troian had no problem advertising their sexual exploits, but I knew that Nikole was a bit more reserved, even if it was just me. "So someone's got a big birthday coming up," Nikole not so innocently observed.

"God. Don't remind me," I groaned.

"Why are you so weird about your birthday?" Troian asked, although I didn't think she expected a forthcoming answer. "I'm still mad at you that you didn't let us do anything for you last year when you turned thirty."

"I just don't like birthdays," I explained with a shrug. "I don't like all the attention."

"Does Hunter know?" Nikole asked.

"No. And she doesn't need to know," I threatened.

"Well, now she does." Troian beamed proudly. My stomach dropped when I saw her phone in her hands.

My own phone immediately chirped with an incoming text message from Hunter: "Your birthday is TOMORROW? Why am I just hearing this, and from Troi?"

I made a frustrated noise and shoved my phone in my bag so I didn't have to look at it. "Why do you do these things to me?" I complained.

"You're ridiculous," Troian clucked. "Who doesn't like birthdays?"

"Just wait until you're an old lady like me," I grumbled.

"Right. Because you're a total hag at the ripe old age of 31." Nikole shook her head.

Thirty one. God, when had *that* happened? I had never understood those women who stopped aging and just kept celebrating their 29th birthday over and over again; or not until it happened to me, at least. But I honestly didn't feel a day over my mid-twenties. If only the date on my birth certificate agreed. I'd made my two best friends promise not to do anything over the top for my thirtieth birthday, and I would make sure my thirty-first birthday was the same.

"This isn't a Hunter thing, is it?" Troian asked. "Are you gonna be super weird this year because your girlfriend was born in the 1990s?"

"You really know how to make a girl feel special." It didn't really matter how old Hunter was; I just wasn't a fan of birthdays. It's not like I'd done anything. It's kind of like when someone compliments your name. I had nothing to do with that; they should be congratulating my parents instead.

"Any cute students this semester?" Troian asked.

I flashed my friend a warning look.

Troian held up her hands, instantly retreating. "What? It's ritual at the beginning of each semester. Just because you're all domesticated now, I don't get to ask that anymore?"

"You can ask; I'm just not going to humor you with a response."

"You got married and became un-fun."

"Whatever," I scoffed. It wasn't the most eloquent retort, but I didn't feel comfortable talking about attractive students anymore, not even with my best friend. I knew my reputation had been slightly tarnished over the fallout from Hunter. Now I felt guilty just admiring female students at the gym or when my gaze lingered a little too long standing behind someone at the drinking fountain.

"You two fight like an old married couple. I swear, sometimes I think you guys are the ones in a relationship." Nikole laughed, showing off a mouthful of straight, white teeth. Troian would have to staple her girlfriend's mouth closed if she wanted to keep the baristas away. "I'm just here for sex and occasional cuddles."

Troian reached across the divide to grab her girlfriend's hand. She brought her wrist to her mouth and pressed her lips against it.

"Well I'm going to take off; I've got some work to do at the greenhouse," Nikole announced, standing from her chair. She directed her gaze at Troian. "When can I expect you home?"

"Soon. I'll probably work from here for another hour; I've got a teleconference call later this afternoon, so I'll take that at home."

Nikole bent down to kiss her girlfriend goodbye. "Ok. See you then."

"Mexican for dinner?" Troian suggested. "I can pick up an avocado on my way home if you grab some cilantro from the greenhouse."

Nikole pulled on her jacket. "Sounds perfect."

"*You're* perfect," Troian countered with a goofy smile. Her grin was so broad and so wide I was almost afraid her head would topple off her neck from the weight of it.

"Puke," I replied.

Troian stuck out her tongue at me, and Nikole laughed again.

"Behave you two," Nikole admonished before she waved and left us to our work.

We spent the next hour lost in our own tasks. Today Troian had writing to do, and I had drafts of essays to provide feedback on. It was nice spending time with Troian because when we had these coffee dates, we knew how to balance socializing with actually getting work done. Sometimes I was actually more productive with her around.

"Professor Graft?"

My reading glasses made it hard to see features at a distance. Normally I couldn't identify people while I wore them, but this student's face was hard to forget even though our class had only met a few times so far.

"Loryssa."

Half Egyptian and half Irish, Loryssa Mubarak had exotic features mixed with a more mainstream beauty. She was model tall, which was accentuated today by her black leggings and long, oversized sweater that drooped on one side revealing an olive-toned, angular shoulder. Her long brunette hair with golden highlights was thick and voluminous like she was the spokeswoman for a shampoo company.

"Hi. I apologize if I'm interrupting." She spoke slightly accented English and looked between both Troian and me. My friend looked up from her laptop screen and openly stared at my student.

"Not at all. What's up?" I shuffled some papers around so she couldn't see all the corrections I had made to one of her classmate's rough drafts.

"I just had a question about the reading for Monday," she said, switching her weight from one foot to the other. "Do we need to have the entire book read?"

"Mhmm," I confirmed, trying not to sound too apologetic. The book was a quick read and students usually gave good feedback on it, so I didn't really have a reason to feel bad about assigning the whole thing. It was college, after all.

Loryssa didn't appear intimidated or disappointed by my announcement. Instead she nodded and thanked me. "Okay. Well, see you in class later," she said, breaking out a blinding smile. I gave her a half wave and she walked away.

"You are such a liar."

I snapped my attention back to Troian. "What?"

"You told me you didn't have any attractive students this

semester."

"Who? Loryssa?"

Troian rolled her eyes. "No. That other gorgeous Glamazon you were just talking to."

I was about to defend myself when I paused, realizing something. "Wait. Is Troian Smith actually admitting that someone besides her girlfriend is *attractive*?"

"I think lots of girls are attractive," she countered haughtily.

"Sure. But they're all celebrities," I pointed out. "That doesn't count."

"You gonna be able to keep your eyes to yourself this semester?" Troian poked, deflecting the attention back on me.

"My girlfriend is smart, funny, and gorgeous," I ticked off with some satisfaction. "It's the Holy Trinity. Neither Loryssa nor anyone else is going to distract me."

Troian continued to openly stare after Loryssa and her long legs as she walked out the front door of Del Sol. "When did *you* get willpower, Bookie?"

My dream from the previous night's sleep flashed into my head. I apparently still had work to do.

+++++

I would have spent the rest of the day at Del Sol, trying to be productive, but I had office hours and an evening class, so I spent the second half of my day on campus. The University was trying to attract part-time students and build an adult continuing education program, so new to this semester I was teaching a 3-hour writing class on Thursday evenings.

Outside my office window the snow was still thick in places, but it was pulled back in other spots to reveal the yellowish-brown grass beneath. It was a depressing time of year when the weather flip-flopped between Winter-like conditions and Spring every other day. I liked snow, having lived in the Midwest all my life, but this time of year made me second-guess my choice in geography.

I took a step back to inspect my work. My doctoral graduation diploma, centered in a dark-stained wooden frame, now hung on my office wall. I had delayed putting anything up on the walls for years after I'd been hired. It had been a strange superstition that if I made the space my own with personal belongings, diplomas, and pictures of the people in my life, that it wouldn't remain my own for long. I often felt like a fraud despite the Ph.D. behind my name, like I'd tricked my University to pick me over all the other potential candidates, a graduate student in professorial clothing.

"New frame?"

I spun on my heel at the unexpected voice. My boss, Bob, the Chair of the English department, stood just outside of my office door.

"Looks nice."

I didn't bother admitting to him my superstition and that this was the first thing I'd ever put up on my office wall.

"How's it going?" I asked.

"You have a minute?"

"Of course." I waved my hand at the vacant seat on the other side of my desk.

"Do you mind if I close the door?" Bob asked, looking uneasy. "There's something...*sensitive*," he said, trying the word out, "that I need to discuss with you."

I felt an uncomfortable twist in my stomach. Maybe I shouldn't have hung up that diploma on the wall. "S-sure," I stumbled.

Bob closed the door and that anxious feeling in my gut turned into full-on suffocation. I couldn't imagine what he'd want to talk to me about that would warrant a closed-office door, but it couldn't be good.

I cleared my throat and fidgeted with the stems of my reading glasses which I'd set on my desk. "What's up?" I asked, trying to keep a cheerful lilt to my question.

Bob looked more interested in the art on my walls, all leftover from the professor who'd occupied the office before me, rather than directly facing me.

"The new Dean called me about you."

"Which one?" We had a bunch of Deans – the Dean of Students, the Dean of the Faculty, the Dean of the College of Arts and Sciences.

"Dean Merlot."

I didn't recognize the name. "Dean Krauss' replacement?" I guessed.

"That would be the one," Bob confirmed. "The Dean, um, is

concerned with how public you're being."

I didn't understand what Bob was referring to at first. I swallowed when I realized what this was about though. "With Hunter, you mean," I said carefully.

Bob nodded, albeit sheepishly.

"Am I being too publicly *gay*?" I spat out the final word without meaning to.

Bob grimaced and squirmed in the chair. If I wasn't consumed with trying to control my anger, I would have felt sorry for him.

I leaned forward. "Did someone complain, Bob?" I demanded. He was kind of my boss, yes, but I was pissed and rapidly losing my composure. I thought we'd hashed this out with my Tenure Review and that it wouldn't be mentioned again.

"Dean Merlot received an anonymous call —."

"Bullshit," I cut him off. "I'm so *sick* of these cowards hiding behind anonymity to tattle on me because my sexuality makes them uncomfortable. It's not against the law to be *gay*, Bob. Last time I checked I'm allowed to hold hands or hug my girlfriend in public."

"Yes, but this is a private university with a religious affiliation," he tried to counter.

"More bullshit," I spat. "The Health Center provides students with contraceptives, the History department teaches History of Sexuality and the Women's Studies Department offers Queer Theory," I ticked off. "Mary Haste in the Psychology department is a single mother. What other so-called 'sinful acts' do I need to call to your attention?"

"This isn't coming from me," Bob said weakly, holding up his hands in surrender. "Believe me, Elle; I wouldn't be talking to you about this if it weren't for pressure from the new Dean. I think it's just about trying to establish authority and boundaries, being new and all."

"Uh huh," I said, not really listening. "And what's the ultimatum? I stop being gay or what? I get fired? I've got Tenure, Bob," I reminded him. "It's going to take a lot more than someone seeing me hugging my girlfriend on campus to get rid of me."

Bob took a deep breath. "Dean Merlot simply asked me to remind you that under federal statutory and constitutional provisions, religious institutions like our school are able to make employment decisions based on the traditions of our faith." He sounded like a robot, and I wanted to strangle him.

I bit into my upper lip to keep from snapping off something about where he could shove those traditions. "Understood," I said stiffly. I stood and opened my office door. It felt like a blast of fresh air to have the door open again, and I took a deep, calming breath. "I hate to rush you off, but I've got a mountain of student writing to look over. I don't want to fall behind so early in the semester. So if there's nothing else…"

Bob stood and pulled on the bottom of his *Cosby-Show* sweater. "No, that's it." He shuffled toward the door and made an awkward passing. "Thanks for your time, Elle. I know you're a busy lady."

I gave him a forced smile. "Never too busy for a chat with you, Bob."

He bobbed his head looking grateful that he'd managed to get through this conversation without losing any limbs.

I watched him walk down the hallway and turn into the mailroom. I shut my office door, closeting myself inside in more ways than one.

+++++

CHAPTER THREE

"Great." I snapped my laptop closed from my seat at Hunter's desk. "Like things could get any worse today." I rubbed at my temples.

Hunter glanced up from her textbook. "Uh oh. What's wrong?"

I'd come straight over to Hunter's apartment at the conclusion of my Thursday evening class. Even though there was more room in my house and I was more comfortable in my own space, I'd been trying to be better about splitting time equally between our respective homes. I had been too selfish early in our relationship by assuming Hunter wanted to spend all of our shared time together at my house.

I flopped down next to her on her bed. "The trade press that was falling all over itself to give me an advanced book contract changed its mind."

I'd been in talks with a popular trade press that had a strong catalog of contemporary short stories. I'd secured a book contract elsewhere for my anthology of stories about individuals with unique powers and abilities just in time for my Tenure Review. It included a short story about Hunter that I'd originally written when she and her winter jacket had first caught my attention. The book was in the copy-editing stage and would go to press soon. But one book was never enough in the world of academia – it was publish or perish. And before the ink had dried on my first book contract, I'd started brainstorming ideas for a second book.

Hunter frowned. "They can do that?"

"Apparently."

"So what does that mean?"

"It means I suck," I pouted.

The reader reports you received from publishing with a University Press made me sick, but working with a trade press wasn't proving to be any easier on my ego. Everything I did for my career – writing and teaching – was subjected to reviews. It would be so nice to do something without an anonymous person judging my best efforts.

Hunter shut her textbook and I felt its weight beside me on the mattress. "Now you're being a little melodramatic."

"I know," I sighed. I rearranged myself so I could rest my head in her lap. Her fingers immediately began stroking through my hair, lightly massaging my scalp, and I felt my stress begin to slip away. "That feels good," I murmured.

She bent over to peck the tip of my nose before returning her attention to my scalp.

"I'll just have to send the book proposal to another press," I said, thinking out loud. "It's not the end of the world; it's just annoying that they requested exclusive review only to reject me at this stage."

"Everything happens for a reason," Hunter reasonably responded. "Your book just wasn't meant to be published with them. It'll all work out."

I hummed in agreement. I had nothing to worry about, really. "I know," I concurred. "It's just an added annoyance to my day." I was still massively aggravated that I'd been confronted about being seen on campus with Hunter.

Hunter perked up on the bed. "Did something else happen today?"

I rubbed my face. I hadn't wanted to tell her about my meeting with Bob. We'd been through enough unnecessary drama because of our age difference and my Tenure Review. I didn't want her to worry; this was out of her control. "I've got a new boss – he's the Dean of the College of Arts & Sciences." I paused, deliberating whether or not to tell her the second piece of information. "And he's a bit of a homophobe."

"What? How do you know?"

I sighed, feeling deflated. "Because he told the Chair of my department to tell me to stop being so gay."

Her eyebrows rose on her forehead. "Really?"

"Well, in so many words." I tried to reign in my emotions as I recalled the conversation. "Apparently someone saw us together on campus yesterday, and they complained to the Dean. That's what Bob told me at least. I think it's more likely that the Dean himself saw us and is hiding behind this so-called anonymous complaint."

Hunter didn't immediately respond. She rose from the bed and sat down at her desk.

"What are you doing?" I asked. I rearranged myself on the bed and propped myself on one elbow.

She flipped her laptop open and pulled up a web browser. "I'm looking him up. What's his name?"

"Uh, Merlot," I said. "Dean Merlot."

Her fingers moved against the laptop's keyboard. "Well, first of all, he is a *she*."

"*She?*" I echoed.

"Yup," Hunter confirmed. "Unless 'Jessica' is a gender-neutral name?" She turned her laptop so I could see the screen better. "Here's the announcement about the new hire on the university's news page."

"Huh." I felt a little foolish for assuming that the new Dean was a man. Some feminist I was.

I patted the space beside me. "Come back? I miss you."

Hunter smiled and shut the lid of her laptop, so she could return to her previous position with my head on her lap.

"Have you figured out yet what you're going to do about your living situation?" I asked. Hunter's current roommate, Sara, was moving out at the beginning of the following week. While I would have loved for us to have this generous apartment all to ourselves, I knew that wasn't practical. Hunter's parents paid for her to live off campus, and I doubted they would foot the bill for the entire apartment.

The hands in my hair paused momentarily. "I think I have to get a new roommate. I don't really want to move just to go to a studio apartment for a semester. I figure if I get a roommate, I'll only have to deal with them for a few months until I graduate. Once I get a job, in theory, I'll be able to afford a place on my own without my parents' help."

"Sounds like you've got it all figured out." I picked at the screen-print letters that said the name of our university on the leg of her sweatpants. I was tempted to point out that she could always move in with me for a few months, but things were really good with us right now. It seemed like an unnecessary complication.

"I guess so," she said wistfully. "Tomorrow I'll put some fliers up in the common areas on campus about looking for a roommate, and then I'll just wait for the calls to come in."

"Have fun with that," I snorted. I had always rented studio apartments in college and in grad school for the sole reason of not wanting to share my space.

"Sara said she'd keep paying her share of the rent until I find a replacement. She's technically still on the lease until graduation, but she feels bad for bailing."

"That's nice of her."

Hunter nodded. "I know. It takes the pressure off. I would have had to get an afterschool job or something to take care of her portion of the rent, and with my licensure exam coming up, plus all the hours I'm already doing at the hospital for my practicum, on top of the internship, it would have stretched me thin." She shook her head. "Isn't senior year supposed to be easy?"

"Sorry, Hunt. I wish I could tell you it gets easier from here."

She kept stroking her fingers through my hair and looked particularly thoughtful. "Do you ever feel different?"

"Different how?" I asked.

"I mean, like when you're kissing me do you ever think 'Oh my God, I'm kissing a girl.'"

"I'm not really thinking much of anything when I'm kissing you," I answered truthfully. "You make me decidedly un-cerebral."

"Such the charmer," she chuckled. She leaned over and brushed her lips against mine. "Why are you so soft?" she sighed against me.

"Are you calling me fat?" I countered, not really meaning it.

"No. Your lips are soft."

"Well, I *am* a girl," I pointed out.

"I don't understand why everyone wouldn't want to kiss girls."

I couldn't argue with her; it was pretty awesome.

"Kissing you is like eating cotton candy," she breathed. She tilted her head and moved to recapture my mouth with her own while her hands softly wandered and explored the contours of my body.

She pulled away abruptly, leaving me wanting more.

"What?" I asked, looking up into her cornflower eyes.

"I just remembered that your birthday is tomorrow. I'm not prepared, and it's your fault. Why didn't you say something?"

"Because I didn't want you to make a big deal about it. It's just another day on the calendar."

She stopped touching my hair so she could cross her arms across her chest. "So you *wanted* me to miss your birthday?"

"Why not?" I asked, reluctantly sitting up. "I missed your 21st birthday," I reminded her.

"You were in California."

"Right. Being a stubborn asshole too afraid to let myself fall in love with someone ten years younger than me."

"It's only 9 years and a few months," she said, starting to look annoyed. "Did you not want to tell me about your birthday because of the age thing?"

"No. I'm over the age thing," I readily dismissed. I'd finally decided not to let our age difference bother me anymore. Hunter was an old soul, and I still had a lot of growing up to do. It all evened out. "I just don't like birthdays," I said for what felt like the hundredth time that day. "I never have. Everyone fusses over you and there's so much unnecessary pressure to make the day go perfect, and I hate all those eyes on you when you blow out your candles, and if you leave three candles lit your friends and family slut-shame you because you have three boyfriends."

Hunter blinked a few times. "I have no idea what you're talking about. You lost me somewhere in that rant."

"Your family never did that to you?"

She still looked lost, so I had to explain: "When you make a wish and blow out your candles, if you leave any still lit, that number represents how many significant others you have at once."

I could vividly remember the horror and embarrassment of my nine-year-old self from failing to extinguish all of my birthday candles in one breath. Extended family members would be huddled around the dining room table, teasing me about having multiple boyfriends when two or three candles remained lit. I was too young to really know what any of that meant or why it mattered; all I knew was to blow out the flames as quickly as possible to save face. It had made me feel like I'd done something wrong. There was too much anxiety that mounted whenever I heard the Birthday Song.

She shook her head. "Sorry, hun. I've never heard of that. You just have a weird family."

"I also twist the stem off my apples before I eat them. And I recite the alphabet with each rotation."

She stared blankly at me, and for a moment I worried I'd revealed too much. She knew I had quirks, like the being-late thing, but she probably hadn't accounted on me being *this* weird.

"And why do you say the alphabet?" she asked in a clear, calm voice. I wondered if she was mentally diagnosing me with OCD.

"Whatever letter I'm on when the stem snaps off is the first initial of the person I'm supposed to marry." I knew how ridiculous it sounded as the words came out, but I didn't care. I ate an apple nearly every day, and without fail I twisted off the stem before eating it to find out who I was going to marry.

She shook her head and smiled. "You'd better be tugging extra hard when it gets to H."

+++++

The next morning, Hunter rolled over in bed beside me. "Morning, babe," she yawned. She sat up slightly in bed and ran her fingers through her unruly hair.

I groaned. "It's too early," I complained. I grabbed a spare pillow and covered my face. It was Friday, which normally was a day off of teaching for me, but today I had to go to campus for meetings. Most semesters it felt like I spent more time doing committee work for the university than actually teaching.

I could hear Hunter's amused laugh. "We went to bed at like 10 last night. Is this what I have to look forward to when I get old like you?"

The seemingly innocent comment about my age rattled me. I removed the pillow from my face and glared. "Don't you *dare* do anything for my birthday today," I warned.

"Ellio, we've been over this," Hunter replied with an innocent smile. "I'm not going to."

"Good," I stated stubbornly. I was annoyed that another birthday had snuck up on me.

Hunter chuckled good-naturedly and ran her palm over my stomach. "Are we going to have a repeat performance of this conversation every year?"

"Unless you can figure out a way for me to stop having birthdays."

"Sounds very vampire-y to me. And no offense, but even if you sparkled in the sunlight, I'm not into necrophilia." Hunter grinned, showing off her deep dimples.

"I'm trying not to judge you for having read those books." When I'd found the paperback trilogy among Hunter's personal library, some works of fiction, but most of them books for school, I'd been horrified.

Hunter smirked. "Doesn't matter," she breezed. "I know you're not in love with me because of my massive brain."

I quirked an eyebrow. "And why exactly *am* I with you?"

"Because of my ass, naturally," she returned, batting her eyelashes comically.

I rolled my eyes. "You're an ass alright." I laid still in bed for a moment, but realizing the morning wasn't going to pause itself just because I wanted an extra hour of sleep, I started to roll out of bed. "I should get ready for work," I sighed.

Hunter remained in her place in bed. "I've never heard of anyone working on their birthday," she replied with a yawn.

"That's because they don't know it's my birthday," I reminded her as I picked up my clothes from the previous day off of her bedroom floor. "Academica is different from a regular work environment. No one pays attention to things like that. Besides, I really don't want *anyone* to make a big deal over it. It's not worth it." I narrowed my eyes slightly. "So if you've got something planned..."

Hunter held up her hands as if retreating. "I swear. It's just gonna be a normal Friday night tonight."

"Good," I said, satisfied that she was telling the truth. "I don't have any classes today, but Penny called an emergency meeting of the Women's and Gender Studies program for some reason. I shouldn't be home too late."

"I've got a full day at the hospital today," Hunter noted. "But I'll meet you at your house later?"

"Sounds good," I confirmed. "We can order in so neither of us has to make dinner tonight."

"Want some company in the shower?" Hunter practically purred. Her lips curled into a smug smirk. "I could scrub all those hard to reach places."

I laughed. "As tempting as that sounds, I can't be late for this meeting; you'd better stay in bed." We'd just had a WGS meeting a few days ago, but Penny's email had sounded urgent.

Hunter gave me a lazy smile and stretched her arms above her head. "Okay," she conceded. As she stretched, the cotton sheets slipped further down her body, revealing more of her toned, smooth skin. "But you don't know what you're missing out on."

Although I should have been immune to the sight of Hunter's naked body by now, I felt my willpower rapidly diminishing. My eyes unabashedly drank in the sight of her tight body.

I scampered out of the bedroom before I got unnecessarily distracted. *Oh yes I do,* I wistfully thought.

+++++

Penny, the director of the Women's and Gender Studies Program, looked around the room. We were in a conference room in the Humanities building; our usual meeting room in the Library was booked, a conflict with the hastily scheduled meeting. "We're just waiting on Kathy, but let's get started."

No sooner had she called the meeting to order when the door to the conference room flew open with Kathy from Sociology on the other side, looking more agitated than usual.

"She did it," she said, slightly out of breath. "I can't believe she actually did it."

"Who is 'she'? And what did 'she' do?" Penny asked gently.

Kathy wiped at her forehead. I wondered if she'd run across campus. "Dean Merlot canceled my summer session to Costa Rica. She said that the funds for the course had been reallocated."

"What?!" Gemma from the Psychology department exclaimed. "She can *do* that? Is that even in her job description?"

Kathy waved a stack of papers she'd been clutching in one hand. "I printed out the emails to show you. I don't even know how she got included on the email thread. I was emailing with the Registrar about opening the course cap so more students could enroll, and suddenly I had an email from Merlot informing me that plans had changed because the funds were no longer available. This is the beginning of the end, people," she ranted. "Once Administration starts telling us what we can and cannot teach, say goodbye to Academic Freedom as we know it."

Penny's aged face scrunched with maternal concern. "But what about the students who've already enrolled and are counting on those credits?"

Kathy sat down in the vacant chair beside me with a dramatic grunt. "Merlot told me I can do the class, but it has to be on campus." She raked her fingers through her short, tussled hair. "I have to completely redesign the course now. How can I do a service-learning class on women's reproductive health issues in developing countries without actually being *in a developing country*?" She made a frustrated sound and threw her hands up. "I've been planning this class for *years*! All the contacts I had to make and the red tape to go through – all for nothing."

"Did the Dean say where the funds had been reallocated to?" my friend Emily asked.

Kathy shook her head vigorously. "No. I asked, but she hasn't replied yet to my emails."

"That bitch," Gemma from Psychology seethed. "Someone needs to yank that stiletto out of her ass."

"Gemma," Penny scolded. "That's not very sisterly of you."

Gemme frowned, but looked properly chastised.

"You should go talk to Merlot face-to-face, Kathy," Emily reasoned. "Maybe there's been a misunderstanding."

Kathy looked wistful, but clearly defeated. I bit my tongue. I wanted to share my own frustrations about the Dean and the thinly-veiled warning that I keep my gay to myself. My own problem felt insignificant, however, compared to Kathy's. At least my classes weren't getting canceled.

Peggy stood up. "Well, I did call this meeting to address a recent outbreak of student plagiarism, but I think we've had enough bad news for one day," she announced. "Who wants donuts?"

+++++

Instead of indulging in donuts and continuing to complain about Dean Merlot, fueled by unnecessary carbohydrates, I hiked up the multiple flights of stairs to the English department offices. I liked bakery pastries as much as the next woman, but in my experience it wasn't productive to simply complain about the administration's decisions. If we wanted to affect change, we needed to take an organized proposal or petition to the faculty senate. And to be honest, my tenure was still too new for me to start rocking the boat.

When I reached the appropriate floor, there was a group of professors hovering outside of the mailroom door, nearly blocking the entrance to the department.

"What's up with the traffic jam?" I asked Thad, one of my Associate Professor colleagues.

"Haven't you checked your email?"

I shook my head. "No. I was in a meeting this morning." *And in my girlfriend's bed.*

"Dean Merlot put everyone on blast," he frowned. "Everyone's teaching is going to be evaluated before the semester is done."

"*Everyone's?*" I asked.

Thad nodded. "Even the full professors. They're all in an uproar." He jerked his head in the direction of the mob of faculty members clogging up the hallway. "Hence the angry villager routine. I think they're getting ready to storm the castle."

"Merlot's at it again." I breathed out a heavy sigh. Kathy from Sociology was going to go postal after she heard about this new development.

Thad ran his fingers through his surfer-boy hair. "Yeah, and it gets worse. We're not going to be given any notice about when the observation is going to happen. Someone can sit in on one of our classes whenever they feel like it."

"That's ridiculous," I snorted. "What's the point of having tenure if the Dean's office is going to monitor us like we're children? *We're* the experts in our subjects," I scowled, "not some administrators who've never taught a class in their life."

I'd already had to go through a rigorous teaching evaluation process to achieve tenure. It was intimidating because often a class's performance was out of your control. If you had scheduled a discussion of a reading for the class period, but the majority of the students didn't actually do the reading, you were stuck and had to think up something on the spot to do instead. One of the perks of being an Associate Professor was not to have those watchful eyes on you anymore.

"So what happens if we get a bad review?"

"The email claims it's tied to performance raises," Thad said. "You get a bad review, you don't get a raise."

I couldn't help rolling my eyes. "So, once again, our tenure is pointless."

He nodded, looking full of remorse.

"Well if the villagers bring out their pitchforks and torches, let me know," I tried to laugh. "I want to watch."

I circumvented the roadblock by the mailroom and walked down to my faculty office. I needed to make a fresh start on my second book proposal while there was a lull in student grading. The disturbance of my fellow faculty and their inspired grumblings floated down the hallway. I closed my office door to shut the voices out so I could get some work done.

I was also curious to learn more about this new Dean who seemed intent on keeping her faculty on a short leash. A web search of her name produced no helpful results – just pictures of nail polish. Typing in 'Dean Jessica Merlot' was even less revealing; the latest news on Paula Dean showed up at the top of the search engine page. When I browsed the university's webpage, my research came up empty as well. Dean Merlot was too new of a hire, and the IT Department was too lazy for the appropriate webpage to have been updated. Dean Krauss's headshot smiled back at me where Jessica Merlot's picture and biography should have been located.

When there was a brisk knock at my door, I hastily closed all the open web browsers as if I'd been caught looking at pornography; it wouldn't have surprised me if the Dean's office had installed spyware on our work computers and knew when we were searching for information on her.

I opened the door, more reasonably expecting to see Emily, Thad, or one of my other colleagues, still fired up about Dean Merlot's recent proclamation. I wasn't prepared to see my student Loryssa though.

"Hi," she smiled affably. She gave me an awkward-looking wave. "Do you have a minute?"

"I, uh, I'm actually not even supposed to be on campus today," I stumbled.

Two expertly sculpted eyebrows rose on her unlined forehead. "So that's a no?"

"Can it wait until Monday?" I winced.

The smile slipped from her face. "I had some questions about the reading for next week, but I suppose it can wait."

A cumbersome guilt settled over me. I couldn't ignore a student request just because I was afraid that my willpower would falter. I was actually pretty proud of myself for reigning in my wandering eyes lately, and I hadn't had anymore inappropriate student dreams in two days. I'd chalk that up to a win.

"No, no. Come in."

She walked into my office and started to shut the door behind her. "You can keep that open," I said, almost desperate.

"Are you sure? It's pretty loud out there." She gave me a peculiar smile. "Are you guys having a party and starting the weekend early? English professors gone wild?"

I shook my head. "English professors don't go wild unless there's a Renaissance Faire or something in town."

She laughed a little too loudly. "I'll have to remember that for the future. Busty wenches, mead, and jousting, right?"

I cleared my throat and moved to sit behind my desk, determined to keep things professional. There was no way I was going to flirt back and let my idiot mouth betray me.

+++++

I unlocked the front door of my house, feeling emotionally exhausted. Even though it was just past 6pm, the sky was already dark due to the late winter month. I'd stayed later on campus than I'd originally planned because of the drama over Dean Merlot's new totalitarian regime. After my brief one-on-one meeting with Loryssa, I'd penned a letter to the Dean's office, protesting the re-allocation of funds for Kathy's sociology course. My words would probably fall on deaf ears, but I'd been inspired to do something to stem this power-trip the new Dean was on. It had been a dismal way to spend my birthday afternoon, but it wasn't as if any of my coworkers knew today had any special significance. The only people at work who had record of my birth date were in Human Resources because it was filed away on my I9s and W2s.

I'd received a few rambling texts throughout the day from Troian teasing me about my advanced age and a simple "Happy Birthday, lady!" text from Nikole, but beyond that I hadn't heard from anyone else. Even though I always vehemently insisted that my birthdays go unrecognized, there was still a tiny part of me that wanted *some* kind of recognition – a balloon, maybe a single cupcake at my desk, a bouquet of flowers. Anything. I'd even entertained the thought that maybe Penny's "Emergency Meeting" had been code for a birthday surprise for me. It was silly though, and I knew it.

I entered the front foyer and was greeted by silence and darkness. I reached around, fumbling for the light switch I knew was there. When I flicked the toggle up, however, nothing happened. I tried again. Nothing.

I cursed and took off my snow boots in darkness. I hung up my jacket and allowed my eyes to adjust to the limited light coming in through the front windows from the streetlamps outside.

"Hunter?" I called out.

I could make out the sound of footsteps traveling down the darkened hallway. Sock-covered feet padded in my direction. I tensed momentarily until I recognized Hunter's familiar gait. As she came closer, I could make out the smiling features of her beautiful face.

"Hey, birthday girl." Hunter greeted me with a warm hug. "How was your day?"

I kept my face buried in her shoulder. She smelled like her coconut body wash.

"Uneventful." I didn't want to rehash all the Dean Merlot drama.

Hunter pulled away and held me at arm's length. "That's a good thing, right?" she asked with a quirked eyebrow.

My mouth scrunched up, and I blew out a deep sigh. "Yeah, I guess so."

"Why is it so dark in here?" Hunter asked, noticing the lack of lighting for the first time.

"I think there's a fuse blown or the bulb in the front hallway burned out," I remarked. "I thought that maybe...maybe you'd planned a surprise party, and that's why it wasn't working."

"But you told me you didn't want me to do anything." Hunter's eyebrows scrunched together. "You also told me you didn't want a birthday present."

"I know," I agreed, feeling unwontedly crestfallen. "I just...I didn't think you'd actually *listen* to me."

Hunter blinked a few times. "I...is this a trick? Because you often complain that I don't listen to you."

"So why'd you choose *today* as the one day to actually listen?" I literally whined.

Hunter chuckled and grabbed onto my hand. "Come on. Your present's in the kitchen."

"Present?" My voice embarrassingly cracked on the syllables. I allowed Hunter to pull me in the direction of the kitchen.

She pulled a small white box out of the refrigerator and set it on the kitchen island. She grabbed a knife out of the butcher block and snapped the twine that held the box closed.

"I was planning on saving this for later," she remarked with a smirk. She opened the top of the white box to reveal a small, circular 6-inch birthday cake. There were no candles, but it would have been a mathematical feat to squeeze thirty-one candles onto the surface of the modest-sized cake.

I immediately swiped my finger along the top of the cake, covering my fingertip with light purple frosting. I sucked my finger into my mouth and licked off the creamy topping.

Hunter cleared her throat uncomfortably. "Is it weird that I'm suddenly jealous of your finger?"

I raised an eyebrow, my finger still in my mouth. I popped the digit out from between my lips. "Because it's covered with frosting or because it was in my mouth?"

Hunter's lips curved into a leer. "Take your pick."

An unorthodox idea filtered through my brain. I must have made some kind of strange face, because Hunter looked confused.

"What?" she asked.

My mouth widened into a grin. "I just figured out what I want for my birthday."

+++++

"But, baby," Hunter complained as she tugged on the bindings around her wrists. "It's *your* birthday. Shouldn't I be the one doing all the hard work?"

I sat atop my tied-down girlfriend, straddling her naked body between my thighs. The fashion scarves around her wrists were soft, but I had tied them securely. The wood slats on my headboard creaked, but gave no indication that they'd break as long as Hunter didn't suddenly turn into the Incredible Hulk.

My lips twisted into a wry smile. I stroked my fingers down the center of her naked body. "Haven't you ever heard the phrase that it's far better to give than receive?"

"Sure, but—."

I placed a finger over Hunter's generous lips, effectively silencing her. "Like you said. It's *my* birthday. So let me have some fun."

Hunter grumbled. "Fine. But can't you at least take off some of your clothes? I'm feeling a little weird being the only naked one."

I smirked and shook my head. "Maybe later. But that's not on the agenda right now."

"Agenda?" She turned her head toward the birthday cake she'd gotten me; it sat on the bedside table. "And what's the deal with the cake?" she asked. "Are you gonna eat me and have your cake, too?"

"You'll see," I sing-songed. I swiped two fingers across the top of the cake. A giant dollop of frosting hung from my fingertips. I smeared the sugary topping across the side of Hunter's neck.

"Oh God," Hunter groaned, as if suddenly realizing why I had brought the cake into the bedroom.

I licked my lips and beamed down on Hunter's vulnerable body. "Happy birthday to me," I murmured.

Leaning over, I licked up the frosting I'd wiped on Hunter's skin. I sat up straight again and wiped at my mouth with the back of my hand. "Good choice on the cake, hun," I approved with a sly smile.

"Uh huh."

I dabbed a smaller dot of frosting behind Hunter's right earlobe and proceeded to paint small dots down her neck and across her collarbone. I bit my bottom lip to keep my triumphant smile at bay. I knew Hunter was going to pay me back for this later. But for now, I was going to have my fun.

I swabbed my tongue across the length of Hunter's jutting collarbone. I sucked on the flesh and bone long after the last remnants of sugar frosting were gone, leaving small red welts in my wake.

"I wanna suck you dry, baby," I breathed across her skin. I suckled my way up to her ear. My breath was warm and it tickled against the strands of hair close to Hunter's neck and ear. I flicked my tongue out at her earlobe and drew the soft flesh into my mouth. When I gently bit down, I heard Hunter quietly moan.

"Wanna taste?" I whispered into her ear.

I gathered more purple frosting on two fingers and offered them to Hunter. She greedily sucked my fingers into her mouth and her tongue cleaned away the sugared topping.

"You can do that to me later," I promised, eliciting another painful moan from Hunter.

I sat back up and collected more frosting. I ran my fingertips around Hunter's tightening nipples, covering the sensitive nubs with more frosting. I sucked one nipple into my mouth and ran my tongue around it, getting it clean. I continued to work on her breasts even after I'd licked away all the frosting. My tongue flicked across a nipple and I gently bit down on it. Hunter whimpered quietly and her barely audible sigh turned into a throaty groan when I used my teeth to tug on the perky nub before releasing it.

I dabbed more of the frosting on Hunter's flat stomach, just below her belly button. Leaning forward, I stopped, my face just an inch above her naked skin. Hunter's stomach rose slightly as she breathed in. My tongue snaked out and touched her. I could feel her flesh slightly quiver as I began to lick up the frosting with long, steady strokes.

Not bothering to pause for more frosting, I licked hard along Hunter's right hipbone. She moaned appropriately; her hips had always been one of her more sensitive spots, and I was certainly taking advantage.

Hunter's breath now came in short, ragged bursts. Her body was sweaty to the touch even though she'd done little more than lay on my bed. I saw her flex her wrists, as if tempted to rip out of the scarves that held her back from participating. But as much as she might have wanted to turn the tables on me and have her own fun, she knew how much I enjoyed this. Plus, I'd probably stop altogether if she destroyed my favorite scarves, and I knew that stopping wasn't something Hunter wanted me to do anytime soon.

I slid down the length of her prone body and repositioned myself between her naked thighs.

"Almost out of frosting," I stated with a hint of a pout on my lips. "Good thing I rationed though," I mused aloud, "or we wouldn't get to the really fun part." I collected more of the sugary stuff and drew purple lines along the inside of Hunter's thighs.

I ran my fingertips along the insides of her thighs and smirked as my touch elicited small jumps and twitches. There was nothing like this rush of rendering my normally in-control girlfriend to such a state. But she wasn't begging though, not yet.

I lowered my mouth to the tender part of her inner thigh. I lightly bit down and I swabbed my tongue along the soft flesh, removing the cake frosting. I bit down harder and sucked. I could feel her tense beneath my ministrations. I nipped and kissed my way closer to her sex, but stopped just short.

I sat up again and collected the final frosting from the top of the cake. I brought my hand between Hunter's thighs and slowly, softly, outlined the curves, dips, and folds of her sex. The sweet cake topping mixed with Hunter's arousal.

"Not that you need to taste any sweeter, of course," I remarked in a low, raspy tone.

Hunter nearly rocketed off the bed when my fingers finally came in contact with her most sensitive flesh. I spread the frosting across her shaven folds, thinly covering her naked pussy lips with the light purple cream. My tongue darted out and with light, quick licks, I cleaned away the frosting. With each flick of my tongue, Hunter's body jolted as if being electrocuted.

I spread her pussy lips apart and slowly lapped at her inner lips, still refusing to touch her clit. I silently mused that I could spend the rest of the evening just like this – between Hunter's spread thighs.

"Please."

The word came out like a strangled prayer.

Our eyes locked, and I wordlessly cocked an eyebrow.

"I need you, Elle," Hunter panted. She strained against the scarves twisted around her wrists. "I need you inside me."

I removed my mouth from Hunter's sex. I swiped the back of my hand across my mouth, wiping away bits of frosting and arousal.

"Well," I mused, "if you insist."

Hunter groaned and pulled at her restraints again, causing the bed to groan and protest. "God damn it, Elle," she cursed. "I just want to cum!"

Hunter was always so patient, so polite, and I loved seeing her like this. But I'd made her wait long enough, I reasoned.

I sat up on my knees between Hunter's thighs. I pressed down lightly on her abdomen with my left hand, keeping her in place. My right hand traveled the distance from her knee, up her inner thigh, and hovered just inches from her desperate sex. I pressed two fingers against her slit.

I bit my lower lip. Her arousal coated the tips of my fingers. Every time I felt her like this I honestly wondered why every woman wasn't gay; I was addicted to this feeling. She rolled her hips and my fingers slid harder against her.

"Oh God," she whimpered. "Please. Keep going."

I could feel her struggling to make more friction and force my fingers inside her. I kept her pinned to the mattress, however, and continued my control. I shallowly dipped two fingertips inside her, just up to the first knuckle. Hunter's sex was swollen, warm, and wet around me, begging for more, but I resisted the primal urge to completely penetrate her.

"More. Please, more," Hunter pled, her eyes screwed shut. She sounded like she was going to die if I didn't fuck her soon.

I flipped her legs over my shoulders, and my slender fingers easily slid deep inside her.

"Fucking Christ," she swore as I bottomed out. Her heels dug into my lower back.

"Is this what you wanted?" I grunted between thrusts. I pistoned two fingers in and out of Hunter's clenching sex in short, rapid bursts.

I reached up with my free hand and twisted and tugged at Hunter's pert nipples. She yelled out into the room, her lips unable to form words. Her eyes closed tightly and her back arched off the bed as the first long-awaited orgasm washed over her.

The room was silent beyond Hunter's heavy breathing. After a moment, I pulled my digits free from her tightened sex.

"Good?" I asked smugly, already knowing the answer.

"Ah, fuck," she managed to pant in response.

I smiled and snuggled against her warm and sticky body.

"So as far as birthdays go," Hunter asked, still breathing hard, "how does this one rate?"

I flicked my eyes towards the alarm clock on the bedside table and grinned mischievously. "It's not done yet."

+++++

CHAPTER FOUR

My right nostril was stuffed and my left nostril kept leaking. My body ached all over like when Hunter dragged me on a run with her. It hurt to swallow and I'd become an unattractive mouth breather. In short, I was miserable. I grabbed another blanket and layered it on top of me. It was no use. No matter how many blankets I piled on top of myself, I was still cold.

Like clockwork, during the second week of every new semester, I got sick. All of those students' germs finally caught up with me. I rarely got sick any other time of the year, but when I did, I fell apart. It was just a cold, but try telling my body that.

I hated being sick. It made me feel weak. I hated anything that prevented me from doing whatever I wanted, when I wanted. My brain could have been urging me to go run a marathon, but so long as my body was in this state, I would only resent this sickness. It wasn't as if I could even run a 5K, let alone a marathon, but I loathed the simple fact that my body was uncooperative.

Hunter bounded down the stairs, a vision in pastels and cottons. How anyone made hospital scrubs look sexy was beyond my understanding. She always looked so put together, crisp and polished, but I think I liked her best in sweatpants and a tank top. It was like I got to see a side of her that no one else was privy to, like she felt comfortable enough around me to let her guard down. I wished I could do the same for her. I stood from the couch to greet her.

"Are you sure you don't want me to call in today?" she asked, grabbing a granola bar from the pantry. "It's not a big deal. It's not like they actually pay me for my time."

"No, no," I said, my voice more nasally than usual. "You should go to the hospital today."

"It's my job to take care of sick people, Ellio," she reminded me.

I waved a dismissive hand and held back a sneeze. "I'll be fine. I'm just going to hang out on the couch and nap."

"*You?* Nap? You must *really* feel sick."

I could only make a pained noise in agreement. All I wanted was to be taken care of, but I was too stubborn and too proud to ask for that. I hated letting anyone, let alone Hunter, see me like this. I wasn't on top of my game. My body was giving up on me and my traveling headache was making it even worse. A sudden cough attack overtook me and I coughed so hard and violently that I doubled over.

"Ellio." Hunter's voice dripped with sympathy and concern.

I waved a hand at her. "Save yourself," I said between the racking coughs.

She hesitated even more. I stood erect finally after the coughing subsided. I wiped the tears from my eyes. "You're going to be late. And if you're late, and it's the reason they don't hire you after graduation, I'll never forgive myself."

That seemed to be the magic combination of words because she picked her backpack up. "Call me if you need anything." She stared at me admonishingly. "I mean it."

I held up my hand in solemn oath, but I dared not speak in case it brought on another coughing attack.

When Hunter left, I threw myself down on the couch with an exaggerated groan. This was going to be a long day. Luckily, I had no place to be, because between the naps and the cold medicine, my brain was in a hazy fog. If my head hadn't been physically attached to my neck, I would have feared it would float away with nothing to tether it to this plane.

I faintly heard the doorbell. I ignored it though, knowing the only people who showed up during the day were solicitors. If it was someone I knew, they'd call my phone.

As if on cue, my cell phone rang. When I saw my mother's phone number flash across the screen, an uneasy feeling that I couldn't accredit to my head-cold settled in my stomach.

"Hey," I said as way of greeting when I answered the phone.

"Where are you?" my mom asked, eschewing any kind of civilized hello. I wondered if this was a belated birthday call. I hadn't heard from anyone in my family, not that I was surprised or disappointed.

"On my couch? Where are you?" I asked carefully.

"At your front door."

Even though my body ached, I threw off my blankets and bolted from the couch to the front foyer. I unlocked and yanked open the door to see my mother standing on my front porch. She had a wine bottle in one hand and wheeled luggage in the other.

"You look like crap," she said.

You know that old adage – a face only a mother could love? That wasn't my mom. I didn't say anything about her own appearance. Her hair was different than I remembered: longer and blonder. She looked a little pinched in the face, too. I hadn't seen her in years. We talked, but not religiously, on the phone.

"I've got a cold." Normally I thought I looked okay. I wasn't a fashion model or anything, but I stayed in shape and dressed professionally and age-appropriately. "My new boss is a homophobe, I keep getting older no matter how much I try to stop it, and my book proposal was rejected by a trade press." I listed off everything that had been weighing on my mind lately. "You didn't catch me on my best day."

My mother made a clucking noise, almost sounding amused at my list of complaints. "Sounds like someone needs a vacation."

My mother was a professional vacation-taker. It wasn't her actual job to go on vacation, but every time I talked to her she seemed to be someplace exotic rather than in my hometown. She took more vacations than anyone I knew. It was silly, but it was one of the things that bugged me the most about her.

"More like I'll be kissing my spare time goodbye since I'll be spending every free moment making massive revisions to my book proposal," I bitterly countered.

She breezed past me, into the front foyer, and slipped out of her jacket to hang it on a hook in the entranceway. "Well, at least you had time to answer your phone. I can't believe you were going to make me wait out there."

I sighed and shut the door.

My mom made her way to my kitchen and began opening and closing the cabinets looking for God-knows-what. She'd never been to my house before, yet she was acting like she lived here.

I shuffled after her and leaned against the kitchen island. "Mom, what are you doing here?" I was in no condition to entertain, let alone be polite.

"Oh, call it a Mother's Intuition," she said in a sing-song voice. "I sensed that you needed me." She patted me on the cheek. "Go get comfy on the couch, dear. I'll make soup."

+++++

"Ellio?" Hunter called out. I hadn't heard the key in the lock over the volume of the television and my mom's tinkering in the kitchen. "I stopped by the Vietnamese place and got you that soup you like." Troian had long ago turned me on to pho to cure everything from a hangover to the common cold.

I craned my neck from my seat on the couch to see her enter, one hand holding a backpack, the other the Vietnamese takeout bag. I was too buried under layers of blankets and afghans and a *House Hunter's* marathon to hop up to greet her. Plus, Sylvia was sleeping on my legs, pinning me to the couch. I knew better than to get up and disturb what was no doubt her seventh nap of the day. When she'd originally curled up on my lap I'd been touched, thinking she must have sensed I wasn't feeling well. But the more I thought on it, she probably just wanted to steal my body heat. Or my breath.

Hunter froze when she spotted a stranger in my kitchen. "Um, hello."

After a brief struggle I was finally able to shed the layers of blankets and hop next to my girlfriend. "Hunter," I said as way of introduction, "this is my mom, Vivian Graft. Mom, this is my girlfriend, Hunter."

"Nice to meet you," Hunter routinely offered.

My mom held up hands covered in sticky cookie dough and gave her a little wave. After the homemade chicken and dumpling soup, she'd launched into making my grandma's chocolate chip cookies. There was something definitely strange going on. My mom had never been any kind of domestic goddess.

"Get comfortable, girls," she announced. "The first batch of these cookies will be ready in about 15 minutes and I'll need some testers."

I obeyed my mother's command and pulled Hunter into the living room where she sat next to me on the couch.

"How are you feeling?" She kept her voice low as if she didn't want my mom to overhear.

I buried my face in her shoulder. "Not so good," I muffled. I breathed in her clean, sweet scent.

When I pulled away, she felt my forehead with the back of her hand. "Have you taken anything today?" she frowned.

"Not unless you count *You've Got Mail.*" Sometimes the only cure is a Nora Ephron movie marathon.

"You like that movie?"

"She doesn't just *like* that movie," my mom cut in from the kitchen. "She *loves* it."

Hunter raised her eyebrows. "You *love* it, huh?"

I pulled the afghan up and closer to my chin. "Don't judge," I whined. "It makes me feel better."

I didn't bother telling her about the time I watched the movie while running on the treadmill. I'd started crying at the end of the movie when Meg Ryan's face crumples when she realizes it's been Tom Hanks the entire time. I wasn't much of a runner to begin with, and crying while trying to run proved impossible. I'd been a sobbing, gasping mess.

"Isn't it about emotional dishonesty though?" she pointed out. "Tom Hanks and Meg Ryan are having an affair over email."

The blanket went even higher until it nearly covered my eyes. It was probably telling and not very flattering that cheating was the central premise of the one movie that never failed to make me feel better.

Hunter kept stealing glances at my mother in the kitchen who was currently humming rather loudly. She had officially become the 900-pound gorilla in the room. I knew Hunter wanted to ask why she was here, but I also knew she was far too polite to blurt out the question when my mom was within earshot.

She stood, stiffly, and walked in the direction of the second-floor staircase. I stared after her, confused.

"Baby, why don't you come upstairs?" she practically purred. She ran her fingers along the wooden banister and even in my cold-foggy state, I imagined them caressing my body. "There's something up there that's even better than cookies."

For the second time that day, all blankets were tossed to the side and I moved faster than my cold normally would allow.

My bedroom door hadn't yet closed before the question was out: "Why is your mom here?" Hunter demanded. She put her hands on her hips.

I held up my hands in defense. This wasn't at all what I'd been promised. I wanted to protest the false advertising. My grandma's cookies were about to come hot out of the oven downstairs, after all. "I have no idea," I said truthfully. "She showed up on my doorstep not long after you left this morning."

"Without warning you first?" Her voice was so sharp, it practically cut me.

I nodded.

"Who does that?"

"My mom, apparently. Didn't you get my text?" Even in my cold medicine-induced fog, I'd still been mindful to text Hunter a warning about my unexpected houseguest.

Her anger faltered, but only momentarily. "I forgot my phone here this morning." Hunter was a rarity in the Millennial Generation. She didn't participate in social media and she still used a flip-phone. I was more technologically savvy than her, and that was saying a lot.

"How long is she staying?" I had never seen her get so worked up. I couldn't understand why she'd be so upset by my mom's unanticipated visit.

"I don't know."

"What *do* you know?" Hunter asked, looking more and more irritated with each unsatisfactorily answered question.

"That I feel like crap," I sniffled, "and I just want to cuddle with my girlfriend."

The former annoyance on Hunter's face faded. "God, you make it hard to stay mad."

+++++

When I came downstairs the next morning I shouldn't have been surprised to find my mother still in the kitchen where we'd left her. Overnight, my kitchen had been turned into a French *patisserie*. Parchment paper covered nearly every kitchen surface. I wondered if she had gone to bed at all or if she'd been baking all night.

"Morning," I mumbled, plopping down on a stool at the kitchen island. My body ached, and I was definitely still sick.

"Coffee?" my mom offered, sunshine in her voice.

"Please."

She poured me a cup. "You still look like crap," she observed.

"I just woke up," I complained. I ran my hand over my face and through my unruly hair. My fingers got caught on a tangle that if left to its own devices might turn into a dreadlock.

My mom returned the coffee pot to its usual place with too much enthusiasm. "That girl. She's your girlfriend?"

"Yes, Mom," I sighed. I didn't bother to hide my exasperation. "And her name is Hunter, not 'that girl.'"

My mom fiddled with the rings on her fingers. Even though my parents had divorced when I was little, she still wore her engagement and wedding ring for some reason. She'd never remarried, had never gone back to her maiden name, and I didn't know if she'd ever seriously dated anyone after splitting with my dad. "I couldn't help noticing how young she looks."

"She's 21." I cupped my hands around the warmth the ceramic mug offered and inhaled its sweet aroma.

"But you're 31," she said, as if I'd forgotten my own age. "Is this some kind of mid-life crisis?" My mom put her hands on her hips. "Do lesbians have those?"

I wanted to tear out my hair. I know you're supposed to love your family unconditionally, but why did she have to make it so hard?

She stared me down. "And I didn't appreciate the way you two skipped away last night. You know it's rude to abandon a houseguest. I thought I raised you better than that."

"You're not a house guest. You're *my mom*."

"Exactly," she clipped. "Which is all the more reason to be polite."

"Sorry. It won't happen again," I said dully. I didn't think I had anything to genuinely apologize for – she was the one who'd shown up unannounced. She should have been happy I'd let her into my house at all.

"Why are you here, Mom? For real." My eyes scanned over the assortment of cookies and bars that covered my countertops. "And what's with all the baking?"

Her erect shoulders now slumped. "I got fired."

My mom didn't have a college degree, but she'd done well for herself. When my sister and I were growing up, she'd bounced from one job to the next, but was always moving up the economic ladder. The last time I'd bothered to ask, she had some fancy development job with the city where I'd grown up, turning abandoned lots into playgrounds and revitalizing the once quaint downtown area.

"You got fired?" I repeated, shocked by the admission.

"It's all politics," she said, waving an unconcerned hand. "The men on the City Council were intimidated by me so they let me go. They want someone in that job whom they can control." She winced. "But now I'm in a tiny little bit of debt," she added sheepishly.

My eyes widened. "All of those vacations?" I guessed.

"I suppose I should have been saving for a rainy day," she said wistfully. "Because now it's absolutely pouring." Her eyes snapped into focus and she leveled her gaze on me. "I need someplace to stay. I had to foreclose on my house."

"Foreclose?" I squeaked. This was getting worse and worse by the minute. "But why me? What about Lauren?" My sister, a few years younger than me, and her husband, still lived in our hometown. We didn't talk or see each other often, but we were on good terms. We just had that kind of relationship where we didn't need to talk religiously. But when we did see each other, it was as if no time had passed.

My mother wrung her hands in front of her. "I didn't want to be a bother. She and Matt just have the two-bedroom apartment, and with the baby on the way –."

"Lauren's *pregnant?*" Maybe I should talk to my sister more often.

My mom nodded. "And she told me that you'd gotten tenure and were living in this big house all by yourself..." she trailed off.

I let my head rest in my hands. My mom dropped a bombshell on me, and I didn't know how to react. I went for addressing the most immediate and visible issue – the baked goods taking over my living space. "What am I supposed to do with all this food, Mom?" I asked weakly. "There's no way the three of us can, or *should,* eat it."

"Can't you take it to school?"

There was nothing undergrads enjoyed so much as free food, especially pizza and baked goods. I myself had had a hard time shaking the habit of reaching for handouts after so many years as a student with little or no money. Even now with a steady salary I was hesitant to spend money. Frugality was a hard habit to break, but luckily I had a girlfriend I loved to spoil, even if she scolded me when I tried.

"Maybe we could have a bake sale," I suggested without thought.

My mother's frown was severe. "I don't find that funny, Elle. My financial situation is nothing to joke about."

No matter how old you are, there's nothing so powerful as a mother's guilt-trip. "I'm sorry," I apologized. "I wasn't thinking. But since you mentioned it, how much debt are we talking about? Is the IRS going to be knocking on my door and seizing *my* assets, too? Did you rob a bank to settle up and now you're on the lam?"

My mother smiled mildly. "You always did have a wonderful, if overactive, imagination. A lesser mother would have put you on medication," she congratulated herself. "Are you still writing?"

"I have to for my job," I nodded. "But even if it wasn't required, I'd still do it." I tapped a finger against my forehead. "There's too many voices in there, competing to get out."

"I wouldn't say that too loudly, dear," my mother said with an easy smile. "Normally people don't brag about the voices in their head."

I swiveled around on the kitchen stool when I heard light footsteps skip down the stairs. Hunter appeared, newly showered and pristinely primped. Instead of her usual scrubs or sweater and jeans, she wore a printed skirt that hit just above her knees and a sleeveless shell beneath a dark blue cardigan. The outfit choice was unsuited for her schedule that day, not to mention that it was well below zero with the wind chill outside. Her legs were going to freeze. I knew the clothes were because my mom was here, making Hunter feel the need to look perfect. It made *me* feel guilty. My favorite moments were when she let that sometimes rigid exterior falter to just be human.

"Good morning," she greeted with a practiced cheerfulness.

I stood and kissed her cheek, but frowned when I felt her stiffen as my arm went around her cinched waist. "You okay?"

She nodded, and as unobtrusively as possible, slid out of my reach. "Just nerves," she insisted, taking a quick sip of my coffee. "I've got a bedside manner test today, and I'm feeling unprepared."

"Why didn't you tell me? I could have helped you study." Normally I would have never let a phrase like 'bedside manner test' pass me by without turning it into a thinly-veiled sexual innuendo, but I held myself back for my mom's benefit and because Hunter already looked so uncomfortable in her presence.

Hunter glanced briefly in my mom's direction before returning her gaze to me. "I'll be fine. I just have to remember to smile more."

"And breathe," my mom offered unhelpfully.

Hunter gave her a forced smile. "Right," she said with a curt nod. "And breathe."

+++++

My phone vibrated for at least the tenth time that morning since I'd arrived at Del Sol. I glanced at the screen, but when I saw my mom's number *again*, I let it go to voicemail. She'd get the picture sooner or later. I shoved my phone into my work bag so I didn't have to see her constant texts.

"So your mom is staying with you?" Troian questioned.

"For the time," I nodded, taking an experimental sip of my coffee. "Although I honestly don't know how temporary this situation is going to be. It sounds like she's dug herself a serious financial hole."

Troian wrinkled her nose over the top of her own coffee mug. "That must make for some kinky sex with your mom sleeping downstairs in the guest room."

I luckily was no longer mid-sip, otherwise I would have spit hot coffee all over my friend. "I will *not* be having sex with my mom in the house."

"How do you pass up sex?" Troian looked truly flabbergasted.

I shrugged. "It's not the only important thing in life, you know."

Troian pointed at me and waved her finger around. "You *so* lose the right to bitch about being sexless from this day forward. So don't complain to me when Hunter stops spreading it for you."

"Ugh." I cringed at her words. "Why are you so crude?"

Troian grinned triumphantly. "Because I love the look on your face when I am."

I rubbed at my eyes. "My brain feels like mush today."

"Student papers that bad?"

I made a noise of agreement. "That and I'm still nursing this damn cold."

"I'm curious," Troian stated, tapping her fingers against her ceramic mug, "what makes a student paper painful?"

"Oh, you know; they do things like add unnecessary words and phrases just to bulk up their word count. Or, my favorite is when they give two thumbs up to a Pulitzer prize-winning author. Like, 'John Updike does a good job writing this novel,' – funny things like that. Plus," I continued to rant, "I see the same stylistic mistakes over and over again until I legitimately start to worry if *I'm* the one who doesn't know how to use commas."

Troian snickered while I made a disgruntled noise.

"And if my writing seminar doesn't pull their weight in discussion today," I continued, picking up steam, "I'm going to lose it. I'll shame them and send them home."

Troian's dark eyes widened a bit. "O-okay?"

"When you were in college, did you ever show up to a class that you hadn't done the reading for?" I asked, feeling myself unraveling. "Would you just *sit there* taking up space and oxygen instead of participating in class discussion?"

"All the time."

I threw my hands up. "Who *are* you people?"

Troian cocked her head to regard me. "Are you sure you're not sexually frustrated, Professor Graft?"

A little. But it wasn't my fault. I challenge anyone to feel sexy when they've got a cold and their mother is staying in their house.

"No. I'm just disgruntled. I'm still pissed about that book proposal rejection and that Dean Merlot thing, and now my mom is staying with me, so every little thing my students do is annoying me."

Troian hid a smile behind her coffee cup. "You know my response. You could always come work with me."

"I know, I know." I roughly ran my fingers through my hair. "But I'm fine. This is just my once-a-semester rethinking of my career choice. I'll get over it."

Despite the unnecessary headaches that working at this school provided me, I still loved teaching. I got a strange thrill of satisfaction looking across a sea of student faces, observing them diligently take notes while I lectured or watching them scribble furiously in their blue books during a final exam. There was something magical happening in that exchange of knowledge, and I'd be lying if I didn't admit to liking the power.

"Speaking of work – I, um, I have some news." Troian set her coffee cup down and regarded me with a serious expression.

"Uh oh. You're pregnant," I joked. "How are you going to survive without caffeine?"

Troian rolled her eyes. "As if."

"Am I supposed to keep guessing?"

Troian smirked. "That might be fun, but no. Nik and I, we're, uh…" She paused deliberately and cleared her throat. "We're moving to California."

I blinked once, taking my time to let the words connect in a meaningful order that actually made sense because what Troian had just said didn't register. "Say that again."

My best friend breathed in sharply. "The Studio tapped me as head writer for a new show they've given the green light. If I want to do a good job, I can't telecommute," Troian explained. "It's an amazing opportunity," she said, almost apologetically.

"What about Nik's business?" I asked. Who was I kidding? Forget Nik's business. *What about me?* I wanted to shout. First the annoyance of Dean Merlot, then the rejected book proposal, then my mom's unexpected arrival, and now *this*?

"We've never really needed the money in the first place, and with the pay bump I'm getting from the Studio, she really won't have to work. But even if she wants to start up a new landscaping business, California has sunshine and dirt to grow plants in, too."

"I can't believe you're leaving me." I felt gutted by this news.

"You're being overly dramatic, Bookworm. I'm moving, not dying."

"But what am I supposed to do when I'm having a nervous breakdown?" I demanded. "Who am I going to talk to?"

"Me, silly," she said, shaking her head. "There's this thing called a telephone. And rumor has it, you can even talk to people over the Internet. I know you're old, but I have faith you'll figure it out."

"I suppose congratulations are in order then." The words came out, but I felt the opposite of celebrating. "When's the big move?"

"End of the month. I've got so much to do between now and then. I've gotta find someone to sublet the townhouse, which, now in hindsight, seems like a ridiculous purchase," she grimaced. "We'll probably lose money, but that's my own fault for buying in this market. Know anybody looking for a two-bedroom condo?"

Both Hunter and my mother came to mind as candidates to sublet, but I knew that neither of them would be able to afford the rental property on their own. Then I thought about them being roommates. And then my head exploded.

"How much were you thinking about for rent?" The gears that worked my brain started to churn. I did some quick mental math. With the jump in title from Assistant to Associate Professor had come a significant raise. Even without the pay increase I had been living comfortably. I had planned on squirreling away the extra money into my savings account, but maybe it would be worth it to finance my mom subletting Troian's condo if it got her out of my house.

"I have no idea. I haven't had time to research comps. Why?"

"I will literally pay you to take my mother off my hands," I said.

Troian quirked an eyebrow. "It sounds like you're hiring a hitman."

"Don't tempt me," I said, only partially joking.

+++++

We hid from my mother that evening in my bedroom like teenagers. Truthfully, nothing made me feel more juvenile than knowing my mother was lurking around downstairs. When Hunter came over after finishing her afternoon at the hospital, I had just gotten off the phone with my sister. First, I'd congratulated her on being pregnant. Then, I'd berated her for telling our mother where I lived.

I buried my face in a pillow on my bed and yelled. It was overly dramatic, it was a pre-pubescent move, but sometimes you just needed to scream. I looked up when Hunter tugged at the pillow; my loose hair nearly covered my face.

Hunter brushed the hair away from my eyes. "Was that about your mom or Troi?"

"Both."

"You're really upset about them moving, aren't you?"

"I am," I nodded glumly. "And I know it's incredibly selfish of me. I should be ecstatic for Troi and this opportunity, not sad for me."

"Your best friend is moving across the country, Ellio. You're allowed to feel sad. You're allowed to feel things."

All of this was too much at once – the Dean breathing down my neck, the book contract falling through, my mom staying with me for who knew how long, and now my best friend was leaving.

"I should throw them a going-away party," I sighed.

"That would be nice of you."

I mentally shook myself. It would do no good to wallow in this. "How did your test go today?"

Hunter laughed softly. "I remembered to smile. And breathe."

I looked away from her angelic face when there was a knock at my bedroom door. My mom stood in the open doorway, looking timid. "Dinner's almost ready."

"You made more food?" I asked, sitting more upright on my bed.

She nodded. "But don't worry; I kept it reasonable. We're not opening a restaurant." She turned her eyes toward my girlfriend. "Hunter, will you be staying for dinner?"

Hunter flashed me a look of uncertainty.

"Yes, she is," I answered for her.

My mother's smile was tight. "Great. I hope you like lasagna."

+++++

I had never sat at a dining room table with my mother and whomever I'd been dating before. I had had boyfriends in high school, but I'd rifled through them so quickly that no one had ever been invited over for a meal. In college the situation had been similar; I hadn't figured out my sexuality until my Junior year, and by then my family and I had become distant.

I pushed my uneaten food around on my plate. There were too many awkward silences, but I couldn't come up with anything to fill the gaps in our conversation. The sound of knives and forks scraping against plates seemed louder than usual.

"So, Hunter...that's an interesting name," my mother not-so-innocently remarked. "If Elle had told me she was dating someone named Hunter, I would have thought she'd gone straight again."

"Mom!" I complained, letting my annoyance show.

My mom didn't look up from her plate and the dainty cuts she was making in the lasagna. "But it's not like you ever call me anymore."

"Whenever I do, you're always out of the country," I pointed out, waving my fork at her. "Besides, you have a phone, too. It works both ways."

"I'm just a little hurt you never told me you were dating someone new. What happened with Cady?" She set her fork and knife down. "I always thought you two would get back together."

"That was a long, long time ago, Mom," I sighed. "Cady and I are better at being friends than girlfriends." I hadn't talked to Cady since Hunter and I had officially started dating; we were barely even friends now.

Hunter cleared her throat. "This is really good, Mrs. Graft," she complimented.

"Thank you, dear. But please, call me Vivian."

Hunter took another bite. "Did you use Italian sausage instead of ground beef?" she asked when she'd finished chewing.

My mom nodded and took a sip of her red wine. "Good catch. I like the subtle kick it provides."

Hunter had been very quiet through dinner, but I couldn't blame her. It was an awkward back and forth between my mother and me. We really should have hashed things out, just the two of us, before I subjected Hunter to a family meal.

I kept waiting for the question – the obligatory origin story of how Hunter and I had met – but it never came. Either my mom had already guessed, or she didn't care, or she was too uncomfortable to ask those kinds of questions.

When we finished eating, Hunter was the first one out of her chair. "I'll clean up," she announced.

My mom started to stand up. "Don't be silly. Guests don't clean up."

My eyes darted between the two women, my mother and my girlfriend, mentally preparing myself for some kind of confrontation.

My mother's choice of words, calling her a guest, didn't appear to faze Hunter, at least not visibly. She picked up her empty plate and grabbed mine as well. "You made a lovely dinner, Vivian; it's the least I can do."

I scrambled to my feet. "I'll help, too."

Hunter waved a hand, shooing me away. "Sit down, Elle. I've got this. Keep your mom company."

I glanced at my mother who arched an eyebrow at me. I sat back down in my chair while Hunter cleared the table and brought everything into the kitchen. The kitchen and living room were open concept, but the formal dining room where we sat was separated from the primary living space. I could hear Hunter clattering around in the kitchen, but I couldn't see her.

I fiddled with the stem of my wine glass.

"She's awfully polite," my mom observed. I couldn't tell if her statement was meant to be a compliment or not, so I simply nodded in agreement. Hunter had impeccable manners, even in the most uncomfortable scenarios.

"She's sweet," my mom continued. She took a small sip of her wine. "Maybe too sweet for you."

I stopped fidgeting. "What's that supposed to mean?"

My mom gave no answer; she just shrugged and continued drinking her wine.

+++++

CHAPTER FIVE

Hunter and I lounged on the couch watching Saturday morning cartoons. Well, *I* was watching cartoons and she was reading out of a cumbersome textbook. She sat beside me with her long legs tucked under her. Unlike the skirted outfit she'd worn earlier, she finally looked relaxed in an oversized jersey sweater that fell off one shoulder that she wore over black leggings. Her feet were bare and her toenails were painted dark blue – the same color as her winter jacket. My attention was split between the adventures of Jake and Finn and the antics of my studious girlfriend. She did this adorable thing when she was deep in thought; she played with the end of her loose braid, running it under her nose like a paintbrush.

"What are you reading about?"

She opened her textbook wider for me to see. "Sexually transmitted infections."

I recoiled when I caught a glimpse of the glossy images in the textbook. "Oh my God. I wasn't ready for that." I crinkled my nose. "How can you study that first thing in the morning?"

She laughed and snuggled deeper into my side.

It was the day of Troian and Nikole's going-away party, but people wouldn't start showing up until late in the evening, so Hunter and I had the morning hours to ourselves. My mom had yet to make an appearance, so for now I enjoyed the time alone. I anticipated that as soon as my mom emerged from the guest room, Hunter would scoot to the opposite side of the couch. She was funny like that. She could stare down strangers who gave us a hard time about being Out in public, but for some reason, my mom's presence was making her shy.

"Why does she bother you so much?"

Hunter looked up from the textbook. "Who?"

"My mom. You turn into robot girl whenever she's around."

She snapped her textbook shut. "I do not," she protested in a stubborn tone.

"Babe, you're practically an ice princess when we're in the same room as her."

Hunter frowned deeply. "I didn't know I was being so obvious."

"You are." I shifted on the couch so I could look directly at her and not the television. It felt like we were about to have a serious conversation, and I didn't want *Adventure Time* to distract me. "So what's up?"

Her front teeth dug into her lower lip. "The last time a mom disapproved of our relationship, we kind of broke up."

Everything became so much clearer to me.

"I can assure you that my mom holds no sway over me."

"How am I supposed to know that?" Hunter asked, her voice rising an octave. "She showed up with chicken noodle soup when you were sick and made baked goods like she was a Little Debbie factory."

Even if I was loath to admit it, my mom's timing had been perfect. I was transported back to my childhood when she used to make me chicken soup with dumplings shaped into little hearts. When you're miserable, sometimes you just need your mom – no matter how old you are or how estranged your relationship has become.

"She likes you," I said.

Hunter snorted, not believing my words. "How can you tell?"

"She told me you were sweet."

"Sweet?"

"Uh huh," I confirmed. "In fact – her words exactly – that maybe you were *too sweet* for me. Hunt, my mom thinks you're *too good* for me, not the other way around."

Her eyes dropped demurely. "Oh."

I grabbed her hand and intertwined our fingers, pulling them onto my lap. She looked so beautiful, ethereal, with the sunshine streaming through the living room windows and reflecting off her honey-warm hair.

The doorbell rang and we both looked in the direction of the front door.

"Expecting someone?" Hunter reached for her oversized mug of coffee that had sat ignored on the coffee table.

"No." I thought maybe Troian and Nikole would show up early for the party, but that was still hours away. And Troian didn't use the doorbell. She knocked with purpose, like she was being chased by zombies.

I unhappily untangled myself from Hunter's long limbs and made my way to the front door. Normally someone unexpected at my house didn't rattle me, but with my mother's recent unannounced visit, I was now suspicious anytime I heard someone at the door. A short list of who it might be filed through my head.

I opened the front door, but there was no one on the other side. I heard a diesel truck start up and saw the delivery vehicle parked in front of my house. There was a small cardboard box on the front stoop. When I saw the return address printed on its top, I knew exactly what it was.

I closed the door behind me and eagerly tore into the thin box.

"Who was it?" Hunter called from the living room.

"Delivery person," I said. "It's my book."

"Your book? It's out?" Hunter hopped up from the couch.

"It's an advanced copy from my editor. It won't be available for sale for a few more months."

Still standing in my foyer, I finished unwrapping the book. Even though I of all people shouldn't have judged a book by its cover, I loved the way the cover art had turned out.

I handed the anthology to Hunter for the first inspection. Her eyes were wide, bright, and eager. She flipped the book open, and I got nervous. I hadn't told her that one of the stories was about her, and I didn't know how she was going to react. If it had been me, I'd probably be equal parts flattered and annoyed.

Her already wide mouth curled up into a warm, approving smile. "You dedicated it to Troian."

I'd nearly forgotten about that. Writing the acknowledgments and dedication page had taken nearly more purposeful thought than the rest of the book. At the time of its writing I hadn't been particularly close with my immediate family and my relationship with Hunter had been very new. Dedicating the book to Hunter so early into the relationship had seemed like the Kiss of Death. We might as well have gotten matching tattoos. Dedicating the book to Troian, however, felt right. Not only was she my best friend, but she was my constant and biggest supporter of my writing.

I wiped at my leaking eyes. The tears were unexpected. I needed to stop being selfish about Troian and Nikole moving. This was an amazing opportunity for both of them. Instead of feeling sorry for myself, I needed to give them the party of the year tonight.

Hunter's arms went around my waist and her head buried into my shoulder. "Don't be sad, baby. This is supposed to be a happy day."

Our arms detangled too soon. "Where are you going?" I complained as she left the foyer to return to the living room couch.

"I've got a new book to read," she called over her shoulder, "and you've got a house to clean."

+++++

I still wasn't in a celebratory mood by the time the going-away party started. Hunter had sent out the e-vites for me because every email I'd constructed read like I was hosting a wake instead of a celebration for my two best friends. Troian and Nikole were the first to show up. Even though it was a party for them, they'd insisted on arriving early to help me set up. Unlike the party I would be hosting later in the semester for the graduating English majors, getting ready for this party had only necessitated buying a lot of alcohol and making a music playlist that Troian wouldn't mock me about. The rest of the party-goers had arrived throughout the evening and I'd been kept busy for the first few hours answering the front door and making sure everyone had something to drink.

It was hard to be a good hostess, however, when Hunter looked so amazing. She looked too good in jeans. They hugged the curves of her lower body so perfectly it was as if the pants had been custom made for her body. It was almost a shame they were going to come off later tonight. Almost.

I watched her talk with someone I didn't recognize – probably one of Nikole's landscaping friends. Nikole often hired students from my university to work for her landscaping company over the late spring and summer months. Sometimes I alerted her to specific students I thought were hard workers and would do a nice job. Just by coincidence, Hunter had worked for Nik the previous summer. I hadn't thought to pass her name on probably because of my massive crush. I'd tended to think that any favoritism when it came to Hunter was inappropriate. We'd only realized our mutual connection through Nik the first time we'd gone out on a double date with my friends.

Hunter laughed at something and tucked a strand of honey-blonde hair behind her ear. Her hair was flat-ironed tonight and fell soft just below her shoulders. She wore light makeup around her eyes and just a hint of blush at her cheeks. Her alabaster skin practically glowed. She used to adorably panic before meeting people in my life for the first time, but tonight she hadn't even consulted me on her wardrobe choice.

"What?"

She'd caught me staring from across the room. I grinned innocently and drank deeply from my pint.

She was the youngest person at the party, but she had a particular talent for making friends in a room full of strangers. She was both warm and engaging, the kind of person you felt comfortable opening up to after just a few moments of talking. I imagined it made for an amazing bedside manner, especially in the pediatric wing of the hospital. Seeing her so engaged and confident, magnetic really, made me fall even more in love. I hadn't wanted to abandon her to a room of mostly strangers, but I had to continually check on things like freshen up the ice for drinks and refill chip bowls. I also didn't want to be one of those couples who couldn't survive at a party without being joined at the hip.

I spotted my mother in the living room, chatting with my ex-girlfriend, Cady. I hadn't known what to do with my mom. I'd suspected that once the tattooed, pierced, gum-chewing freaks started showing up that she'd slip away to the guest bedroom for the night. I'd also thought about giving her some money so she could go see a movie or something, but I knew her personality too well. She'd pretend to be wounded and play the martyr. I was happy that my mom had someone to talk to, but it made me uneasy to see her talking so genially with my ex-girlfriend. Cady and my mom had gotten along when we'd dated, probably better than my mother and I got along.

I had also waffled on the decision to invite Cady to the party, but she'd been close with Troian and Nikole when we'd dated and had maintained a friendship even after we broke up. It was unsettling to have my current and former girlfriend in the same room, but I knew it wasn't uncommon in the lesbian world. It was probably more unusual that it hadn't already happened.

Cady and I hadn't talked yet, but we'd at least made eye contact to acknowledge each other's presence. I hadn't talked to her in some time, actually – not since Hunter and I had started dating, at least. She'd been one of the first people I'd told about Hunter, but we'd lost contact since then.

I walked over to them out of a sense of hostess obligations, but I was also curious what my mom and Cady had been talking about with such intensity. I got a few steps away and heard my mother's voice. "Well, Elle has questionable taste."

"And an extremely supportive mother," I interrupted.

I tried not to appear too ruffled, but my mom didn't have the decency to appear chastised that I'd overheard her talking about me. Instead, she took a sip of her drink. "It's rude to barge into someone's conversation, Elle," she sniffed. "I didn't want to mention it, but your manners have gotten sloppy."

Cady laughed, warm and invitingly familiar. I hadn't realized I missed that laugh.

"Hey, you," I greeted, feeling awkward about the distance that had grown between us. "Glad you could make it."

Her hazel eyes regarded me over the top of her party cup as she took a drink. "I was surprised to get an invite to be honest."

"Why wouldn't I invite you?" I frowned. "You're friends with Nik and Troi, too."

Cady took another drink and hummed, but made no other comment.

"Cady was just telling me she got a promotion at work," my mom chimed in.

"Congratulations," I said. I saluted her with my drink. "Are you still at the bookstore?"

Cady nodded. "Yeah, so it's not really a big deal. More like they were just rewarding me for not leaving. I hear you got tenure though," she noted. "That's really great, Elle. I'm proud of you."

"Thanks," I returned uneasily. I wasn't comfortable with the compliment, not from her. When we were dating, I'd been married to the job. If she complained about me prioritizing work over her, I'd always promised her that things would change for the better once I got tenure. Now that I had tenure, however, it did her no good.

Cady's voice dropped conspiratorially. "Whatever happened with that student? You know the one..."

I scratched the back of my neck. "We, uh, we're dating."

"Oh, really?" she said in a falsetto voice. "Tenured professor *and* a young, nubile girlfriend? It's good to be you."

I cleared my throat uncomfortably and glanced in my mom's direction. She seemed disinterested in our conversation. Her gaze traveled around the party, looking for someone more interesting to talk to, no doubt.

"Which one is she?" Cady asked. Her hand fell on my forearm and my eyes glanced down at the touch that seemed too familiar. "No, wait. Let me guess."

She scanned around the open floor layout of the living room and kitchen. I wondered if she'd guess right.

"Ah ha." She grinned mischievously. "Leggy brunette by the built in."

The brunette description immediately told me she was wrong, but I was curious to see what kind of girl Cady thought I'd go after. Standing near my built-in bookshelf was a tall, slender brunette I didn't recognize. I guessed she was one of Nikole's employees who were, like Hunter, on the younger side. She was attractive, long limbed with an upturned nose.

"Nope."

Cady smirked. "She's blonde, isn't she?"

"Why aren't there men at this party?" my mom butted in.

I kind of stared at my mom incredulously. She shrugged and stirred her cocktail. "Just because you're gay doesn't mean you couldn't have invited someone for me to your party."

I rolled my eyes and turned my attention back to Cady. "Yes, she's blonde."

"I should have known," she smirked. She had her next guess ready. "Short stuff by the fireplace."

I turned on my heel to look in the direction of the fireplace where a pixie sprite of a girl whom I recognized from the crowd at Peggy's stood.

"Strike two."

"Good." Cady barked out a laugh. "I call dibs."

"She's all yours."

"Well, I'm out of guesses. Where's this perfect co-ed of yours?"

I quickly scanned the room and spotted Hunter having an animated exchange with Troian. There was another conversation I wanted to eavesdrop on. "She's talking to Troi over by the island."

"Very pretty," Cady murmured approvingly. "And look at those legs. It *is* good to be you."

"How about you?" I asked, feeling uncomfortable. Maybe Nikole and Troian had been right about not being friends with exes. "Dating anyone?"

Her nose wrinkled. "I was seeing this one girl for a few months, but it wasn't meant to be."

I didn't want to pry because I'd lost that privilege, so I didn't ask any follow-up questions about the break up. "I should get back to the party. Don't want to neglect my hostess duties," I excused myself. "It was good to catch up though. I'm glad you could make it."

Cady nodded. "It was good to see you, Elle. It's been too long."

I exhaled all the way back to the kitchen where I busied myself refilling the sink with ice and beer.

"That seemed to go well," Nikole observed. She fished a new beer from the sink, which was serving as my beer cooler. "No hair pulling at least. Very adult of you both." She congratulated me with a slight tilt of her bottle.

"Well, the night is early," I remarked, letting my gaze travel back in Cady's direction. She had moved on to the pixie-featured blonde from the bar whose name still eluded me. "It could still end in disaster."

Nikole shrugged. "I was never able to stay friends with exes, but you've made it into an art."

"You give me too much credit," I dismissed, shaking my head. Cady and I weren't friends anymore. It would take a conscious effort to rebuild what had been lost.

Nikole took a quick pull from her beer. "Does Hunter know who she is?"

At her name, I glanced in Hunter's direction. "No. But something tells me it wouldn't faze her. She'd probably go introduce herself and start swapping embarrassing stories about me."

Nikole beamed. "You've got a keeper there."

I leaned against the countertop. "I do, don't I?"

I excused myself to go say hi to my girlfriend. While Hunter reconnected with people she had worked with under Nikole, I had tried to keep my distance, not wanting to Out her to anyone she had known before we'd started dating. It was ridiculous of me though – Hunter had never shied away from letting people know she was dating a woman whether it was dancing at Peggy's, looking at cuddlefish at the aquarium, or having an awkward dinner with her family.

She and Troian were still chatting, and as much as I loved my best friend, seeing her engaged in a one-on-one conversation with Hunter made me nervous. She'd been the one to spill the beans about Ruby and my past; who knew what other dirty laundry of mine she was exposing.

I slid my arm around Hunter's waist. She instinctively pulled me tighter. "Having a good time?" she murmured in my ear.

"I think so." I had been too busy playing hostess all night to really enjoy the party myself. Everyone else looked to be having a good time, so I supposed the alcohol was working. For myself, I'd stuck to beer; if I let things get out of hand I was sure I'd turn into a weepy drunk, and that wasn't a good look on anyone.

"You're not sure?" Her pale blue eyes regarded me with new concern.

"I'm fine," I sighed a little. "Just being weird again. Plus I'd rather be spending time with you than making small talk with people from the bar."

Hunter's gaze left my face to appraise the living room. "It *is* an interesting mix of people."

The invitees were an odd assortment – people we'd met from being pseudo-regulars at Peggy's, a few women from writing workshops and book clubs, and people from Nikole's landscaping jobs, long-time clients and employees whom I didn't know.

"I wanted to give them a big party," I shrugged.

I'd stopped just short of inviting members of the English Department who'd had Troian guest-speak in their classes over the years. It was probably a smart move on my part. Some of the faculty like my mentor Emily would have been fine, but I couldn't imagine people like Bob or any of the Dinosaurs mingling with the lesbian bar crowd.

"Well, I think you succeeded."

"Are *you* having fun?" I turned the question back onto her.

Hunter nodded and took a sip from whatever concoction was in her red Solo cup. I'd thought about hiring some of the bartenders from Peggy's to be mixologists for the party, but then I didn't want to hurt anyone's feelings because I'd asked them to work the party instead of being a guest. Most everyone had stuck to beer or wine anyway.

"Yeah, it's been fun reconnecting with people I haven't seen since I worked for Nikole last summer."

Troian tottered over to where we stood. "Break it up you two."

"Have you been drinking?" I grabbed her glass and inspected its contents. The distinct aroma of rum greeted me.

She shrugged, all arms and shoulders. "It's my party, isn't it?"

I narrowed my eyes in concern. "You're not going to, like, go into shock and I'll have to stab you with an EpiPen when we re-enact the Uma Thurman scene from *Pulp Fiction*, right?"

"Nothing so dramatic, Bookie."

"Well that's a relief," I joked.

"Hey, did you ever tell Hunter about the Winter Jacket thing?"

I froze and the playful smile on my lips faltered. *No.*

Hunter, innocent, turned to me. "What winter jacket thing?"

"Giirrrrllll," Troian drawled. "She hasn't told you how obsessed she was with you when you were her student?"

Hunter arched a curious eyebrow and looked back and forth between Troian and me. "Obsessed?"

"Obsessed is a strong word," I protested.

"Whatever," Troian snorted. "Nearly every day she'd wax poetic about you; about something you did in class or some silly little interaction the two of you had that day," she continued. "It was gross. I'm glad she got over that."

"Why did you call it the winter jacket thing?" Hunter asked.

I covered my face with one hand. Was this really happening?

"Because that was your name," Troian clarified as if it was the most rational explanation ever. "That's what we called you."

"I still don't get it. Winter Jacket?" Hunter's confusion was writ on her beautiful face. "Why?"

"Because you kept your jacket on in class," I mumbled between the cracks in my fingers. This was horrifying. Why was Troian spilling the beans? I was never letting her near the alcohol again.

"Oh, so you mean like the Professor Skirt thing."

I slowly lowered my hand from my face. "What?"

Hunter shrugged, looking more amused than creeped out. "I may or may not have done the same thing about you with a few girls in the nursing program. I annoyed them all semester long with my pining over a devastatingly charming and gorgeous English professor with a penchant for short skirts and knee-high boots."

Troian's lip curled up. "You two are so cute it makes me want to puke."

"Sure that's not the alcohol making an encore appearance?" I teased, although I was seriously a little concerned because she'd been drinking. Because I didn't have children or messy pets, I could have white throw-rugs in my living and dining room. I didn't need her to make me regret that decision.

"Love you," Hunter said. She pressed her lips to the corner of my mouth. "I'm gonna go mingle and make new friends."

When she did things like that I wanted to wrap my arm around her and pull her in for a more thorough kiss. But I was mindful of our place and the mixed audience.

Hunter wandered off, and Troian leaned her head on my shoulder. She didn't have to duck or stoop; her head was exactly at shoulder-height. When we hung out we probably looked comically mismatched. Me, tall and broad shouldered with Anglo-Saxon features and she small-boned and Asian.

"Hey, thanks for doing this. I didn't want anyone to make a big deal about the move, but I'm glad you did."

"Any time."

"I'm gonna miss you, Bookie."

"Nuh uh," I chastised, wiggling a finger at her. "Don't you even start with that. You'll make me mess up my makeup."

Nikole chose that moment to join our conversation. "I hate to interrupt this Hallmark moment, kids..."

Troian wiped at her eyes. "I don't know what you're talking about," she denied.

Nik smiled knowingly. Troian and I had a unique friendship.

Someone less secure might have thought it suspect, but Nikole had always accommodated our oddities.

"What's up?" I asked.

Nikole grinned, broad and not a little bit mischievous. "Um, I think your mom might be flirting with Leah from the bar." She subtly pointed in the direction of the fireplace.

Even from this distance I could see that my mother was standing too close to Leah, or maybe it was the other way around. I wondered if my mom even realized that Leah was a girl. She was tall and built, with short, peroxide-blonde hair she usually wore spiked into a faux-hawk. Tonight she wore an open grey vest over a fitted white t-shirt and skinny black tie. My mom must've known though. Leah had the most feminine voice I'd ever heard. It was a startling contrast to her soft butch exterior, but it was that paradox that made her so popular at the bar.

They conversed with heads bent suspiciously close, my mother touching Leah's forearm, and every now and then Leah would erupt with too loud of laughter. My mother was no comedian. She was either spilling embarrassing stories about my childhood or Leah was being suspiciously polite—or something else altogether was unfolding before my eyes.

"Oh, hell no."

I abandoned my two friends and rushed across the room.

"Mom. Mom. Stop," I said when I reached her side.

She waved me off, annoyed that I'd interrupted whatever was happening. "Your friend Leah and I are in the middle of a conversation, Elle. I really thought I'd raised you better." Her eyes looked unfocused to me and her speech had become audibly slurred.

"Mom, I think it's time to say goodnight."

I flashed a look at Leah, both pleading and apologetic.

I tried to pry the wine glass from my mom's hand, but she slapped my hands away. She'd been drinking cocktails all night and I didn't know when she'd made the switch.

I looked back to Leah for help – she had to deal with drunk women all the time – but the traitor had slipped away, probably to go hit on some co-eds from Nik's company.

"Please, Mom," I implored.

"I'm fine," she sourly insisted. "Worry about yourself."

"Your mouth is purple," I told her. "At least brush your teeth and tongue so you're not so obvious."

She made a frustrated noise and spun on her heels to storm away, but at least she was storming away in the direction of the guest bathroom.

I scanned the crowd for Hunter and found her talking to Nikole and Troian. I caught her eye and motioned that I'd be right back.

The bathroom door was closed and I got no response when I lightly knocked. I tried the door handle and, finding it unlocked, went inside. My mom was leaning against the bathroom sink. The faucet was turned on and she had a toothbrush in one hand. She seemed to have forgotten why she'd come in here though. Her head was tilted down and her hair obstructed her face from my view.

"Mom?" I reached for the faucet and turned the water off.

She looked up and I saw her face through the reflection of the mirror over the sink. Under the unforgiving glare of the bathroom lighting her practiced mask had slipped away and I saw the sadness, regret, and worry that she'd worked so hard to hide.

"Did I embarrass myself out there?" she asked her tired reflection.

"No, you're fine, Mom."

"Your friend must think me an old fool."

"Leah would be only so lucky to have a woman like you hitting on her."

My mom brought her hands to her face and hid. Her boney shoulders slumped forward. "How did I get here? How did I get to this place in my life? Why don't I have it figured out by now?"

I had no answers to comfort her. I placed my hand on her shoulder and she looked up from her hands. "Why don't you try to get some sleep?" I gently coaxed.

She nodded somberly and set her toothbrush on the countertop, unused.

I helped my mom pour into bed. The first floor bathroom and the guestroom were only steps away, so we didn't have to make a scene when we left the bathroom. She didn't bother changing into pajamas, and I didn't point that out to her. I knew how she felt. Sometimes you needed to skip that step.

I took the time to get her a glass of water and a couple of aspirin and set them on the bedside table where she'd be sure to find them in the morning. I didn't know her alcohol tolerance, but after drinking all that hard liquor and enough wine to stain her mouth, I was fairly confident she'd be thankful for them in the morning.

I stood in the doorway with my hand on the light switch. Buried under layers of blankets my mom looked so small, almost childlike. I instantly felt guilty. I had seen her arrival as an annoyance to my routine, but she was just asking for help.

When I finally turned off the light I made a silent vow to myself to help her get back on her feet. We hadn't been close for a decade or more, but I was going to try to change that.

+++++

CHAPTER SIX

The next morning was rough. Hunter had left early because she said she had laundry to do. I privately thought that perhaps she just wanted to avoid my mom, but I also knew she had just taken on a new roommate she needed to bond with, too. I was glad she'd been able to find someone to take over Sara's part of the lease so easily. She didn't need something else to worry about in her final semester.

It was nearly noon when my mother finally emerged from the guest bedroom. I was in the kitchen, using the island as a desk as I worked on lesson plans. Normally I would have hidden away in my back den to work, but I had to confront my mom after what had happened the previous night.

My mom pulled one of the kitchen stools around the island so we sat across from each other. I poured two cups of coffee and set one in front of her.

"You can stay as long as you need to." I didn't really want to talk about what had happened the previous night. Even though I'd returned to the party with little incident after putting my mom to bed, I was still embarrassed for the both of us. "You always have a place here with me."

My mom's eyes filled up. When she blinked, a wall of tears fell from her eyes and landed on the front of the shirt she'd slept in.

"Mom, don't cry." I knew from experience that that was the worst thing you could ever say to someone on the verge of a breakdown, but the words still came out. My mother's face crumpled up and her chin quivered.

"Mom," I soothed. "It's gonna be okay. We'll figure this out."

"I'm a grown woman with grown daughters," she openly lamented. "I'm going to be a *grandma*," she added, her voice pitching up. "This shouldn't be happening. I should have things figured out by now."

I was out of encouraging words, so I patted the top of her hand.

"What am I going to do about a job?" she worried. "How am I going to get out of debt?"

"I'll ask around on campus and see if there's a job opening," I offered. "Maybe you could answer phones in the Admissions Office or reshelf books in the library."

Her sobs turned to sniffles. "You think they'd hire an old woman like me?"

I didn't hold my eye rolling back. Even at her lowest point, my mom could still fish for compliments. "You're not old, Mom." I said the words I knew she wanted to hear.

"Maybe I should take a page from your book and find a student to date. I could be a Cougar, couldn't I?"

I took that change in conversation as my cue to leave. I stood from the stool and put my half-empty coffee cup in the sink. "I'm going over to Hunter's now," I announced. "I'll see about finding you a job on campus tomorrow."

I left my mom sitting in the kitchen looking thoughtful and excited about new possibilities.

+++++

I was surrounded by Hunter's belongings; her delicate scent enveloped me like a comforting blanket. My head was on her lap and she was leaned over, her long hair falling forward and creating a space for just the two of us, like a weeping-willow tree. Her lips were warm and soft and we indulged in lazy kisses passed back and forth. It was just simple kisses at this point, but I knew if I applied more pressure against her mouth it could quickly escalate to more.

"Is your roommate home?" I asked. I still had yet to meet the girl who was now sharing Hunter's space, but she hadn't mentioned much about her, so I assumed the co-habitation was going smoothly.

"Maybe," was my girlfriend's response. Her addictive mouth curled at the edges. "But I don't want to share you." Hunter's lips found mine again.

It was easy to take for granted these quiet, intimate moments. With my mom always around, wandering around my house without purpose now that I'd put a stop to her compulsive baking, Hunter and I hadn't had much opportunity to be close like this and just enjoy each other's company. My mom's steps were purposely heavy and she cleared her throat a lot to announce her presence to avoid walking in on anything that might offended her virginal eyes, I supposed.

"Everybody decent?"

My entire body went rigid when I recognized the voice and the face that poked around Hunter's partially closed bedroom door.

"Hi, Professor Graft."

I immediately sat up and my hand went to my hair to smooth down the flyaways.

Loryssa?

Shit. *Of course* she'd be my girlfriend's new roommate. I shouldn't have felt so blindsided, but I was. It was a small school, after all; there had always been a good chance that whoever answered Hunter's roommate advertisement would be a former or current student.

Loryssa stepped into the room. Her hair was up in a bun, her face freshly scrubbed and free of makeup. She wore pajama pants low on her angular hips, and I couldn't help but notice that she was braless beneath her thin tank top. When I realized that, I immediately cast my gaze down to the tiny flower print of Hunter's sheets.

"I just wanted to say hi and goodnight," she said in her careful diction. She bounced on her toes. "I'm in for the night; I might watch a movie on my laptop or something."

I didn't think Hunter realized anything was off with me. "Ok. Have a good night," she cheerfully returned.

Loryssa gave us both a quick wave and a dazzling smile before spinning on her heel and disappearing from view. When she was gone, I still couldn't relax. My body tensed with every creaky footstep I heard as she went to her bedroom.

"She knows you." It wasn't an accusation, but I heard the question and confusion in her voice.

"Because she's in one of my writing seminars this semester."

Hunter's eyes went wide. "Oh, God. I should have asked if you knew her before she signed the lease. Is this going to be a problem?"

"Only if my Dean finds out," I said, feeling defeated by the coincidence. "She'll probably accuse me of recruiting undergrads to start my own lesbian harem."

Hunter's features squished together. "But Loryssa isn't gay. She's got a boyfriend. His name is Eric. He seems nice."

I shook my head forlornly. "That doesn't matter, Hunt."

Hunter's mouth twitched. "So I guess this means you won't be staying over anymore."

I sighed. "Not this semester at least. I'm sorry."

"No, I get it. You can't be parading around in your underwear when one of your students is my roommate." She shook her head. "I knew I should have asked, but what are the chances?"

The way that my luck was going this semester it would have surprised me if Hunter's new roommate *hadn't* been a current student.

"Don't go," I objected when Hunter stood from the bed and walked toward her bedroom door.

"I'll be right back," she chuckled at my reaction. "I just need to finish getting ready for bed."

It was still early – too early for sleep, but I slid under the covers of the bed, regardless. When Hunter returned from the bathroom, she snuggled in close and pressed her mouth against mine; she tasted extra minty, like she'd rinsed with mouthwash.

Her hand snaked beneath the covers. When her hand reached me, she laughed. "Why is your shirt tucked into your pajama pants?"

"I was cold!" I protested. I hated that moment when you first got under the covers and it took a while to warm up the bed. I loved the feel of chilly cotton sheets against my skin at the apex of summer, but not in the middle of February in the Midwest. Hunter's apartment was habitually frigid despite the radiant heat. It was an older building that lacked energy efficiency. Precious heat escaped through the ancient windows that rattled with every violent gust of wind.

She roughly tugged my t-shirt free from my elastic waistband. "I'll warm you up, baby," she reassured. Her fingers slipped beneath my shirt and traveled up to palm my naked left breast. I sucked in a sharp breath as she slowly dragged her nails against my hardened nipple. She wasn't one for empty promises; my temperature instantly spiked.

Even though I wanted nothing more than for her to continue "warming me up," I was also acutely aware that her new roommate, one of my current students, had a bedroom on the other side of the apartment. I should have removed myself from the situation and gone home as soon as I found out about Loryssa. We might as well have been at my house with my mom. It actually would have been preferable because the walls were better insulated and the guestroom where my mom stayed was on the first floor.

I laid my hand over hers on my breast. "We shouldn't..."

I heard her sigh. "I know." Her hand slid out from beneath my shirt and rested innocently on my hip. "God, this is frustrating," she groaned.

"Believe me, I know," I said through grit teeth as her hand resumed its less than innocent intentions. Her fingertips danced softly along the narrow strip of exposed flesh between the waistband of my pajama pants and where my shirt had ridden up.

"When are we going to have a space to ourselves again?" Hunter asked quietly.

Between my mom staying at my house and now a current student as Hunter's new roommate, I feared we'd never truly be alone again until I found a more permanent living situation for my mom.

I closed my eyes and exhaled deeply. "Not soon enough."

+++++

I was running late the following morning, and my shower had been lukewarm. It left me feeling cranky and unclean. It had been an oversight on my part that there were now *three* people who needed to get ready with only one bathroom to share. Prior to Loryssa, if Hunter was monopolizing the bathroom and I needed to get ready, I could just walk in while she was showering or blow-drying her hair. Now, however, I had to be patient; a difficult task when I didn't have the luxury of being late for a class waiting on my arrival.

I was out the apartment door with no time for breakfast and only a fleeting kiss to my girlfriend as I hustled to make my first class of the morning. I could feel myself start to perspire as I drove because of my phobia about being late, rendering my shower useless by the time I made it to campus. I ended up being only a few minutes tardy to my first class, but that hurried and unsettled feeling followed me all morning.

My second class of the day was the writing seminar with Loryssa on the roster. She strolled into class a few minutes early and smiled in my direction as she sat down at her desk. I forced myself to look back down to my lesson plan and mentally prepare for that day's class. I really didn't know what to expect from her in light of her new living arrangement. I only looked up when I sensed someone's presence.

Loryssa stood in front of me with only the teaching podium between us. Her skyscraper heels made her slightly taller than me that day. "Did you have enough hot water this morning? I have a bad habit of taking too long of showers."

At her words I reflexively darted my eyes around the room. Her voice wasn't particularly loud, but the question itself was a shade scandalous.

"I-it was fine," I said curtly.

She leaned against the front podium and drummed her fingernails against its top. "Do you want to carpool to campus sometime? Hunter rarely has to come to campus for her classes, but I thought maybe you and I could."

"I won't be spending the night in the future."

Loryssa's carefully crafted eyebrows knit together. "Are you guys fighting?" she frowned.

This wasn't the time or place to have this conversation. I had a class to start and the last thing I needed was someone listening in on this conversation and having more rumors spread on campus.

I dropped my voice low to lessen the chance of being overheard. "Hunter and I are fine. But you're my student, Loryssa, so it's inappropriate to be having pajama parties."

Her concerned frown deepened. "But you and Hunter—."

"Didn't date until after I ceased being her teacher," I cut her off. "And if you'll please take your seat, I have to begin class now."

I saw her hesitate; I could tell she wanted to say more, but thankfully she followed my cue and returned to her seat.

I glanced up at the classroom clock and then out to the dozen and a half students who populated the class. Nothing seemed amiss, so I tried not to let my conversation with Loryssa consume my thoughts.

"Let's start with a free-write this morning," I announced to the class.

"Everyone take out paper, or those of you with laptops, open up a new word document."

I started to write a question on the board that students would respond to. I liked to use these free-writing exercises, particularly on a Monday morning, because it jumpstarted students' brains.

The door to the classroom swung open as I continued to scrawl on the chalkboard. I expected to see a student coming in late, but I didn't recognize the woman who came through the door. She was older, maybe in her late 40s or early 50s. Her black hair contained streaks of grey, pulled back in a severe bun. Her black suit was shapeless and her boots were unattractive.

"Can I help you?" I practically snapped.

"I'm from Dean Merlot's office, Professor Graft. I'm here to observe your class today." She purposefully traversed the entire length of the classroom, as if claiming the space as her own, to sit down at a vacant desk in the back corner of the room. I watched her set her briefcase on the floor near her chair. She pulled a yellow legal pad from her bag along with a pen. "Please continue," she instructed me, clicking the writing utensil to life.

Shit.

It wasn't a surprise that Dean Merlot planned to observe our teaching by proxy; I'd thoroughly read the email after Thad had warned me about it. But I hadn't expected to be personally evaluated so soon. I wasn't sure how I managed to remain focused for the remainder of the period between Loryssa and Dean Merlot's micro-manager both glaring at me. But by some miracle, the class period passed with minimal awkwardness. Once I reoriented my focus, I was able to block out the external distractions and teach.

I felt dizzy with stress by the time the class period came to a close. I dismissed the students and took a moment to take a few cleansing breaths as I collected my materials. Loryssa approached me, but I held up my hand before she could say anything.

"I don't want to turn this into a big deal," I said. "You're my girlfriend's roommate, but you're also a student in this class. So until one of those statuses changes, I won't be staying over and you and I will maintain a rapport appropriate for professors and students. Understood?"

She bit her lower lip and nodded.

I tried to give her a friendly smile to lighten the moment, but it felt strained. "Do you have any questions for Wednesday's class?"

"No, you've been perfectly clear, Professor." Her caramel colored eyes regarded me coolly and she shouldered her bag. "Have a nice day; I'll see you Wednesday."

The rest of the students filed out and the Dean's spy came to the front of the room when we were alone. "What was that about?"

I had no idea what she'd overheard. "Nothing that concerns my teaching evaluation."

She looked a little taken aback by my response. I hadn't intended for my words to have such bite, but this day was wearing on me and it wasn't even lunchtime.

"Are we done here?" I tried to keep my tone civil, but everything that came out of my mouth sounded like I was pissed off. I threw my papers into my messenger bag. "I have another class to get to shortly."

The woman flipped through the notes she'd taken on her legal pad. "No, I uh, I have all I need."

I walked toward the classroom door, intending to make a silent, yet dramatic exit.

"One last thing, Professor Graft." Her words made me pause in the doorway. "The Dean wanted me to let you know she received your email concerning Professor Wagner."

I'd nearly forgotten about the letter I'd sent Dean Merlot's office the Friday of my birthday to protest the re-allocation of funds which had forced Kathy from Sociology to abandon her experiential course on women's reproductive issues and rights.

"Is that why you're here?" I demanded. "Because of that email?"

The woman looked flustered. "Of course not. Everyone will be evaluated."

"Uh huh," I threw back, not believing anything from her mouth. "Have fun with that."

+++++

I sat in my office, staring blankly at my computer screen. I had a mountain of emails to respond to, but I wasn't inspired. It had been a long week for me mentally. I'd successfully avoided a stack of student essays. I'd even written 'grade' on my To Do list and had crossed it off without ever starting the task. I congratulated myself for being so rebellious.

I was supposed to be meeting with a student in my 20th century Literature course about a paper she had "written" that was copy-and-pasted from Spark Notes, but I was being stood up. Plagiarism *and* missing a meeting – this student obviously did not want to pass my class.

"Knock, knock." Hunter's beautiful face beamed at me through my open office door.

"Hey, you." I stood from my desk to greet her. "Is everything okay?" Based on my morning classes, I expected the worst.

"Of course it is. I just thought I'd bring lunch to my favorite professor." She waved a wax-paper bag which I knew contained a sandwich from my favorite downtown deli. "I know you missed breakfast."

She leaned across the desk, waiting for a kiss hello. I glanced at the open office door. Who knew how many of Dean Merlot's spies might be lurking out in the hallway? I hated that the thought even came to mind. I shouldn't have to look over my shoulder every time I wanted to kiss my girlfriend. But I also hated the conference Bob had had with me about it. It had felt like getting called into the principal's office, but I'd done nothing wrong.

I kissed her, tight lipped and brief. If it was unsatisfactory, she didn't say as much.

"Question," I posed as she settled down into the chair across from my desk and began to unpack our lunch.

"What, hun?"

"When Loryssa called you about the apartment, did she know who you were?"

Hunter's brow knit. "No, we'd never met before."

"I mean, did she know you were Professor Graft's girlfriend?" I tried to clarify. It felt unnatural to refer to myself in the third person, but I had a purpose for asking the question.

She looked thoughtful. "I didn't post my name on the flyer, just my number. She called and we met for coffee, and since she wasn't a socially awkward mutant, I brought her by the apartment to give her a tour. I may have mentioned I had a girlfriend named Elle, but I really can't remember."

I felt a twinge of jealousy that Hunter hadn't mentioned any of this to me before now, but I calmed myself. She hadn't done anything wrong. It wasn't infidelity to have coffee.

Hunter frowned. "You're thinking she sought me out to get special treatment in your class?"

"Maybe? I don't know." I sighed and fell back into my office chair. It sounded so egotistical when actually voiced, but I was still suspicious. "She just acted so...*unsurprised* to see me in your bedroom last night."

Hunter made a thoughtful noise. "You make a good point."

"Well, regardless of her intentions, it won't be a problem now," I noted. "I had a talk with her after class today about boundaries, plus it's not like I'll be running into her anymore when I'm brushing my teeth."

"Are you *sure* you can't stay the night anymore?" Hunter openly lamented.

"It'll only be for a little while," I promised. "It's practically Spring Break, and then the semester will fly by."

She sighed and looked disappointed. "Okay. You're right. Once the school year is over, things will be back to normal for us."

I thought about my interaction with Dean Merlot's teaching evaluator, and I wasn't quite so sure.

"I was thinking about going to the track after work today," she said as she bit into a ham and cheese sandwich. "Do you want to come?"

"Only if you don't make me run."

Sometimes we went to the local high school track after work. Usually Hunter ran while I sat in the bleachers and read, wrote, or graded papers. She was like a gazelle, long legs striding like she was hardly exerting any effort. Her leg movement was so fluid and languid she looked like she was barely moving except when there were other people on the track and she strode past them. I'd discovered that runners were a different breed of person with their own culture. She'd gotten to know a few of the people who also religiously ran at the track, and listening in on some of their conversations was like observing aliens.

She'd dragged me on a few runs and had even helped me pick out a new pair of running shoes, but I just wasn't mentally tough enough to go more than a mile or two without my mind convincing me I was going to die. I'd thought myself mentally tough or at least in shape enough to keep up with her, but I'd sorely overestimated my own abilities. But she didn't tease me; she was just gently encouraging throughout it all. She said she'd get me to run a 5K race with her some day.

"Hey, you want to get a drink tonight?" My friend Emily walked into my office without knocking. "So sorry!" she exclaimed when she noticed I wasn't alone. "I didn't know you were meeting with a student." She turned crisply on her kitten heels and walked straight out from where she'd come.

I practically leapt from my chair. "Emily!" I called out to her.

She paused and came back. "Yes?"

"This is Hunter." I didn't spend much time off-campus socializing with my co-workers, so I hadn't felt the need to introduce Hunter to everyone in the Department. Emily was different though.

"Oh!" Emily exclaimed, recognition coloring on her face. "I'm so sorry I called you a student. I had no idea." She flashed a reproachful look at me. "*This one* never puts up any personal belongings in her office, let alone a picture of her girlfriend."

"It's okay," Hunter dismissed easily. She abandoned her sandwich and stood up to greet my friend. "Technically I *am* still a student for a few more months."

Emily was silent while she took in Hunter's presence. Her eyes narrowed perceptively. "So you're the reason my dear colleague has put up with so much grief this past year."

"Oh, lord. Emily, that's not fair," I chastised.

"I'm sorry," Emily said with a mischievous grin. "I couldn't help myself." She continued to look between the two of us with that same impish grin. "We'll have to do dinner sometime," she offered. "There's a new Indian place I've been wanting to try."

Hunter was doing her best impression of a robot beside me. I kept my hand firm against the small of her back as a stable, reassuring presence. "Sounds great," I said. "We love the stuff."

"Henry's IBS might not," Emily commented with a snort, "but maybe he'll just have to stay home and we'll have a girls' night." Emily was a Rhodes Scholar and I bet she'd never before uttered the phrase "Girls' Night" in her life.

With a promise that we'd get together soon, Emily left us to our lunch. Hunter flopped down on the extra chair in my office. "Do you really still get a hard time about dating me?" She sat up more erect in the chair. "Tell me the truth."

"Emily was exaggerating," I insisted. "Everything's fine." Even though the words came out, I couldn't help but glance back at the open office door and wonder when my next run-in with Dean Merlot would be.

"Is this something that's really going to happen? Dinner with her and her husband?"

"Probably not," I admitted. "Not because of you," I was quick to add. "I think Emily was just being polite. She's never invited me and my significant other out for dinner with her husband before. I've actually never even met the man. I'm kind of convinced he doesn't exist."

Hunter looked more at ease. "I guess I didn't think about what dating a professor would really mean. Everyone's so *smart*. Like, total brains. I wouldn't even know what to talk about."

"You hold your own with me," I assured her.

"But you're different, Ellio. You're not like a regular professor."

I didn't know if that was meant to be a compliment or not. "What's that supposed to mean?"

"It's a good thing," she insisted. "You're not The Job; you don't talk about literature and sentence structures constantly. Plus," she added with a cheeky grin, "I'm not sleeping with them."

"You'd better not be," I playfully growled.

"Although…" Hunter stroked her chin, looking thoughtful. "Emily *is* pretty attractive for an older woman."

"Now we're *definitely* not having dinner with her."

+++++

CHAPTER SEVEN

It was raining the day Nikole and Troian left for California. The weather appropriately matched my mood. Rain splattered against the bay window in the open-concept kitchen where I'd had many a dinner with my two closest friends. They hadn't owned the townhouse for very long, but we'd collected memories in this place in a short time.

The rain accumulated on the kitchen window, distorting the view outside of a small, green park. Down in the complex parking lot was a modest-sized moving truck. They weren't bringing their large furniture with them in the Uhaul because they still had to find someplace in the Los Angeles area to rent. Troian's employer was putting them up in company housing until they found something more permanent.

Because of that, the condo itself didn't look much different; it would have been hard to tell that whoever lived here was moving away unless you knew where to look. Various mementos and knick-knacks had been packed away and all of Nikole's houseplants were gone. She was taking a few with her, but most of them were going to friends' houses, including mine. I'd inherited an adolescent banana tree that I would unintentionally kill as soon as they crossed the first state line.

Hunter leaned against me and we looked out the window at the dreary landscape together. "I've always liked this place. I bet it sells fast," she mused. She'd volunteered to help Troian and Nikole pack up the last of their things with me. She'd already helped her old roommate Sara pack up her things earlier in the month. She was a living saint.

"Maybe," I murmured. There was a person playing with a large black dog in the park despite the wet weather.

"Don't forget I'm having dinner with my parents later, so you'll have to fend for yourself tonight."

I made a noncommittal noise that originated from deep in my throat.

"Are you gonna be okay, Ellio?"

"I'll get through it," I sighed, turning from the window.

I was so incredibly proud and happy for Troian and this new career opportunity, but I couldn't help feeling sorry for myself. It was ridiculous, but I couldn't restrain my emotions. I was losing my best friends. That never got any easier.

Friendships had been easy growing up in a small town. You couldn't be picky – if someone went to your school and did a lot of the same clubs and activities as you, you were friends. I had a few friends on the faculty, and I guessed I could call some people who worked at Peggy's my friends, too, but I had far more acquaintances than people I considered close confidants. And I balked at the idea of making new friends. I wasn't naturally gregarious or outgoing. I could be stiff and standoffish, reserved and private, when meeting someone new.

The front door opened and Troian walked in looking a little damp. "I guess that's everything," she said, speaking as somber and as serious as I felt.

"Pack up all the sex toys and torture devices?" I half-heartedly joked. "Your realtor might get the surprise of her life if she finds your stash."

Troian laughed, but it sounded hollow. I wondered how she felt about the move. She and I hadn't talked extensively about it, and it made me feel like I'd shirked my Best Friend responsibilities. I think we'd both been trying to deny that this was really going to happen.

Hunter and I followed Troian outside. The rain had mostly stopped. The ground was saturated, but the rain was just a mist now.

"You still have your keys in case I need something shipped to me pronto, right?" Troian asked me as we made our way down to the moving truck where Nikole waited.

I touched my hand to my jacket pocket where the keys resided.

"Yep." I'd also promised to keep an eye on their condo until it sold.

"And if your mom starts driving you crazy, the offer still stands to let her stay at our house until she gets back on her feet," Nikole noted.

"We will definitely consider that," Hunter laughed. She bumped her hip into mine and I smiled for the first time that day.

Nikole opened the driver's side door of the moving truck. "Time to get on the road. We've got a long couple of days ahead of us."

I hugged my best friend. "Call me as soon as you get there."

Troian pulled back from the hug and gave me a goofy grin. "Sure thing, Mom."

I dismissed her with a growl. "I worry. I've seen you drive."

Nikole laughed. "Don't worry. I'm only letting her drive when we get to the flat states where the only thing she has to worry about is cows in the streets."

Troian stomped her foot. "Enjoy it while you can, you two. This is the last time you get to gang up on me for a while."

Normally her choice of words would have brought a quip about threesomes to my lips, but instead the truth sobered me. "When am I going to see you?"

Troian's features became serious as well. "When can you come out to LA?"

"I don't know," I said truthfully. "Maybe we can find a long weekend soon that works."

Troian nodded. It would have to do.

I gave my best friend one final hug. Nikole and Hunter shared a brief embrace as well. Troian walked over to the passenger side of the vehicle, wiping at her eyes. I could only imagine the emotions she must have been feeling. Change like this was exciting, but also scary. Even Nikole, the more stoical of the two, looked a little frayed at the edges.

The rain picked up again and Hunter and I stood back under an awning as Troian and Nikole climbed into the moving truck. Hunter's hand found mine. Our fingertips brushed against each others' before she took a more forceful hold of my hand. We watched and waved as our friends began their grand adventure.

+++++

It continued to rain all evening. It was my least favorite time of year when everything gets covered in old, crusty snow or mud. At least the constant rain would help wash that away. I ached for warm spring days when I could sit on my front porch with a cocktail in one hand and a book in the other while gangs of chickadees chirped in the distance. Spring was too short in the upper Midwest. It was either winter or summer – spring usually lasted a long weekend when tulips began to poke up through the just recently thawed ground.

I was caught up with grading and course prep, so I enjoyed a rare moment of free-time. I could have used the break from course work to work on my next manuscript, but instead I was rewarding myself by re-reading an old favorite, *Wuthering Heights*. I'd read all the similar classics when I was in 8th grade, just for fun, but I'd been too young and naive about the world to truly understand the predicaments of characters like Catherine Earnshaw or Lizzie Bennet or Jane Eyre.

I heard a key in the front door lock and the sound of the door swinging open. Hunter was having dinner with her parents tonight, so I knew not to expect her until later. There was a slight jangling of keys and then the frustrated grunt that belonged to my mother.

"How was your first day of school?" I smiled.

Even though the Monday morning after Troian and Nik's going away party had been hell for me between confronting Loryssa and having my writing seminar evaluated, I'd kept my promise to my mom and had stopped by the university library to see if they had any job openings. I knew most of the circulation and reserve librarians from everyday interactions and the head of library services from being on a number of committees together. They were probably the one support-staff team I was closest to because of our mutual interest in books. They usually hired students to fill the more mundane tasks like working the circulation desk or re-shelving books, but I'd hoped they could accommodate my mom. She needed a reason to get out of bed every morning so she'd leave my wine rack alone.

"My head is so full of number and letter combinations, it might explode." She dropped her purse on the kitchen island and sighed. "I need a glass of wine."

I laughed, standing up from my seat near the fireplace, and went to the dining room where my wine rack was located. I returned to the kitchen with a bottle of Chardonnay.

"So did you not like it?" I asked as I poured my mother a glass of wine. I started out conservative until she raised an expectant eyebrow as if to say, 'that's all I get?'

"It was fine," my mom conceded. "The work is a little brainless, so it's obviously not my dream job, but the people seem nice enough."

"And the wages are more than fair," I noted. When I'd originally seen the hourly pay, I'd considered hanging up my teaching shoes to become a librarian instead. Thinking about spending my days surrounded by all those books and words was like an English Professor's erotic dream.

My mom nodded and took her first sip of the overly generous wine pour. "It'll do for now until I figure out what I'm supposed to be when I grow up."

I saluted her with the wine bottle I had no intention of drinking. "Join the club."

"What are you talking about?" my mom scoffed, sounding almost offended. "You've always wanted to be a professor." She set her wine glass on the kitchen island.

"I know," I agreed. "And for so long my goal had been to get tenure. But now that I've got that, I don't know what to do with the rest of my life."

I had always had an immediate goal in mind to guide me through my professional and private life from graduating high school to graduating college to getting my doctorate and my first teaching job. Then I'd been focused on publishing and getting tenure.

"Well, what's the next step? How do you go from Associate Professor to Professor?"

"Keep doing a good job teaching and publish another book," I said. "But I don't have to worry about that for another six or seven years; they won't consider me for another promotion until I've met that next milestone."

"Wow. I had no idea it took that long," my mom said, shaking her head. "And what happens after that? After you get to be a full professor?"

"I don't know," was my honest reply. I didn't have the typical trajectory for my life — there wasn't the goal to get married, buy a house, and have a couple of kids. I already had the house, I wasn't sure I ever wanted to get married, and I was sure I didn't possess a single maternal bone in my body. "I don't know what's next."

My phone rattled on the kitchen island with an incoming email to my campus address. The subject line made my breath catch in my throat: "Your Teaching Evaluation."

I rushed to the back of the house to the den where my computer resided, leaving my mother sitting in the kitchen without an explanation. I didn't bother turning on an overhead light as I headed directly for my laptop. My stomach churned as I waited for the campus email program to open.

I hadn't thought much about the woman who had come to observe my writing seminar earlier in the week. She hadn't mentioned when I might receive feedback or the format through which it would be communicated, and I'd been too annoyed that day to ask. Student evaluations at the end of each semester were stressful enough; although the majority of student comments were always positive, I had a tendency to linger too long on the rare negative review.

I opened the email with its attached document and briefly scanned its contents. The evaluation itself was surprisingly brief for the Dean to have gone out of her way to even bother with the observation in the first place. The review commended my level of instruction with minimal criticism. To me it seemed like an inadequate tool if it was truly going to be used to assess merit raises.

"Is everything okay, Elle?" My mom hovered in the doorway of the den. The light from the hallway spilled around her silhouette and into the dark room. I could understand her concern; I'd run out of the kitchen without a word to her like my hair was on fire.

I stared at the words at the bottom of the email: *Based on classroom observation and previous history, it is recommended that Professor Graft be reminded about professionalism in the workplace.*

"Yeah, Mom," I said. The words were tight in my throat. "Everything's fine.

I laid in bed that night, listening to the soft rain clatter against the tin roof of my house, thinking about the conversation I had had with my mom. What did I want to be when I grew up? What were my goals now that I had an amazing girlfriend and had achieved tenure? Had I plateaued? Was this all I could hope to achieve in life?

Thinking about Troian and her brave decision to move across the country was making me second-guess the trajectory of my own life. Did I want to teach for the rest of my working life? Would I still find satisfaction championing the Oxford Comma and drilling the 5-paragraph essay into undergraduates' heads 10 years from now? What about 20 or 30?

Sometimes I found myself being contemplative as I watched a group of students struggle over a midterm or final exam. Who would they become after graduation I wondered. Would they go on to do great things? Would they ever remember the skills they had learned in my classes?

The Dean's evaluation did nothing to assuage the worries currently bouncing around in my brain. My teaching itself was irreproachable – the observation had said as much. But the final recommendation was weighing heavily on my mind. *Professionalism?* The statement had been too vague for my liking. Was she referring to my disrespect toward the evaluator? Had she overheard my conversation with Loryssa? Or, did this have to do with Hunter still? She'd be graduating in a short time, and in theory that would signal the end of a conflict. But with this new Dean at the helm, I wasn't going to take anything for granted.

I looked over at my girlfriend, blissfully asleep beside me. She'd come over after dinner with her parents. Her lips were slightly parted and she made a kind of whistling noise when she exhaled. Sometimes I hated sleeping; I could stay awake and watch her all night. She still reached out for me while she slept. It wasn't uncommon for her hand to find my shoulder, my bicep, or the neckline of whatever top I was wearing to bed. Every few moments I would feel her fingers flex and tighten around my arm, but they were all involuntary movements. It should have felt smothering, but it didn't; it comforted me. It tethered me like a stable anchor.

My brain refused to quiet itself for a long time that night. When it finally shut down so I could fall asleep, I still had no satisfactory answers.

+++++

CHAPTER EIGHT

"Paging Hunter Dyson," a woman spoke into the receiver of a black phone. "Hunter Dyson, come to the nurses' station."

I waited and tapped my fingers on the front counter to give me something to do. Being still for too long made me more anxious than usual. I gave the woman who sat at the nurses' station a tight smile. She returned the receiver to its cradle and stared back at me without emotion.

Down the hallway a set of double doors pushed open, erratically swinging on their hinges. Hunter appeared, worry written on her delicate face. Her normally alabaster features looked flushed, red cheeked, and her pale blue eyes darted anxiously around the main lobby. Her hair was different than when she'd left this morning. Instead of being loose and touching the tops of her shoulders, it was now pulled back into a ponytail, meticulously parted on one side. Her salmon colored scrubs clung to her slight curves as she hustled out the double doors to reach the nurses' station. How anyone could look so edible in that shapeless uniform was nothing short of a miracle.

I saw her in scrubs nearly everyday, but seeing her in that outfit in the context of this environment made my knees buckle. She looked so grown up, so...*natural* in these surroundings. I lamented that this was the first time of me visiting her here. I had resisted until now because of my aversion to hospitals, although I didn't think many people actually *liked* hospitals.

This moment felt important though; it felt like the rest of my life was playing out before my eyes – not of her visiting me at my campus office, but of me bringing her pre-packaged sandwiches at the hospital to share over the lunch hour.

When our eyes met, the worry erased from her face. "Hey you," she greeted. She tugged a little at the v-neck of her top and flashed a quick smile in the direction of the woman behind the desk who observed our conversation. "Hi, Tonya."

The woman grunted a non-verbal greeting and turned away from us to attend to some other task.

Hunter grabbed my hand. "What's up?" I looked down at our enjoined hands. It still gave me heart palpitations to see and feel how well we fit together.

"Nothing, really," I admitted. "I had some free time today – well, all this week actually because I'm on Spring Break – and I wanted to see you, maybe bring *you* lunch for once." I lifted the wax-paper bag I'd been given at the local deli. Inside were two sandwiches and obscenely large Kosher pickles. "I probably should have talked to you about it before though because you might be totally busy today, or maybe it's unprofessional for an intern to have their girlfriend show up at their place of work, and now that I'm thinking about it, I should probably just go before I get you into trouble."

I heard her laugh and then her mouth was stopping my unexpected ramble. I wanted to give in to the way her lips were moving against mine, but when I felt the tip of her tongue touch my bottom lip, seeking entrance, I pulled away instead of deepening the embrace.

I coughed and ran my hand roughly through my hair. I flicked my eyes around to see if anyone had seen our kiss. The area where we stood was relatively empty and everyone in our area appeared too distracted by reading charts and inspecting patients' vitals that we went unobserved.

"Ellio, you don't have to be nervous," she insisted, expertly deciphering the reason for my modesty. "Nobody cares."

I didn't think myself closeted, but maybe Dean Merlot was getting into my head. And when it came to Hunter, I got nervous; I didn't want to make things harder for her where she worked if she didn't want to be Out. But once again I was reminded of my girlfriend's fearlessness.

"Wanna see something?" she asked. Not waiting for my answer, her hand tightened around mine and I found myself being tugged down the corridor.

"Is this allowed?" I asked, looking around as she pulled me through the set of double doors from which she'd originally appeared. The words "STAFF ONLY" were printed in vibrant red paint on the doors, and they yelled at me to stop and turn around.

"It's fine," she claimed. "Turn off your alarm system, Professor Graft."

After traversing a series of hallways and taking so many right and left turns that I would never find my way back to the main lobby, we stopped in front of a large window. On the other side of the glass were a dozen or so newborns, tightly swaddled like tiny burritos in their little boxes. Cribs, I guess they're called.

"Okay, now I'm *positive* I'm not supposed to be in here," I murmured, feeling myself sweating from anxiety.

Hunter waved at a woman who stood inside the nursery, checking on charts and other official-looking hospital things. She smiled pleasantly and waved back at us. Apparently this was okay.

Hunter leaned against the ledge above the window. "Do you like kids?"

Our surroundings made the context of the conversation obvious, but I still wasn't prepared for that question from her. "I don't know," I answered. "I haven't really been around kids, unless you count Troian."

"I won't tell her you said that," Hunter smiled.

I allowed myself a laugh, even though I was still wary about being in this part of the hospital. "That's probably for the best."

It still made me a little melancholy to think about my best friend. I had to continually remind myself that she wasn't dead; she just wasn't available for coffee at Del Sol anymore. I had thought about visiting her during my Spring Break, but she was still finding her footing at work and in Los Angeles, so I didn't want my visit to be one more complication to her acclimating.

I pressed my palms flat against the large window and peered through the glass. "I never really babysat for anyone growing up, and I made the conscious decision to teach college and not elementary school," I remarked.

"So you don't want kids someday?"

"I don't *not* want kids," I said, mindful of my words. They felt as unstable as an incendiary bomb. "I just haven't been in a situation career-wise or relationship-wise where it's ever been on my radar."

"Just to be clear, I'm not pushing you one way or the other," Hunter noted with a small smile. "Babies aren't on my radar either. I've still got a lot of living to do before that time ever comes."

"It's funny," I said, feeling wistful as I continued to lean against the glass partition. "My sister's pregnant. It's weird being at an age that when people get pregnant, it's considered a *good* thing."

"You have a sister?" Hunter sounded surprised, and I couldn't blame her. I supposed she'd been stunned to learn I had a mother and father as well for as little as I ever talked about them.

"She's a few years younger than me. We're not close – it's not a feuding family thing," I explained, "we just haven't been very good at keeping in contact."

"Where does she live? Is she married? What does she do?"

My eyebrows rose at the rapid fire questioning, and Hunter blushed prettily. "Sorry. I just want to know about my girlfriend's life."

"Hunter?" An unexpected male voice interrupted our conversation.

"Dr. Green!" Hunter practically yelped. She grabbed at the fabric of her top, just over her heart. "You startled me!"

I snapped my gaze away from the nursery. My heart throbbed in my chest, too, but more from the worry that we were breaking some kind of rule instead of being surprised as Hunter had been.

"Sorry." The man who looked far too young to be a doctor lifted a shoed foot. "It's hard not to sneak up on people in these shoes." He seemed to notice my presence for the first time. "Good afternoon," he greeted with a bob of his perfectly coifed head. His voice took on a more formal tone than the one he'd used to address Hunter. "Are one of those yours?" he asked, nodding toward the burrito babies.

"Oh God, no," I blurted with probably a little too much eagerness.

Hunter's hand rested on my forearm. "This is my girlfriend, Elle. I'm just showing her around."

He didn't miss a beat. "Don't let Amanda see you back here. You know it's not allowed."

Hunter nodded. "I'll be sure to hide Elle in a storage closet if she comes around on rounds."

He grinned, broad and plastic. I decided I didn't like him or his teeth. "Be good." He waved at us both before turning and walking down the hallway.

"Who's Amanda?" I asked when the doctor was out of earshot.

"Dr. Amanda Sharron," she said. "She's head of pediatrics. She's also a stickler for the rules." Hunter nudged me in the ribs and gave me a playful grin. "You two would get along famously."

"And that guy?" I asked, nodding after the retreating doctor. "Dr. Green? What does he do?"

"He's an ER doctor, I think."

"What was he doing in the maternity ward?"

Hunter shrugged. "Looking at the babies like us?" she guessed. Her gaze went back to the nursery and the tidy rows of tiny newborns. "It's a popular place around here. If a doctor's having a bad day, sometimes they'll hang out in the pediatric wing to emotionally recharge."

"He likes you."

"He doesn't have any reason *not* to like me," Hunter noted with an arched brow. "My manners are impeccable, and I work hard."

"No, I mean he *likes* you, likes you," I clarified.

Her nose wrinkled adorably and she shook her head. "You're imaging things."

"I didn't imagine him checking out your ass."

"Whatever," she dismissed. "I said you were my girlfriend."

"He heard you call me 'your girlfriend,' but his Man Brain translated it as 'friend who's a girl.'"

A particularly pleased smile spread across her face. "Are you jealous, Ellio?"

I snorted. "Hardly." I knew I was transparent.

"Don't be jealous, baby. You know I'm into skirts." She looped her arm through mine and rested her chin on my shoulder. "Besides, I don't need him. I've already got a Doctor."

"I'm not a *real* doctor though." I sounded pouty, even to my own ears.

"Neither is he. He's just a Resident."

"Wanna play doctor when you get home?" I said, wiggling my eyebrows.

Hunter looked exasperated. "Why would you put those thoughts in my head?" she huffed. "You know I have four more hours of my shift today."

Between a current student living with Hunter and my mom staying at my house, there hadn't been much opportunity for us to be intimate without worrying that someone might overhear us. But Loryssa had gone to visit her parents in the Twin Cities for Spring Break, so we had the apartment to ourselves for the first time since she'd become Hunter's roommate. It would be the first time we would have a space to ourselves, period, ever since my mom had shown up on my front porch.

Things had gotten much better between my mom and me since I'd found her a job at the university library. She continued to save money by eating my groceries and she'd sold her car and was now carpooling with me to campus or using my car on days when I didn't have classes. She'd promised to look after Sylvia so I could spend all of Spring Break with Hunter at her apartment.

I smirked and leaned into her personal space. "I just want you mentally prepared for what I have planned tonight." I heard her sharp intake of air and something stirred within me. I leaned in further so my lips brushed against her ear as I spoke. "And since we'll finally be alone, don't you dare hold back if you need to scream."

I jerked away from my girlfriend when I heard someone tapping on the glass that separated us from the nursery. The woman from before smiled indulgently, but shook her finger at us. My face grew hot; I'd completely forgotten where we were.

Instead of being horrified like myself, Hunter giggled. "Let's have lunch," she said, grabbing onto my hand and tugging me away from the nursery. "And hopefully we'll run into Dr. Sharron on the way to the cafeteria."

"Why would you ever want that?" I implored, recalling the name.

"So I can have my way with you in a supply closet, obviously."

+++++

I propped up the tablet to see Troian's face better. It was a little strange talking to her disembodied head and carrying her around with me. I used to tease her about being a pocket-sized lesbian, but now she was truly portable.

I stood in Hunter's kitchen with an alarming amount of groceries and cooking supplies covering the modest counter space. I didn't often assemble an intricate meal, but when I did, I tended to create chaos around me. Dinner tonight consisted of homemade ravioli and steamed vegetables. I had never attempted to make pasta before, but this seemed the time to try. If it went badly, that's what Chinese takeout was for.

"I never knew you were Betty Crocker," Troian observed from her California location. "You were holding out on me."

"I'm really not," I said, conferring with the recipe yet again. "This could be an epic failure."

"What's the special occasion?"

"Nothing. I just wanted to do something nice for Hunter. I have the week off for Spring Break and I feel bad that she still has to work at the hospital every day."

Troian stuck out her tongue. "You should have ditched your girlfriend and come to California to hang out with me."

"You talk a big game," I snorted. "Like you'd ever go on vacation without Nik."

"I know," Troian sighed. "But I wouldn't have any fun without her."

"That's exactly what I told Hunter when she suggested I go on Spring Break without her."

Troian pressed her lips together. "You really like her, don't you?"

"Um, yeah?"

"Don't take this the wrong way," Troian started carefully. "I just...you don't have the best track record, you know? And even though you're not this wildly mature, esoteric person, I wondered how Hunter would keep up with you intellectually, or at least keep your interest."

I knew I shouldn't feel offended. Troian hadn't said anything that wasn't true, and if my best friend couldn't tell me these things, who could? I was notoriously fickle and had a short attention span when it came to relationships. It had begun long ago in high school – I'd figured my disregard for monogamy had been the lack of being attracted to my boyfriends, but then that behavior had continued in college with girls. Cady had been my longest relationship, and we'd just barely made it over a year. Compared to Troian and Nikole's decade of being together, I was an amateur at long-term relationships.

But I couldn't help feeling a little annoyed. Sure, Hunter and I hadn't been together for very long if you compared us to Troian and Nikole, but I'd put my career on the line to be with her – that had to count for something, right?

My annoyance must have been transparent.

"Bookie, I just want you to be happy."

"Hunter makes me happy," I snapped, cutting her off.

Troian held up her hands. "I know she does – you didn't let me finish."

"Sorry."

"I just want you happy," she tried again. "And when you're not over-thinking or sabotaging your relationship, you've been the happiest I've ever seen you." She sucked in a deep breath. "So what I guess I'm trying to say is fuck what everyone else thinks, including your Dean. Don't let one narrow-minded bully make you give up on that girl."

I felt a guilty twinge at Troian's mentioning of Dean Merlot. I had confided in my friend about the recent wave of tyranny and my concerns regarding my teaching evaluation. "I haven't talked to Hunter about that."

"What? That's like Relationship 101 stuff, Elle," Troian scolded me. "You don't keep the important stuff from your partner."

"I know, I know. I just don't want to make a big deal about it, that's all," I tried. "And if I tell Hunter, it officially becomes a big deal."

Troian looked unconvinced by my weak logic. I didn't blame her – even I knew this had the potential to blow up in my face.

"Bob's right though – they can dismiss me for not fitting in with the university's faith traditions. And I don't fit."

"Why would they have given you tenure then?" Troian pragmatically stated. "They knew you were gayer than a unicorn long before they found out about Hunter."

"This is a new Dean," I said. "The old Dean, Dean Krauss, signed off on me. Dean Merlot did not."

"I bet he has a secret life – *everyone* in the Midwest has a secret life," she grinned. "Want me to do some digging? I bet I find dirt."

"He is a *she*," I corrected my friend, "and no, no digging is necessary." I could practically see the gears churning in her head. "I mean it, Troi," I warned. "Stay out of this."

She grinned, but I didn't trust her for a second.

I heard the front door unlock. "Elle?" Hunter's voice wasn't far behind.

"In the kitchen!" I called back.

She walked to the back of the apartment where she found me, elbow deep in homemade pasta dough. I must have been a sight because she let out a belly laugh.

"What are you doing?" she asked between giggles.

"I'm making dinner."

"Is that what it's called?" She slung her bag on the ground and came over to me. I couldn't do much with my hands and much of my forearms covered in sticky dough. Her arms went around my neck and she pulled me in. Her mouth pressed softly against mine and I moaned a little when I felt her tongue flick against my bottom lip.

"Get a room!" Troian called out, mid-kiss.

Hunter leapt back. "Jesus!" It was a good thing she was young and healthy – it was the second time today she'd been startled. She pushed me away. "You could have warned me that Troian was here."

"In Elle's defense, your tongue was down her throat before she had the chance," Troian retorted.

Hunter hid her face behind her hands. "I'm going to take a quick shower and wash off this embarrassment."

"Bye, Hunter!" Troian chirped. "Nice seeing you!"

Hunter waved a hand as she disappeared down the hallway, mumbling, but I couldn't make out the words.

"That wasn't nice," I complained to my friend.

"Then don't force me to watch your homemade porno," Troian laughed back. "I know exhibitionism is your thing, but don't subject me to it."

Why I ever confided in Troian my personal-brand of kink was still a mystery to me. "As if you and Nik haven't done 100 times worse in front of me."

"Whatever, Bookie," Troian scoffed. "My girl and I are hot; you'd be only so lucky to get a free show."

"As fun and as traumatizing as this conversation has been, I gotta go," I said, wiggling dough-covered fingers at my tablet. "I need to finish dinner." I still had to get the dough the right consistency, roll it out thin, and put the filling of ricotta cheese and spinach inside.

"Check ya later, loser," Troian cheerfully signed off.

Hunter reappeared shortly after I said my goodbyes to Troian. She toweled off her hair as she walked out of the bathroom. She looked refreshed and relaxed in her tank top and sleep pants. Her cheeks were flushed from the heat of the shower or else she had yet to recover from the embarrassment that was Troian.

She stopped in the hallway. "Is it safe to come in?"

I waved to bid her to come closer. The dough was done, and I was rolling it out with the wine bottle I'd brought to have with dinner. Hunter's kitchen supplies were impressive for someone still in college, but she didn't have a rolling pin. "Troian's gone now."

Her steps were still hesitant despite my assurances. "I promise it's just us," I laughed good-naturedly. "I'm sorry I didn't warn you about her. She was keeping me company while I prepped dinner."

"What's for dinner?" she asked. She hung her damp towel on the back of a dinette chair. There wasn't a formal dining room in her two-bedroom apartment, but the kitchen was big enough for a small two-person table and chairs.

We would have had a lot more space at my house, even with my mom being there, and everything was more updated and upscale than at the apartment, but the food would taste the same and there was something cozy about us kind of 'roughing it' in Hunter's apartment. I imagined us building a fort out of blankets and couch cushions and streaming movies on her laptop later.

"I'm attempting homemade ravioli. I've never tried making it before though, so I can't promise anything. It might be a disaster."

She swooped in close to observe my cooking. I was spooning filling onto what would be the bottom layer of my stuffed pastas.

"I've got bread from the bakery and wine, too."

"Wow," she admired. "What's the occasion? Did I miss a milestone?"

"Troian asked me that, too. I just wanted to make dinner for you."

"That's awfully sweet." I was rewarded with a quick kiss near my temple.

I wasn't normally very good at romantic gestures and being

thoughtful. But being with Hunter made me want to be a better girlfriend.

A short while later we sat at the kitchen table. Tiny tea lights illuminated the table for two. "You first," I urged. "And remember, I'm not making any promises."

Hunter's fork hovered in the air with a ravioli attached to its end. "Mmmm," she hummed when her fork slipped past her lips.

"Good?" I asked, waiting for confirmation that I didn't need to order pizza.

She nodded enthusiastically. "*So* good, babe. These ravioli are like perfect little pillows."

With Hunter's stamp of approval, I too dug into the food on my plate. It *was* good; she wasn't just humoring me. I hadn't even thought to test it before serving her. I wasn't an expert in the kitchen, but now I could add homemade pasta to my small repertoire.

Hunter made an eerily familiar, sexual sound with her second bite.

I arched an eyebrow. "Should I give you and your pasta some privacy?"

She covered her mouth as she chewed the rest of her bite. "Sorry," she mumbled, coloring a bit.

"Don't apologize. You're adorable," I approved. "How was the rest of your day?" I asked, stabbing a few ravioli on my fork.

"It was good. Pretty standard. I basically followed around Marcie on her rounds in the pediatric wing."

"Which one's Marcie? Have you told me about her before?" I reached out to top off our wine glasses. They were actually juice glasses with snowflakes etched on the glass, but they served their purpose.

"Maybe. She was the nurse we saw in the nursery today."

"The one who caught us..." I trailed off, feeling a blush as deep as the color of the wine.

Hunter popped another ravioli into her mouth and grinned at me around the mouthful.

I cleared my throat, still embarrassed by the memory. It struck me strange that being intimate in front of strangers or acquaintances didn't bother Hunter – she seemed to revel in it. But when it came to being seen by someone she knew, like my mother or even Troian, she became more modest.

At the end of the meal, Hunter stood and cleared my plate before I could stop her. I grabbed her wrist and ran my thumb across the fine bones. "Why don't we leave that for tomorrow, Hunt?"

Her smile was lazy, but knowing, and her eyes slightly lidded. "What would you rather do instead?"

+++++

CHAPTER NINE

It was dark in Hunter's bedroom, but I could tell she was looking at me.

"Tell me your fantasies," she breathed.

I rolled onto my side. "My what?"

"Your fantasies," she repeated. Her features were obscured with only the moonlight filtering through her bedroom windows. "What kind of sexual fantasies bounce around in that giant brain of yours?"

I didn't answer her immediately. I had been able to do certain things, many of them degrading and humiliating to past partners, especially Ruby, because I wasn't in love with them. I had had no desire to nurture or protect anyone before being with Hunter, and so I had been comfortable playing the role of dominatrix or, when I rarely switched roles, of the reluctant submissive.

"You under my desk, pleasuring me with your mouth while I try to maintain my composure during a meeting or a phone call," I said, treading lightly.

The mattress shifted under her weight as she moved closer to me. "Naked from the waist down?" she continued my scenario, "Legs spread for me?"

"Mmhm," I confirmed.

"That doesn't sound very dom-like," she observed.

"No, I suppose I'm more into exhibitionism than BDSM," I admitted to the space above my head.

"Like when you fucked me in the bathroom stall at Peggy's."

Hearing curse words come out Hunter's mouth did all kinds of

116

things to my libido. Her apartment tended to run on the cold side, but I was feeling anything but that right now.

"What else?" she pressed.

I hesitated, but only briefly. "Tying you up and cutting off your clothes."

I could see her eyes widen, even in the dark. "Like with a knife?"

I shrugged, not wanting to make a big deal about it. "Scissors work, too. You'd be amazed at how good cold, metal scissors feel against your skin."

She regarded me with a serious look. "Why haven't we done any of that?"

I didn't have an answer for her. I couldn't call Hunter unkind names or inflict even mild physical pain. I restrained myself with her, but the sex was still amazing; she made my heart *so* happy. But I wondered how long it would take before my cravings and darkest fantasies pushed beyond my purposeful checkpoints.

I kissed her solidly on the mouth to derail the conversation. One hand went to her hip while the other got tangled in the hair at the base of her neck. Her hands mirrored my own. She squeezed my hipbone with one hand while the other wrapped around my loose curls. Her breath came in bursts against my lips as our bodies pressed together. My hands went to her pert backside and I grabbed onto her, pulling her more solidly against me. She moaned into my mouth, a noise that originated in the back of her throat to hum against my lips.

Her fingers toyed with the bottom hem of my v-neck shirt. I lifted my arms so she could free me of the garment. I made short work of her sleep clothes, first pulling off her tank top and then slipping off her pajama pants until I'd stripped her down to her pink cheekster underwear. I licked my lips and drank in the view. They looked impossibly sexy against her pale skin, the satin finish with black lace on the edges contrasting nicely.

I curled my fingers beneath the waistband and Hunter lifted her backside off the mattress to help, but I had other plans. I pulled my hands out of her underwear.

Her face was flushed just from the brief activity. "What's wrong?"

"I'm really sorry, Hunt." I faked a yawn. "I think being a housewife today really took it out of me."

She looked so horrified and frustrated, I had to bite back a laugh.

With the apartment finally to ourselves we didn't have to worry about anyone overhearing us except maybe the nosey neighbors.

"But...but you promised. At the hospital."

"I know I did." I rolled onto my side and propped myself up on my elbow. "But you could always finish the job yourself?" I suggested, unable to resist a smug smile.

Those pale blue eyes widened. "I don't think I can do that."

"No?" I trailed my fingers down the center of her chest, between her naked breasts, and down to the lace trim of her underwear. "You masturbate, right?" My fingertips slid beneath the elastic band to play just beneath the surface. "How would this be any different?"

Her pale blonde eyelashes fluttered when my fingers dipped a little deeper beneath her underwear. "But I've never had an audience."

I peppered her neck and up to her temple with soft kisses. "I can give you some suggestions if you don't know how to start," I offered. I made sure my words were warm and wet against her the shell of her ear. I knew how sensitive that spot was on her.

I felt her shudder against me, letting me know her reluctance was crumbling.

"We'll go slow," I assured her, leaving my fingers just beneath the elastic band of her panties to innocently play. "Start with your breasts. Palm them and feel how soft and full they are."

I hummed approvingly when she followed my instruction with little hesitation. Her hands slowly moved to cup her own breasts.

"Does that feel good?"

She didn't verbally respond, but her breathing had become more shallow.

"Squeeze a little," I urged. "I want to see you make your nipples hard for me."

"Th-they already are," she stuttered.

"*Harder.*"

She whimpered, a noise just barely audible to my ears. Her eyes were shut as she scraped her fingernails over her nipples. She pulled and tweaked the hardening buds until they stood up stiffly, contrasting with the soft fullness of her full breasts.

"Good girl," I murmured my approval. I slid my fingers out of her underwear. "Now, touch yourself over your underwear."

That demon inside me surged as I watched her right hand slowly move from resting on her right breast to hover just above her underwear.

"What next?" came her shaky question.

My heartbeat quickened in my chest. "Rest two fingers on top of your clit. But don't move them," I commanded. "Just feel their weight against you."

I heard the shaky intake of air as she did what I requested.

"Now, lightly press down."

Her hand repositioned as I started to push her beyond her comfort zone. Unbidden by me, she began stroking herself over the material of her underwear.

"Just like that," I encouraged. My eyes never left the movement of her hand. I didn't want to miss a thing.

"Touch your clit through your underwear. Focus on how good it feels when the material rubs against you. Keep teasing yourself," I pushed. "I know you want it harder, baby, but not yet. I know you want to feel your pussy without anything in the way."

She made a small noise like a quiet grunt.

"Slide your panties to the side," I ordered. I wet my lips as I watched. "I want to see you."

She moved the material covering her sex out of the way so I could better see her. She was wet and dark pink, flushed and ready. I bit back a telling moan.

"You can touch your pussy now," I allowed. "But don't touch your clit anymore."

Her fingers fluttered against the shaved skin and she sighed when her fingers finally made direct contact.

"Now run a single finger up and down your slit," I continued my instructions. "Get yourself nice and wet."

A single digit divided her folds and she quietly sighed. She opened her hips and her legs fell apart; her self-consciousness slipped away with each new command.

"Are you wet?" I asked. I began to toy with her nipple, pinching and rolling it between my thumb and forefinger.

"Uh huh," she whimpered back.

"Do you want more?"

"Yes," she hissed. She pressed down harder against her opening, just moments away from slipping inside. I grabbed her hand to stop that from happening. "Not yet," I said, my tone gruff. "I'll tell you when you can."

I was never so forward or aggressive in my everyday interactions. I didn't even consider myself an extrovert. Only in the classroom, looking over a room full of students, each eagerly writing down everything I said, did I find an equal thrill. It was probably one of the reasons I'd always been resistant to Troian's urging that I give up teaching to work for her.

"Please, Elle," Hunter panted. Her hips rose off the bed and she made a frustrated sound.

"Please what? What do you want?"

She looked away, but her fingers continued their ministrations. "I want...I want to cum." Her wiggling and arching became more noticeable.

"And what do you need in order to cum, love?"

"In-inside," she stuttered, her eyes meeting mine again.

"So soon?" I taunted.

"Please?" she gasped.

"One finger," I allowed, making myself look cross at her impatience.

A look of relief passed over her features. Her initial timidity had been banished in favor of desire. She cupped her sex fully in her palm before slowly inserting her middle finger inside.

"Better?"

She whimpered and nodded.

She looked so utterly licentious; her left hand continued to paw her bare breasts while she penetrated herself with her underwear still on. I wanted to remove her hand and replace it with my own to feel her sex swallow me whole, but a larger part of me wanted her to see this through to her completion.

"All the way in and all the way out," I told her.

She began pulling and pushing her single finger in and out of her. I could hear how wet she was. Her arousal clicked in my ears.

"Can you do three?"

Her single finger stalled as she considered my question. She bit her lower lip and nodded. I sucked in a sharp breath as I watched two more fingers disappear. It wasn't the easiest of maneuvers, especially because she still wore her underwear.

Her head tilted back and her eyes closed, mouth hanging slightly open. Her breath came out in short, staccato breaths.

"Keep your eyes open. Look at me when you make yourself

cum."

Her eyes fluttered open and she stared back at me, now bold and challenging where once she'd been hesitant and shy. "I'm close."

"Fuck yourself, Hunter." My nostrils flared, taking in the scent of her arousal. "I want you to cum."

Her eyes shut on their own accord and her head lifted from the pillow. I could have stopped her for disregarding my command, but I wasn't so cruel as to interrupt her orgasm. Her mouth fell open and she breathed out sharply with a strangled cry.

"Fuck." Her blue eyes blinked rapidly. "That was...*intense*. I-I've never gotten off like that before."

I kissed her forehead, now slick with sweat. "You did so good, Hunter. So very, very good."

+++++

There was a mountain of dirty dishes awaiting me in the morning. I found a bottle of dish soap in the cabinet beneath the sink and I started the hot water. Hunter's kitchen wasn't equipped with a dishwasher, so that job fell to me. But believe me – it had been well worth it. A smile, unbidden, reached my lips when I thought about the previous night.

"You're doing my dishes?"

I turned my head and saw Hunter, already dressed for work. She had another full day at the hospital. I privately thought they were taking advantage of my girlfriend as it wasn't even a paid internship, but I kept my opinion to myself. Her hard work would be rewarded and she was getting invaluable experience. "Correction. I'm doing the dishes *I* got dirty yesterday."

"From making us dinner," she continued to protest.

"I've got this one, hun," I assured her. "It's a small price to pay after the performance you gave me last night."

She ducked her head and made for the pantry. "I still can't believe I did that," she mumbled. She seemed to be hiding behind her box of Cheerios.

"Are you okay with last night?" I worried aloud. "I didn't...it wasn't too uncomfortable, was it?"

She grabbed the milk from the fridge and sat down at the kitchen table with her breakfast. "I was embarrassed at first," she admitted. "I've never done that before with anyone. I felt so...*vulnerable*. But then I kind of got into it." She dunked her spoon up and down in the bowl, drowning individual pieces of cereal. "I wouldn't mind if you wanted to do it again."

"Good," I beamed with relief. She'd pressed me as to why we hadn't traveled far into the realm of my sexual fantasies, but I didn't want to pressure or least of all traumatize her. "I wouldn't mind if it happened again, either. That was fucking sexy." I wrinkled my nose at a sauce pan that refused to get clean. "But next time remind me to presoak these dishes first."

Hunter's spoon scraped the bottom of her bowl. "Maybe…maybe I could tell *you* what to do next time."

I frowned and reflexively ran my fingers through my hair. I scowled when I realized my hands were covered in wet soap suds. "I don't really *do* that."

She arched an eyebrow. "Masturbate?" she guessed.

"Take orders."

"Not even from me?"

"I…maybe," I said tentatively. "Maybe we should talk about it later; another time when you don't have to immediately run off to work," I proposed.

She bobbed her head in agreement. "What do you have planned for today?"

"A big fat nothing," I admitted. I abandoned the dirty dishes for the time being and sat across the table from Hunter. I had all day to clean them.

"No work?"

"I could do some writing, but I don't have anything to do for school. I've taught the writing seminar and U.S. Literature so many times, I could teach those in my sleep."

"Do they always make you teach those classes," she asked around a mouthful of Cheerios, "or could you teach something different?"

"I'm low professor on the totem pole until a Dinosaur retires and they hire someone new," I explained, "so I usually get stuck with the writing seminar." I made a thoughtful tilt of my head. "But, I suppose I could ask Bob for something different – maybe propose an entirely new class."

I hadn't proposed a new class since I'd been hired. I'd been resigned to teaching the general education writing seminars because they'd also let me add a creative writing class that was popular with the English majors. But I was starting to get bored of the same classes each and every semester; maybe proposing a totally new class would reinvigorate my passion for teaching.

"You. Are. Brilliant." I leaned across the table and kissed her soundly on the mouth. She tasted like honey.

She popped another spoonful of cereal into her mouth and grinned. "I have my moments."

I was still sitting at the kitchen table when the front door opened a few hours later.

"You're home," I astutely observed.

Hunter set her bag down in the hallway and slipped out of her ugly nurse shoes. "It was slow at the hospital, so they let me go early."

She padded back in her stocking feet to the kitchen. "Have you eaten today?" The dirty dishes from last night's dinner continued to sit in the sink, but she didn't point that out. I was sure she'd noticed though. My girlfriend was more Type A than even me.

"No. I've been working on course proposals," I said, gesturing to the yellow legal pad in front of me.

"Think you can take a break for a picnic? I just have to clean up a bit and then we can go; a baby threw up on me."

I looked out the kitchen window which overlooked the street in front of the apartment building. It was overcast outside, and it might have been drizzling or at least misting. Not exactly picnic weather. "It's a little chilly for a picnic, isn't it?"

She gave me a carefree smile as she shed her scrubs and disappeared into the bathroom. "Not where I'm going to take you."

While she was in the shower I took the opportunity to change out of my pajamas. I used to have a drawer in Hunter's bedroom wardrobe, but because of Loryssa, I'd brought those items home since I wouldn't be staying over until she wasn't one of my students anymore.

Gathering up all the things I'd been keeping at Hunter's apartment – clothes and toiletries and even a few books – and throwing them in a duffle bag had felt like breaking up. I'd been trying so hard to create equity about which home we spent our time together, but with Loryssa as Hunter's roommate, the balance had been spoiled once again.

Hunter emerged from the bathroom wearing a fitted cotton sundress with a matching three-quarters length cardigan.

"Wow," I openly admired. "This must be a fancy picnic. I should probably change."

I was just in jeans and one of Hunter's running tops. I hadn't brought over many clothes for this stay-cation because I always looked for opportunities to wear Hunter's things. I'd always found something intimate about wearing your partner's clothes, even if it was just an old t-shirt or oversized sweatshirt. I loved it when she wore my sweatpants with my alma mater screen-printed on the leg. It made it feel like we'd always been together.

"You look perfect, Ellio." She ran her hands down the front of the dress's skirt to fix a stubborn pleat. "I'm only wearing this because it's still too cold for a bikini."

I arched an eyebrow at her words. Now I was even more curious about this picnic. But she only gave me another secretive smile as she grabbed her keys and we left the apartment.

Hunter's car was immaculate, inside and out. You might expect a 21-year-old's vehicle to be littered with fast food wrappers, but Hunter didn't eat that garbage for one, and she was too particular to leave her car a mess. She'd ended up getting a new vehicle when one of the university's faculty had t-boned her Honda civic on campus last semester. I probably owed the guy a thank you card since the accident had been a bridge to reconnecting with Hunter after I'd basically broken up with her because of a disastrous dinner with her family.

She pulled the car to a stop in a densely forested area. Her tires crunched on the rough gravel of a makeshift parking lot. I unfastened my seatbelt and climbed out of the car. I recognized this place. Troian had brought me here when they'd first bought the property. But I couldn't understand why Hunter was bringing me here.

"This is Nik's greenhouse," I said, thinking out loud.

Hunter's hand found mine and she wordlessly pulled me in the direction of the front entrance. She singled out a key on her key-ring and unlocked the door to the glass-encased structure. When we stepped inside, I was greeted with that thick, muggy air one finds in a greenhouse or bio-dome. The plants were tall and green and vibrant.

"Nikole had planted the seedlings before Troian got the job in California," Hunter explained. She suddenly looked shy. "She didn't want them to die, so she asked if I'd keep an eye on them."

"You did all of this?" I turned in a slow circle.

I didn't have a brown thumb, but it certainly wasn't green. I always said I had a yellow thumb. I could keep houseplants alive, but they weren't always thriving.

Hunter hung back as I walked deeper into the structure. "I've just been checking in on them between work and classes."

"It's beautiful." I felt the need to whisper. It felt like we were in a sacred space that I didn't want to spoil by talking too loudly. "It's like a tropical oasis."

"Exactly." Hunter's smile grew. "Which is why we're here. I know you were disappointed we didn't get to go anyplace warm or exotic for Spring Break because I had to work. So I thought this might make up for it."

I turned to her. "Why are you so amazing?"

She ducked her head and tucked a lock of hair behind her ear – her go-to move when she was embarrassed. "It's nothing special."

"It's amazing," I corrected her. "I love it, Hunt. I love *you*."

She hugged herself, looking privately pleased that she'd been able to surprise me. "I hope you're hungry. I packed enough food to last us a week."

We laid on our backs on a blanket in the center of the greenhouse, bellies full and bodies content.

"Do you ever think about timing?" I said to the space above my head.

"Like what?" Hunter asked, twisting just slightly to look at me.

"Like what it took for you and I to meet."

"Give me a for instance."

"Well, for example, I went straight through from undergrad to grad school even though I'd thought about taking some time off to re-charge my brain after graduation. If I had done that, I wouldn't have finished my Ph.D. in time to apply for the job I have now. More than likely I'd be teaching someplace else. We wouldn't have ever met."

Hunter made a thoughtful noise. "I think about things like that sometimes – like if I'd taken the writing seminar earlier, instead of Junior year."

"You might have still had me as a professor," I pointed out. "Everyone has to take that class at some point."

"Maybe, but you wouldn't have pursued a relationship with a Freshman."

"You're right about that," I agreed. "It was hard enough going for a second-semester Junior."

"Well, I'm glad you did." I saw the adoration in her eyes. It made my heart swell.

"I'm glad I did, too," I said softly. "This may be my favorite Spring Break ever."

Hunter reached for me. Her fingers curled around my forearm and she squeezed. "Even without me in a bikini?"

"Oh, I'm still gonna get you in a bikini, love," I assured her.

+++++

CHAPTER TEN

I spent the remainder of Spring Break working on two course proposals and helping Hunter study for her upcoming licensure exam. Before we'd started dating, I hadn't known anything about what it took to be a nurse, let alone knowing the difference between those who went to programs that lasted two years or less and students, like Hunter, who received a Bachelors of Science in the field.

I was actually excited about my new course syllabi and thinking about all the great books I'd be able to teach. One course was designed as an American *bildungsromans* or coming-of-age literature course, and the other I'd titled "The Minority Voice in Literature." I was thrilled to be able to incorporate some of my personal favorites like Danzy Senna's *Caucasia*, John Okada's *No-No Boy*, or Anzia Yezierska's *Bread Givers*, along with undisputed classics from authors like J.D. Salinger, Harper Lee, and Maya Angelou. Getting to talk about great literature with students who loved books as much as I did would be just the thing to yank me out of this teaching funk.

After Spring Break ended, the rest of the semester went by quickly as it usually did when the weather started to get warmer. My mom was still working at the library, but she'd recently moved into Troian and Nikole's condo, which was still up for sale. My friends were letting her live there rent-free, minus utilities, so she could keep saving money to pay off her mountain of debt. I would have been fine letting her continue to stay with me — we'd gotten into a comfortable routine and she had become appreciatively adept at making herself scarce Friday nights when Hunter stayed the night – but it was awfully nice having my house back to myself. I felt like an adult again.

The television was on and Hunter and I were reclined on the couch. There was a glass of red wine on the coffee table next to a stack of abandoned flashcards, but all I could really focus on was the strip of naked skin where Hunter's long-sleeved t-shirt had ridden up to expose her flat stomach and chiseled hipbones. I licked my lips before I realized what I was doing. I loved women. I loved women's bodies. I loved the fragrance of their soft skin. And I loved this woman most of all.

Sylvia stared at me from the loveseat across the room like she was planning on eating my face later. She was probably upset that I was taking up space on the couch that she believed belonged to her. I looked away, unwontedly intimidated; only Hunter had the patience to win a staring contest with my cat.

I picked up a handful of flashcards from the coffee table and thumbed through them.

"Have you given more thought to that thing we talked about over Spring Break?" Hunter didn't look away from the television.

"What thing?" Hunter's normally pale features were tinted pink, which gave me a pretty good indication of what she was referring to.

"If you can't say it, Hunter," I said, returning the study cards to the coffee table, "we can't do it."

Those penetrating blue eyes that had pulled me in so many months ago now stared me down. "I want to Switch."

"Where did you hear that word?" I asked gravely. "Was it Troian?"

Hunter wet her lips. "No. I...I did some research."

Hunter knew too well about my sexual adventures in previous relationships. Well, Ruby wasn't exactly a relationship; it had been more like mutual loathing with benefits. If I could have kept that part of my past hidden from her, I would have. I wasn't embarrassed about it, but I guess I wanted to shield her from anything that might bring her discomfort or make her feel inadequate as a partner. Sex was important, but every encounter didn't need to be unorthodox for me to find satisfaction.

"Think of it as a graduation present to me."

My emotions flared at the mention of her graduation. It was supposed to be an exciting moment for both of us – for her, the culminating celebration of four years of hard work, and for me it meant that I'd no longer be dating an enrolled student from my university. But instead of bringing relief, it was only causing anxiety.

"Ellio," she nearly whined. "I want you there."

"I will be there," I stated matter-of-factly. "All the faculty will be there, dressed up in our academic regalia."

Her eyes narrowed. "That's not what I mean and you know it."

"I don't want to make things awkward," I explained. "This is supposed to be your special day."

"Exactly. Which is why you should be there."

I sighed and my shoulders slumped. "Your family hasn't exactly brought out the welcome wagon for me, Hunter."

"You haven't given them the opportunity," she countered. "We had that one disaster of a dinner with my mom and brother and nothing since then."

Hunter had reconciled with her parents after our ill-fated dinner months ago, but I had yet to see them again. Every once in a while she would make a casual comment about us getting together again, but so far I had successfully avoided a second meeting.

"We're having dinner at the hibachi place after the ceremony. You love hibachi."

Some people might think it a little over the top and cheesy, but there were few things that entertained me like a flaming onion volcano. "Who else will be there?" I tentatively ventured.

"Just my parents and my brother, Brian."

I visibly cringed.

"It could be worse," she noted with a wry grin. "My 82-year-old grandmother could be coming along, too."

"Grandmothers love me," I said, shaking my head. "I'm a good eater. It's your parents who worry me."

"Give them a chance to get to know you better, Ellio. I mean, look at what happened with me and your mom," she pointed out. "Once they spend more time with you, they'll love you, just like I do."

She looked at me with such intensity and apparent desire, that I wanted to say yes. But I could only give her halfway. "I'll think about it."

+++++

I had submitted my new course proposals to my boss, Bob, on the Monday we'd gotten back from Spring Break. But now, a month and a half later, I still had not heard back from him. On the final week of the semester, I finally summoned enough courage to knock on his open office door.

"You have a minute?" I asked, poking my head into the room.

Bob paused, mid-bite, and set his sandwich back on its wax-paper wrapping. "Sure."

I hesitated with my hand on the door, not sure if I should close the door or not. I opted for leaving it open. I had nothing to hide, after all.

I sat down heavily on the chair opposite his desk and crossed my legs. "When do you think I'll be hearing back about those course proposals? It's been a while."

Bob's eyes dropped from my face down to his desktop. "I'm sorry to be the bearer of bad news, Elle."

I leaned forward in my chair. "You're rejecting them? *Both* of them?" I couldn't believe it. I'd known I'd kind of thrown them together last minute, but I hadn't thought them so bad that Bob would reject them altogether. "Can I make some revisions and you'll re-evaluate them?"

Bob frowned. He turned in his chair and pulled out a metal drawer from his storage container and produced a thin folder. He set the folder on his desk and pushed it toward me.

Inside the folder were hardcopies of my proposed course syllabi. I turned the folder to read the handwritten note scrawled across the top of the first syllabus. I didn't recognize the handwriting; it didn't belong to Bob. I knew his writing well. His was a small, precise script that always looked as if he'd used ink and quill. This was a sloppier, nearly illegible print, more reminiscent of a physician's writing on a prescription pad.

I was pretty good at decoding handwriting from grading thousands of Blue Book exams over the years. Despite the near illegible handwriting, I could just make out the following statement: *Based on the required book selection, I do not recommend adopting this course.* I flipped to the second syllabus and found the same sentence, in the same handwriting, tattooed across the top.

I looked up at Bob. "Who made these recommendations?" At a larger school there would have been several levels of bureaucracy, but at my small, liberal arts college, course selection was generally left up to the Chair of the Department.

Bob cleared his throat. "Turn to the required reading section."

I grabbed my syllabus on the Minority Voice in American Literature and flipped to the third page where the required readings were listed. Claire Morgan's *The Price of Salt* was highlighted. I immediately reached for the other syllabus, the one on American coming-of-age stories, and scanned until I found the required reading listed there. Rita Mae Brown's *Rubyfruit Jungle* was similarly highlighted in a bright neon yellow. Both books dealt with lesbianism.

I slapped my hand on the file folder in frustration. "Merlot." The name came out like a growl. "So academic freedom doesn't apply at this school anymore." It wasn't a question; it was an accusation.

Bob squirmed in his seat. He probably never imagined when he'd accepted the position of Chair of the Department that he'd have to be the middleman in this kind of campus politics. I still didn't feel sorry for him though; he was allowing this bullying to happen when he should have had my back.

"How did she even see this?" I asked. Another accusation. There was no reason for Bob to be sending the Dean my course proposals unless he was in on this, too.

Bob cleared his throat. "It's a new policy; I have to send her everyone's course proposals. She wants to be updated on the content of courses our students are being exposed to."

I felt the anger slip through me. "This is all because of me, isn't it? All this new red tape?" I rubbed at my face.

Bob gave me a sympathetic smile. "I wouldn't say that; rumor has it, Doug Witlan in the Biology department is a Socialist."

"Yeah, but it's not like Witlan's going to be assigning *The Communist Manifesto* in Biology 101."

"Probably not."

"What if Emily had proposed this course? Would it have gotten Dean Merlot's approval?"

"Emily wouldn't have proposed this course; she teaches British literature."

"You know what I mean, Bob," I growled. "I can't teach queer literature because I'm gay. Dean Merlot thinks I've got some gay agenda and I'm going to corrupt my students."

Bob opened his hands, palms up, and looked like the man he truly was – helpless and powerless.

"Then I guess I'll just have to take this up with the Dean," I clipped. I snatched the printed copies of my syllabi from Bob's desk and stormed out.

I couldn't remember if I technically said goodbye to Bob or not. My flight across campus was a blur, too. If anyone had tried to stop and say hello, I ignored them, blinded by indignation and beyond frustrated by the roadblocks this woman had put up between me and job satisfaction. It was time I met Dean Merlot, face-to-face.

Unfortunately for me, I should have called ahead.

"She's out of the office today," her administrative assistant told me, "but you're more than welcome to leave a message, and she'll get back to you right away."

It was probably for the best. By the time I'd stomped across campus from the English department to the building that housed the administrative offices, I was practically foaming at the mouth. It had taken every ounce of willpower not to take my frustrations out on the Dean's executive assistant.

So instead of complaining to the Dean about her new neo-Nazi regime, I did the next best thing – got loaded and called Troian to vent.

"It's got to be karma. The university is taking a giant crap on me this year for all the bad things I've ever done," I complained to my best friend. As soon as I'd gotten home, I'd poured myself a generous serving of bourbon and had called Troian. I was thankful that even though we lived in different time zones now, she'd been available to listen to me rant.

"I don't know if I can take anymore rejection this year, Troi." I sat at the kitchen island and pushed my unruly hair out of my eyes. "I've had all my ego and my heart can take. And the rejection doesn't get easier; I just get more numb."

"Just remember that everything happens for a reason," Troian tried to rationalize.

"You're about as helpful as a fortune cookie," I glowered.

"That's racist."

"It has nothing to do with you being Asian – it's a known fact that fortune cookies are useless."

"Just for that," Troian sniffed, "I'm not going to tell you my news."

"Is it good news?" I drank deeply from my tumbler. The alcohol burned the back of my throat.

"*I* think it is."

"Let me guess," I said snidely. "You did such a great job that they want you to be CEO of the Studio now." It was annoying sometimes to have such an accomplished friend.

"No," Troian clipped. "I'm getting married."

I nearly dropped the phone. "*What??*"

"I got a ring. I got down on one knee. And I proposed to Nik."

"And she actually said yes?" I squawked.

"You're such an asshole," Troian scowled over the phone. "Why did I even tell you?"

"Because you're freaking out about planning a wedding, and you need your Best Woman," I said matter-of-factly.

I could practically hear her shake her head. "There's got to be a better name for that by now."

"I don't care if there is." My desire to get drunk dissipated with Troian's news. "We're totally going with Best Woman."

"What says I even want you to be my Old Maid of Honor anyway?" she scoffed.

"Whatever. Don't kid yourself. I'm your Best Woman."

"That's still not a real thing."

"Uh huh," I said, dismissing her complaint. "So tell me everything," I urged. "I want all the gory details. You seriously got down on one knee?"

"Of course I did," Troian huffed. "You know I'm a romantic."

"I know you are, but isn't it a bit redundant? I mean, you just standing up is like a normal person on one knee."

"I don't need this abuse. I should just ask my cousin to be my Best Woman."

"See? We're totally making that a thing," I couldn't help but crow. "So when do you want me out there so we can start planning?"

"I don't know. When can you get out here?"

"How about after Hunter's graduation?" I suggested.

"Really?"

I shrugged even though I knew she couldn't see me. "It'll be summer and my new classes got rejected, so I don't have any course planning to do. What else do I have going on?"

"See?" Troian smiled through the phone. "Everything happens for a reason."

"You're an idiot."

I could hear Hunter's voice outside with someone else. She'd probably gotten trapped on her way inside by the little old lady who lived next door. She was a sweet woman, but she had the tendency to talk your ear off. I was able to evade her in the winter months, but now that the weather was getting warmer, she'd be unavoidable. She was always very friendly, if a tendency to over share. I didn't think she knew that I was gay — there was really no reason for her to think that — it's not like I flew a rainbow flag from my front porch. I did wonder what she thought of me, though — the university professor who lived alone with her cat, but was never short of female friends.

"Hunter's home," I told Troian.

"I'd better let you go properly greet your woman then," came my friend's reply. I could practically hear the waggle of her eyebrows.

"Let's talk soon about me coming out there," I said. "And give Nikole my condolences."

"You're such an ass," Troian said, but I could hear the amusement in her tone. Nothing, not even me, was going to ruin this day for her.

Hunter tossed off her shoes when she came in through the front door. "I've got news," she announced.

"Me too," I said, pouring the rest of my drink down the sink. I was done with that for today.

Hunter bounced into the kitchen, but the hop in her step faltered when she saw the bottle of alcohol on the countertop. "Were you drinking?" She picked up the bottle and inspected the label. "Alone?" Concern troubled her features. "What's wrong?"

"What's your news?" I deflected.

Normally she wouldn't have let me distract her so easily, but her face couldn't contain her grin. "I got offered a job, full time, at the hospital. I start right after graduation."

"You did? That's *amazing*, Hunt."

I would have hurdled the kitchen island to hug her if I were more athletic, but I had to settle for walking around it. I wrapped her up in my arms and drew her close.

"It's not really that big a deal."

I pulled back. "Not a big deal?" I echoed, raising my voice. "Hunt, don't be so modest. These days *no one* gets hired straight out of college doing something they actually went to school for. Plus, you haven't even graduated yet and you're set. This *is* a big deal. I'm so proud of you."

She smiled then, still shy, but I could tell she was proud of her accomplishment as well.

"So what do you want to do to celebrate?" I posed.

"Switch." Her answer came without pause.

She hadn't hesitated, but I did. I hadn't been expecting that response. "I was thinking more along the lines of a fancy dinner or a long weekend away," I said carefully.

Her shoulders visibly slumped and she looked disappointed. Acting quickly I grabbed both of her hands and brought them up to my mouth. "I'm sorry," I apologized, letting my lips brush against her knuckles. "I know we've been flirting with the idea, but I didn't know you were serious about wanting to do that."

She gave me a half-hearted smile, and I felt like a jerk. "What's your news?" she asked.

"Oh, yeah." I shook my head, remembering. "It's kind of mixed. My proposed classes got rejected and Troian proposed to Nik."

Hunter's face fell. "Oh no."

"Troian's not *that* bad," I said with a forced laugh. "I'm sure she'll be a great wife."

"That's not what I meant," she said crossly.

"I know," I sighed.

"What did they say about your classes? I mean, did they at least give you any explanation for why your new courses got rejected?"

I hated to show vulnerably and this failure made me look and feel weak. "I really don't want to talk about it," I deflected. "Not right now, at least."

"You're really good at avoiding topics you don't want to talk about." Hunter folded her arms across her chest. "First Switching, and now this. We *are* going to discuss this," she asserted.

My whole body sagged. "It's the gay thing again. Dean Merlot rejected the classes because I had queer literature on the list of required readings."

"If you took those books off the syllabi would she let you teach the classes?" she stated reasonably.

"That's not the point, Hunt." I shook my head hard. "I shouldn't have to censor material I want to teach. I'm a university professor – having Academic Freedom is like, I don't know, our version of the Hippocratic Oath." I struggled to find an appropriate comparison that would help her understand. "And it's not like the books are even pornographic. They just happen to have main characters who are gay."

Her lips twitched, but she didn't say more. I wondered if she thought I was being unreasonably stubborn.

"So besides *Switching*," I changed the topic with a meaningful look, "what else do you want to do to celebrate the new job?"

"Well, I kind of organized an impromptu party – nothing big, just the girls in my program – and I want you to be there."

I opened my mouth with a protest ready on my lips.

"Before you say no," she quickly interjected, "I've already checked with my friends, and none of them have you as a professor this semester."

"But there's still Loryssa," I rreminded her.

"Who is actually older than me, so it's not like you'd be condoning any laws getting broken if she drinks. Plus, I don't even know if she'll be there. She has a weird schedule."

"I don't know…" The semester was almost over, but I was still reluctant to put myself in that situation.

"*Please*, Elle." She grabbed both of my hands and her thumbs stroked my palms. "I really want you to meet my friends before we graduate and everyone moves away. Can you bend your rules just a little this time?" She batted her heavy eyelashes at me.

"Okay," I relented with a heavy sigh. "I'll come."

She squealed in excitement, but it felt like I'd just made a big mistake.

+++++

CHAPTER ELEVEN

I've never felt so awkward in my life. Loud rap music thumped out of the speakers of Hunter's laptop which sat on the kitchen table where we'd made a meal of homemade pasta just a few weeks ago. I didn't mind the music — I liked most genres, including rap and hip-hop — but it struck me as odd. Hunter preferred indie bands and singer-songwriters.

I nursed my beer and watched the house party unfold before me. It brought me back to my own undergraduate years. I hadn't been a big partier; I had predictably spent more time in the university library than on Fraternity or Sorority Row. I did have a high alcohol tolerance, however, which had earned me a reputation for being able to out-drink even the most seasoned Greek-life student.

I tried not to hover around the alcohol station in the kitchen because I didn't want to look like the disapproving parent every time one of Hunter's friends refilled their party cup. At first blush, Hunter's friends didn't strike me as particularly sophisticated or mature, but I tried not to judge them too much. They were early 20-somethings I had to remind myself, and even though Hunter was their peer, she was the exception to the rule.

I reached for my phone when the awkwardness consumed me. "Help me," I sent out into the ether.

My screen flashed with a text message from Troian: "I'm sitting poolside in Hollywood. Where are you?"

"I'm at a house party with about a dozen co-eds," I replied.

Her response was prompt: "Keep it in your pants."

"Thanks for the advice."

"Are you serious about being at a party?" Troian's next message asked. "Because WORST IDEA EVER."

I couldn't agree more, but since I wasn't yet ready to Switch for Hunter, I saw this as a compromise. I tried to reason with myself that the school year was practically over and Hunter had assured me that, with the exception of Loryssa, none of the people in attendance were my students.

"Is there shrimp cocktail?" I texted back, trying to block out the party around me. Some of the girls were dancing on each other and it made me feel more awkward than ever. "It's not a Hollywood party without prawns."

"How does your girlfriend put up with your weirdness?"

I smiled at the phone in my hands. "Must be my talented tongue."

"Gross, Bookie. You're not allowed to talk like that."

"You still cool with me coming out there after graduation?" I wrote her.

"Of course!" was Troian's response. "I can't wait to drag you around this city. I hope you can handle it, old lady."

I'd recently booked my flight to go to California for a week, my first visit to see Troian and Nikole since they'd moved to Los Angeles. It would also be the first time Hunter and I would be apart for any extended length since we'd started dating. Although I wanted her to be able to come on the trip, she couldn't take the time off. Because she'd just started working at the hospital as a paid employee, no longer a student intern, she hadn't yet accumulated any vacation time.

I slipped my phone into the junk drawer so I wouldn't be tempted to be on my phone all night. I was sure Hunter would be disappointed if she caught me on my phone instead of trying to bond with her overly loud, overly drunk nurse friends.

The ringleader seemed to be a gregarious girl named Cheryl. She actually put off a gay vibe, and I wouldn't have been surprised to see her on the dance floor at Peggy's. She was short and sturdily built with cropped brown hair, dark eyes, and a laugh too big for the galley kitchen where Hunter and her friends were lining up shots of apple pucker. I didn't know if they were all of legal age, but I didn't ask. It would have added more unease to an already uncomfortable situation.

Building on my discomfort, Loryssa came home close to midnight when the party was well underway. She waved at Hunter on her way through the kitchen and disappeared into her bedroom. It put me slightly at ease to think that maybe she was going to spend the rest of the night in her room. After our talk, there had been no unusual interactions in or outside of class between the two of us, but I didn't know if that would translate back to the apartment as well.

A low rasp was close to my ear. "How long until they're doing body shots?"

I jerked to attention. I had been so preoccupied with my thoughts I hadn't noticed Loryssa's return.

I gave her a strained smile and self-consciously clutched my beer. "I don't think it's *that* kind of party, is it?"

She grabbed a plastic cup and made herself an unmeasured drink of vodka and orange juice. "You haven't met her friends before, have you?" She chuckled at an unspoken joke.

I shook my head and took a nervous pull from my beer. "No. This is my first time."

Her lips curled into a queer smile. "I might be wrong, but half of them are in love with your girlfriend."

"Really?"

Her eyebrows raised as she took a long drink from her cup. "You know how it goes, I'm sure," she said, coming up for air. "It's almost graduation, they want to experiment before their time in college is over, and Hunter is the only lesbian they know."

I *did* know; too well in fact. I'd gone to a similarly small school as an undergrad and, being one of the only Out people on campus, I'd been cornered and propositioned quite a few times by bi-curious women in the final semester of school. It surprised me that Loryssa was privy to that kind of information though.

"What year are you?" I asked.

"I'm a Junior, but I didn't go to college right away. I took a few years off after high school to pursue modeling full-time."

"Wow," I openly admired. "That's brave."

She shrugged and took another long drink. "I had done some work for a local agency in the Twin Cities, and I thought I was going to be the Next Big Thing. I moved to Chicago with a pathetic portfolio and found out it wasn't that easy."

"Why'd you choose this school?"

"They gave me a scholarship," she admitted. "I'd basically spent all my savings when I was trying to make it as a model, so I couldn't be too picky."

"Do you still model?" I asked.

"I don't entertain ideas of grandeur anymore if that's what you're asking," she lightly laughed. "But I've done a few photo shoots and runway work to make some extra cash for rent and ramen noodles."

"I'm sorry if I was short with you before." I blurted out. I felt the need to apologize.

"No, no. The fault was mine." She shook her hands in front of her. "I need to learn to respect barriers better. It was totally out of line for me to be so flippant with you in class that day. But you have to agree, this is a pretty unusual situation."

I allowed myself a laugh. "That's an understatement."

"You're different than you are in class." I felt her curious gaze regard me. It made me feel like an insect under a magnifying glass in the hot summer sun. "You seem so, I don't know...proper all the time. I was honestly surprised when Hunt said you were coming."

"If I seem stiff, it's just me trying to maintain boundaries. I've gotten mistaken for a student so many times, it's given me a complex."

"And the Hunter thing can't make things any easier, huh."

"Another understatement." I felt myself sag. "But once Hunter graduates, things will get much easier." It was a mantra that was the only thing getting me through this semester from hell.

"Less boundaries to maintain," Loryssa mused.

I happened to look in Hunter's direction at that moment. Her friend Cheryl was laughing and unabashedly hanging around her neck. I bristled at the view; it didn't sit well with me.

"Speaking of boundaries...I think I need to go rescue my girlfriend," I said out loud, more to myself. I turned briefly to Loryssa. "I'm glad we got to talk."

Loryssa raised her plastic cup to me. "Go mark your territory, Professor," she chuckled.

Hunter wasn't drunk, but Cheryl clearly was.

"Okay, someone is cut off," I said, grimacing as I peeled the sloppy co-ed off my girlfriend. "I think Cheryl's met her limit," I murmured in Hunter's ear.

She nodded, agreeing.

"Let me have some of that, Cher," Hunter said, coaxing the red plastic cup out of her friend's hand. She surrendered her drink willingly, which didn't surprise me, especially if she had a crush on Hunter as I suspected.

Instead of waiting to see if Hunter would return her drink, Cheryl reached for a half-filled bottle of vodka. Her hand-eye coordination was off, however, and she only managed to knock the bottle off the kitchen counter. We could only watch helplessly as it plummeted and shattered on the linoleum.

"Oh no!" Cheryl cried out. She reached for the broken glass, but Hunter stopped her just in time before she could slice her hand on the jagged shards.

"Why don't you have a seat, Cher," Hunter said gently. "Don't worry about this mess. I've got it."

I grabbed a broom and dustpan to take care of the broken glass and a pile of paper towels to start mopping up the wasted alcohol.

"What are we going to do with this one?" I asked, nodding in Cheryl's direction. She now sat on one of the kitchen chairs, slumped forward and moments away from passing out.

Hunter's face scrunched. "What are we going to do with *all* of them?"

That's when I noticed that somewhere between my texting with Troian and my conversation with Loryssa the party had taken a turn for the worse – or at least a turn for the drunk.

The kitchen counter where the alcohol had sat was in disarray, hard liquor bottles empty or nearly so. The music was conspicuously louder than when things had started for the evening, and the party-goers, Hunter's friends from school, were in various stages of undress. One more bottle of Malibu and a pillow fight would break out, or there'd be projectile vomiting. I could see it going either way.

"I'm in Hell," I muttered.

Hunter's sensible voice brought me back. "They'll just have to sleep it off here."

She strode over to her laptop and turned the music down. The action was met with a chorus of boos, and if I wasn't so annoyed by the prospect of babysitting half a dozen drunk co-eds, it would have made me laugh.

If Hunter had started to let the alcohol she'd consumed chisel away at her pragmatism, all traces of that disappeared once Cheryl had knocked the vodka bottle onto the floor. She methodically began to put away the remaining alcohol and replace it with glasses of water.

Loryssa hovered close. "What can I do?"

Hunter brushed some hair out of her eyes. "You don't have to stick around. I've got this. They're *my* sloppy friends, so I'm responsible for cleaning up after them."

"What about me?" I half-teased. "I didn't sign up for this either." I had just finished cleaning up the mess from the broken vodka bottle. I threw the broken glass in the nearly overflowing kitchen garbage bag and put the broom and dustpan back in their closet.

Hunter gave me a reproachful look. "I need you to grab some extra pillows and blankets from the linen closet. And then take all this trash down out back to the dumpsters and recycling."

I mock saluted her, and she stuck her tongue out at me.

When I returned from my assigned duties, Hunter's friends were sprawled out on the living room furniture and floor with extra pillows and blankets. Some brainless reality television show was on the TV and the few who hadn't already passed out were quietly watching and rehydrating.

I found Hunter in her bed. I stripped out of my jeans and pulled on a pair of her sleep shorts that I found on the floor.

"You did a nice job out there," I approved, snuggling into her side. "Everyone looks like they'll survive the night, and no one's puked yet. I'd call that a win."

"I'm good at taking charge," she murmured. Her hand rested of my stomach. "You just never give me the chance."

"Well, maybe I should take a backseat more often then," I replied unthinking.

Her gaze inspected me in the darkness of her room. "You might actually like it, you know."

Somehow the conversation had come back to Switching. I closed my eyes instead of rehashing the discussion. Something told me I might like it *too much*.

"Is it weird between you and Loryssa because of me?" I asked her.

I still felt guilty about potentially souring her relationship with her long-time friend and former roommate, Sara. I didn't want the same thing to happen with her new roommate.

"No. I really don't see much of her," Hunter said. She slipped her hand under her head like a pillow. "She keeps strange hours – out all night, gets up late. She's apparently a model, so when she's not at school she's at a photo shoot or something."

"That doesn't surprise me."

"You're not supposed to say that." Hunter's lips twisted. "I might get jealous."

"Speaking of jealous, what's the story with that Cheryl girl?"

"Story? Jealous?" Hunter echoed.

"She's totally gay, right?" I posed.

"Not that I know of." Hunter sounded confused.

"Oh, c'mon, Hunt," I goaded. "I know you're new to this, but she doesn't ping your gaydar even just a little bit?"

"Be nice; she's the reason you and I are together."

My eyebrows rose to my hairline. This was a story I needed to know.

"The night I saw you at Peggy's wasn't the first time I'd been to the bar; but it was the first time I'd actually stayed."

"What does that mean?" I rolled onto my side to face her.

She stared at the ceiling. "I tried to go a few other times before, but I chickened out when I got inside. This one time I tried to buy a beer, but a woman at the bar said to me 'who are you trying to fool?' I didn't know if she was talking about me not being 21 yet, or if I didn't look gay enough. I ran right out of there, totally embarrassed, and I vowed never to go back."

"But Cheryl made you go back?"

"She wanted to go dancing," Hunter explained. "And Peggy's is like the only place you can go dancing if you're under 21 in this town. I figured if I was going to try out Peggy's again, that was the time to do it, surrounded by friends."

"And that was the night I was there."

I made a mental note to thank this Cheryl person.

"Enough talking for the night. Come here and cuddle like you mean it," Hunter instructed sternly.

I wiggled closer; we were nearly the same height and size, she a little smaller in frame and me broader in the shoulders, but she fit perfectly with her backside snuggled up to my front. I draped my arm over her waist and she grabbed onto my wrist and pulled so that my forearm was practically nestled between her bra-less breasts. I pressed my lips against her bare shoulder blade.

"I love you," I whispered into her skin.

The hand still wrapped around my wrist tightened affectionately. "I love you, too, baby."

+++++

Today was an anniversary of sorts – it had been exactly one year ago when I'd summoned my courage and had talked to Hunter at the English Department's end-of-the-year party. I'd caught her digging around in my home office, after Sylvia had scattered student papers all over the floor. Thinking back on it though, Hunter had been the truly brave one for showing up at the party in the first place. It was intended for faculty and staff, graduating seniors, and English majors – all of which she was not.

Hunter was making herself scarce this evening, however. As a graduating senior, she would have probably known some of the students who would be in attendance, but I could understand her reluctance to come. I already felt on display on campus even when Hunter was nowhere in sight. Also, she probably sensed my increased anxiety about the prospect of Dean Merlot being in my house. The English faculty always came to the party, but very often administration showed up as well. Dean Krauss had been at last year's party, and I was nervously anticipating that Dean Merlot would take the opportunity to throw her weight around on my turf.

The cheese and cracker plates were set out and the wine bottles opened, but I had largely ignored my hostess responsibilities tonight to spend the majority of the evening talking to my colleagues, Thad and Emily. Sucking up to the Dinosaurs was less pressing now that I didn't have an impending tenure review. I used to avoid Thad at all costs because he frequently found a way to flirt with me. That bad habit had somewhat faded now that he knew I wasn't interested in men. Sometimes it only encouraged men, but Thad was a smart guy.

I might have been paranoid, but it seemed like there weren't as many faculty members in attendance as there usually was. The student numbers were the same though – all crowded around the food tables and giving sideway glances to the open wine bottles set out on the dining room buffet.

A woman I didn't recognize had cornered Bob, the Chair of my Department. He looked ill at ease despite his surroundings. I wondered if he got tongue-tied around attractive women, too. The woman's hair was long — chestnut brown with honey blonde highlights — and curled into loose corkscrews that framed a tan, heart-shaped face. She wore a sharply tailored suit, pencil skirt, and blouse. It was similar to something I might teach in, but I would have foregone the formal jacket. Her legs were long, trim, and tan like the rest of her.

"Do you know who that is?" I asked my friends. I gestured to the corner of the living room as unobtrusively as possible.

Thad peered over the top of his glasses that I was convinced he really didn't need. "That's the new Dean."

"*That's* Merlot?" I nearly choked on my tongue.

Emily made a noise of affirmation. "The Great Dictator herself."

I didn't know when she'd shown up because I'd been stationed by the front door with Emily and Thad for most of the evening.

I froze when I saw the Dean look in our direction. Emily leaned in close to me. "Incoming," she murmured before abandoning me. I continued to stand like a deer in headlights as Dean Merlot crossed the living room.

"You're dangerously empty." Thad pried the nearly empty wine glass from my hands. "Let me get you a refill," he said, scattering as well.

"Dr. Graft?"

I nodded, a little dumbfounded. No matter how old I got, I still became tongue-tied around attractive women — and Dean Merlot was most definitely that.

To say I was surprised by her appearance would have been a gross understatement. Unlike most other Deans I'd known during my time in academia, this woman was young, maybe just a few years older than myself. Most people didn't get to be Dean of a college until they'd taught for decades and then made the move to upper administration. It also annoyed me to admit that she was attractive. It was far easier loathing someone's existence from behind a computer screen if you didn't actually know what they looked like and could instead imagine them as some dried-up old crone.

She held out a slim hand. "Jessica Merlot," she greeted as I took her hand. Her fingernails were as manicured as the rest of her. "It's nice to finally put a face to a name."

Somehow I had a hard time believing she hadn't at least looked me up on the English department's webpage like I'd tried to do to her. Plus the fact that she'd walked right up to me and had known me, suggested she wasn't being entirely forthright.

"Your home is charming," she complimented.

"That's kind of you to say," I returned, feeling unnaturally formal. Maybe Hunter's defense-mechanism was starting to rub off on me. "I'm glad you were able to make it to our little end-of-the-year gathering."

She nodded and absently plucked a red grape from a bunch on a fruit platter. "I've been trying to make the rounds to the departments," she said, popping the grape into her mouth. "but it's taken some time to get acclimated to a new school. I swear" she said, chuckling and shaking her head, "I think I spent all of January and February in my office, staring at my computer, and trying not to feel overwhelmed, or giving myself daily pep-talks that the Trustees hadn't made a mistake when they hired me."

I nodded, not sure what to say. Ever since Bob had instructed I tone down my gayness, I'd wanted to march into this woman's office and pontificate, throwing around acronyms like HRC and ACLU. Self-preservation had kicked in until the next personal insult, having my proposed courses rejected. But now that she was in front of me, delicately picking at the fruit plate and almost making me feel sorry for her, I didn't know what to do but be polite.

"I've no doubt the Trustees made an informed decision."

She nodded, looking wistful. "I suppose only time will tell." She rubbed her hands together as if brushing away invisible crumbs. "Well, Dr. Graft, I should probably let you go attend to your other guests. It was a pleasure finally getting to meet you."

"Elle," I choked out awkwardly. "Please, call me Elle."

The Dean's eyelashes fluttered. "Well, Elle," she murmured lowly as if getting to call me by my first name was a secret between the two of us, "thank you again for having me in your home. I'll have to repay the favor soon."

Dean Merlot sashayed away, leaving me feeling bewildered and not a little bit blindsided. I hadn't known what to expect from our first meeting, but I certainly hadn't expected such a civil, nearly flirtatious conversation. It felt like a trap.

Emily reappeared at my side almost as quickly as she had made herself scarce. She held a bottle of red wine in one hand and shoved a topped off glass toward me. "You survived."

I nodded, watching the Dean continue to make her rounds. "What just happened?" I blinked.

"She killed you with kindness, Professor Graft," she snorted over the top of her own wine glass. "You don't get to be a Dean of the College of Arts & Sciences at her age without knowing how to charm and bullshit your way through a conversation."

"So that was an act?" I openly marveled.

"Don't let that doe-eyed pantomime fool you, Elle. She's a pit bull behind closed doors."

"Why is she touching all my stuff?" I quietly hissed. I watched her stand on tiptoe to inspect the books on the top of my built-in book shelves. I felt like she was judging my life with every item she casually picked up and inspected. "Is she just trying to torture me?"

"I'm pretty sure this is what's called Marking Her Territory," Emily remarked. "She's an Alpha and she wants you to know it."

I continued to stare after the Dean, letting my gaze unabashedly travel the length of her long legs. "Do you ever think about what you'd be doing if you weren't teaching, Emily?"

"Painting coconuts for tourists on a remote island oasis," she said without hesitation.

"You sound like you've thought about this," I laughed, returning my full attention to my friend.

She ran a finger along the top of her wine glass. "Nearly every semester," she sighed.

+++++

CHAPTER TWELVE

It was a beautiful Spring day in the upper Midwest; the perfect day for a college graduation ceremony, but the scent of sweet, fragrant flowers in the air did nothing to appease my sour stomach. Emily sat next to me at the ceremony. It was a tradition from when I'd first been hired. We were in charge of nudging each other to keep from falling asleep during the long and often tedious event. From where the faculty sat on an elevated platform, we roasted in our heavy academic regalia under the heat of the sun above. The speeches were long, and I felt Emily's elbow in my side a few times throughout the ceremony. But when it came to the conferring of degrees, I was alert.

The Dean of Students, a kind-faced woman named Nancy with whom I'd interacted a few times, stood at the podium and read off each student's name alphabetically. When she called out Hunter's name, Emily nudged me in the ribs. I bit back a complaint; Emily was a thin woman and her elbows were sharp. I watched with joint pride and adoration as Hunter walked across the stage to shake hands with the university president and accept her diploma. From out in the crowd of family and friends, I heard a voice above the polite claps.

"Yeah, Grunt! Way to go!"

I smiled privately, recognizing the nickname Hunter's brother had given her.

Hunter ducked her head, embarrassed, and waved at the crowd without really looking at them before stepping off the graduation stage to return to her chair.

"Congratulations, Elle," Emily leaned in to murmur in my ear. "You're no longer dating a student."

Having a last name that began with the letter D, Hunter's name was one of the first called. I settled back in my chair and tried not to think about the dinner I was supposed to have with her family later that day. Instead, I retrained my focus on the rest of the students as they received diplomas, waving at a few English majors as they caught my eye before crossing the stage.

I always became a little nostalgic on the last day of classes, but especially at graduation. It was a small school, less than 2,000 full-time students, so chances are I would see many of my students again on campus either in another class or just randomly at the cafeteria or walking to and from one class to another, unless they were graduating. Teaching is hard for people who hate goodbyes. You get to know students and they you, and then at the end of the semester you go from seeing them 3 to 4 times a week to never again.

When the ceremony ended, I ditched my robes in my office and quickly freshened up so I didn't look like a wilted flower when I had to meet Hunter's family. My heels clicked in the empty halls of the Humanities' building. Just before exiting, I stopped at a drinking fountain to stave off the dehydration from sweating in the sun that afternoon. I congratulated myself for being responsible, but really it was just another delay before I had to face Hunter's mother for the second time.

"Dr. Graft."

At the greeting, I stood upright and turned. Dean Merlot stood behind me. She too had changed out of her academic regalia and was wearing what I assumed was her signature outfit – an immaculately tailored power suit. It was a little too much clothing I thought for a late Spring afternoon.

I wiped the water from my chin. "Oh, hi."

I hadn't realized anyone else was in the building. I'd thought everyone was still outside or had gone home already. It didn't make sense why she was in this building, which housed classrooms and the offices of humanities faculty like myself; her office was on the other side of campus.

Her eyes seemed to slowly take in my form. I'd changed into a light cotton dress, cinched high at the waist with a thin belt that accented my thin waist. "It's a lovely day, isn't it?"

"It is," I acknowledged with a nod.

"Hunter Dyson participated in today's graduation, did she not?"

I bristled. There was no reason for Dean Merlot to know my girlfriend's name. She hadn't called her my girlfriend, per say, but there seemed no other reason for her to single-out Hunter as a student who had just graduated. I wondered at Dean Merlot's need to research. "She did."

"Congratulations," the Dean said, bobbing her head and rocking a little on her stiletto heels.

"Thank you." I didn't know how else to respond.

She looked like she wanted to say somewhat else, but deciding against it, she turned and walked away. Her heels echoed in the hallway until she walked out of sight.

I pushed through the double doors to the outside to escape Merlot before I could go after her and say something I'd come to regret later. I might have been able to check my emotions at the departmental party, but I was still angry; it felt like this woman was going out of her way to single me out. I loved my job and my co-workers, and the students were bright and friendly and polite, but Dean Merlot had made this my worst semester ever.

I shielded my eyes as I first walked out to let my pupils adjust to the lighting change. The sun was still bright and hot above in the cloudless blue sky. I scanned the campus green, trying to find Hunter or her family. Robed faculty, graduates, and their friends and family littered the lawn, but the crowds had begun to disburse now that the ceremony was over.

I spotted my girlfriend standing near an ancient maple tree, surrounded by an assortment of similarly blond and pale people whom I took to be relatives. She was originally from the suburbs, and it looked like her entire extended family had made the commute into the city to support her. She had a small, blond, curly-haired child on one hip, a younger cousin perhaps. She looked at ease, and most importantly – happy.

And I hesitated.

I wanted to walk over to them, but she looked so happy, so

carefree; I knew that the second I interrupted their family moment things would become uncomfortable. I didn't want to ruin this day for her. She would be disappointed, but in the end, this was for the best.

I turned down the sidewalk, away from campus, and began my walk back home.

+++++

I was on the couch watching *You've Got Mail* when Hunter returned from dinner with her family. As soon as I heard the key in the lock, I tensed. I buried myself under blankets and tried to focus on Tom Hanks bringing daisies to Meg Ryan in a trench coat even though every noise coming from the front of the house put me on edge.

I heard the front door close and Hunter lock the door behind her. Tom Hanks was making tea for Meg Ryan. Hunter took off her shoes and carefully set them in the front foyer, lining them up with the other shoes and sandals in the entryway.

She dropped a doggie bag on the kitchen island. I could smell the distinct aroma of chicken fried rice even sitting in the living room.

Her feet creaked on the wooden floor as she walked from the kitchen to the living room where I sat.

She stood behind me, hovering over the couch. "Why are you watching your sick and sad movie?" Her voice sounded detached, void of any emotion.

Tom Hanks was tucking Meg Ryan into bed.

I made a noncommittal noise before I dared to look up at her.

"You disappeared." The corner of her mouth twitched. "My parents asked where you were. I had to lie to them about a family emergency."

My stomach twisted uneasily. "I'm a coward, Hunter. That's my only explanation. I wanted to be there, but I thought it would be for the best if you went to dinner with your family without me."

"Stop it. I don't want any more of your excuses." Her nostrils visibly flared. "I want you upstairs."

"What?"

"Go upstairs to your room," she commanded. "And don't make me wait."

+++++

I was on my back on my bed, and Hunter was straddling me between her thighs. This would have been Heaven except that she was currently tying me to the headboard. I should have been distracted by the perfect view of her sundress inching up her toned thighs, but instead, I was about to have a panic attack.

"Shit," she uncharacteristically swore. The curse word sounded ugly coming from her mouth.

"What's wrong?"

"Your clothes." She bit down adorably on her lower lip and rested her weight on my stomach. "I should have planned ahead." She stood up and hopped off the bed.

"Where are you going?" I lifted my head with difficulty.

"I'll be right back," she called out as she disappeared.

I clenched and unclenched my hands a few times, testing the strength of the bindings around my wrists. I didn't know where she'd learned to tie knots so well. Maybe her father took her boating when she was younger because the knots were efficient and capable of keeping me in place. There was a tiny knot that dug into the inside of my wrist every time I tugged at the restraints.

"You're not trying to get free are you?" came Hunter's sing-song-y voice. "I wouldn't have tied those just so you could wiggle out of them."

My eyes trained on the location from where Hunter's voice floated. She walked through the threshold of my bedroom. She had changed out of her sundress and was now wearing little more than lace and a smile.

Once again, however, my perfect view was corrupted when I saw the scissors in her hand.

"Wh-what do you need those for?" I asked in a tight voice.

She flashed a wide smile at me, her temporary captive. "To cut off your clothes, obviously. I can't take off your clothes if your arms are tied to the headboard. And there's no way I'm untying you until I'm satisfied." The cheerful tone in her voice was in stark contrast to the gleaming sheers she held in her hand – like a sunshine-y serial killer. I'd be lying if I said it didn't turn me on.

Hunter swung her right and then left leg over my own, straddling my lower body. She gently sat down on the tops of my legs, pinning me to the mattress even more so than the bindings that held my wrists.

"Hunter –." I wanted to reassure her that we didn't need to do this, but my words were cut off with the end of the scissors, gently resting against my lips.

She smoothed down my hair with the fingertips of her free hand while the other hand continued to grasp the scissors' handle. "Relax, Ellio. It's just for your clothes."

"But I just bought this dress," I whimpered.

"Then you shouldn't have stood me up," she said quietly. "You know, just because you're beautiful doesn't mean you can do whatever you want. It really hurt me that you didn't come to dinner with my family and me."

"I know, baby. And I'm sorry." I wasn't just saying the words out of routine. I genuinely felt horrible for what I'd done. At the time it had seemed like the right thing to do, but now I saw it for the self-centered act it was.

"Quiet," she said sternly. The honey warmth was gone from her tone.

A nervous giggle stuck in my throat. I wasn't laughing at her or the situation, but I was disoriented. I was a natural top, so I had a hard time letting go of control or letting myself be vulnerable like this. I trusted Hunter, and I wanted to be able to give in to her request to Switch, but taking orders or being a pillow princess was unnatural for me.

She drew the scissors' blades down my lips, the sharp tips lightly brushing against the skin of my neck, collarbone, and down to a covered nipple. With two quick motions, she cut the thin straps that held my dress affixed to my shoulders. With my hands securely bound, I was helpless to do anything but watch as Hunter slowly peeled the top of my dress down over my breasts.

"Oh, Ellio," Hunter murmured, as if in a trance. "We should have done this a long time ago."

The scissors clattered as she set them down on the bedside table.

"Now," she announced. "What to do...what to do..." She fluttered her fingertips over the tops of my breasts, feeling the goosebumps that rose on my skin.

"You could always use those scissors to cut me free?" I suggested. I jerked a little at the bindings around my wrists. The wooden slats of my headboard creaked. I could probably get out of this position, but it would mean breaking my bed.

Hunter continued to straddle my waist, resting her slight weight on me. She leaned forward and her blonde hair, even blonder now from sun exposure, fell forward like a waterfall. The ends of her hair tickled at my exposed collarbone and her cleavage swelled beneath the confines of a black lace bra I'd never seen before; I forgot all about trying to escape.

She traced her tongue along the hard line of my mouth, requesting access. She gently nibbled at my bottom lip. I closed my eyes and could only sigh, my resistance crumbling.

Hunter trailed kisses down my neck, leaving a wet path in her mouth's wake. "Fuck," she mumbled into my skin. "I've wanted to do this since the moment I saw you, Professor," she rasped.

"Oh God." I groaned at the sudden sensation of Hunter gently biting on my right nipple through the thin lace of my bra. I could feel her smile around the hardening bud, as my body instantly responded. I moaned lowly, arching my back and pushing my chest desperately at my girlfriend. Hunter made a disapproving noise and placed her palm on my sternum to gently, but forcibly, push me back onto the mattress. She continued to lavish attention to the two tight nubs through the delicate material of the undergarment and it took all my willpower to stay still.

The scissors reappeared. Their metal flashed against the extinguishing sun streaming in from outside. "Is this really necessary?" I was already out a new dress; I really liked this bra, too.

"Sorry." Nothing in the way her mouth formed that word sounded like an apology. Using the tip of the scissors, she pushed the lace material across my sensitive bud and we watched together as my nipple slowly became more visible with every touch of the blades.

I tensed when the cold blades slide across my skin. The scissors were sharp and with a few loud snips, my bra was separated from my body.

Hunter wet her painted lips and slowly sank into the newly exposed flesh. She took my right nipple into her mouth and let her tongue lash back and forth against the pink skin. I felt my reserve continue to melt away and couldn't help releasing another quiet sigh when Hunter tenderly enveloped the left bud as well, bathing the skin with attention and with her tongue.

She left my breasts shortly to place light kisses on my bare stomach. She continued to pull my dress down until it bunched at my waist. Her lips waltzed down the skin as though we'd spent a lifetime practicing for this moment. She paused briefly to dip her talented tongue into my shallow belly button, and despite her stern exterior, she allowed herself a small smile when she heard my sharp intake of air.

She lightly skimmed the tips of her fingers down my bare legs and up the insides of my sensitive thighs. Despite the bindings at my wrists, I leaned my weight on my elbows, slightly sinking into the soft mattress beneath me to prop myself up. Hunter's mouth was parted slightly and she swabbed her tongue across her full bottom lip. My breath caught in my throat as I watched her slowly inch the skirt of my dress up.

With deliberate and painfully slow movements, Hunter inched the material up my legs, increasing both of our anticipation. The soft cotton material brushed against the increasingly sensitive skin of my inner thighs. My eyes fluttered of their own accord.

Hunter continued pushing the soft material up, bunching the cotton skirt at my hips. She inched her fingertips closer to her goal. She ran two fingers down my panty-covered slit, pausing to gently rub my swollen clit through the material of the cotton barrier. I gasped when I felt her teasing touch and I rolled my hips, silently pleading for more.

Hunter crawled on her knees, bringing her face just inches from my covered sex. Her breath was warm against my inner thighs. I could feel the heat of my sex burning like a warm campfire, and she'd hardly touched me. I tried to not wiggle around too much, but I kept thinking about how good her mouth would feel when it made contact with my most sensitive skin.

"Please," I whispered almost inaudibly.

She wet her lips and sucked her bottom lip into her mouth, contemplating. My inner thighs quivered around her ears as I watched her lean forward to brush her thick tongue against my panty-covered clit. She slowly tongued my aching sex through the thin material of the undergarment. She sucked on the material, rubbing it lightly against me. I cried out in frustration when I felt her tongue push into me as far as it could go with the panty barrier still in place.

Hunter took her time. She wasn't rushed or desperate; she didn't act tentative or unsure; it was as if she intended to use all the time in the world to torture me this way. That she would make a talented Top shouldn't have surprised me. She was much better at taking bold risks and putting herself out there than me. She had been the one to come uninvited to the end of the school year party, she'd approached me at Peggy's and offered to buy me a drink, and she had shown up on my front porch in the middle of a rainstorm to declare her attraction to me. She'd been the gutsy one all along, the aggressor, and I simply the lucky recipient of her forwardness.

"Hunter," I sighed.

She looked up at me from between my thighs. "Yes, Ellio?"

"Thank you."

Her head cocked to the side. She wasn't in my head; she couldn't know what I'd been thinking about. "For what?"

I bit my lower lip. "For putting up with me."

"Is this a trick?" She rested her chin against my stomach. "Are you still trying to get me to untie you?"

My lips curled and I shook my bound hands for affect. "Do your worst."

Her wide mouth curved up. "Gladly."

With renewed vigor, she hooked her thumbs along the elastic waistband and slowly slid my underwear off; the damp material slightly stuck to my most intimate places. She paused to contemplate the skirt still lewdly gathered at my waist, but she appeared content to leave me in a state of disheveled half-dress.

Returning to her previous position, Hunter breathed in deeply, inhaling the scent of my arousal. She stretched out her tongue, and I hissed at the first touch. Her tongue, but just the very end, ghosted along my shaved sex. It felt good, and kind of tickled, but it wasn't the pressure I needed to get off. But I knew I would have to be patient. This wasn't about my immediate pleasure. This was about control. This was about power.

Hunter gently lapped at my shaved sex, the flat of her tongue dancing over the sensitive skin. She ran the tip of her tongue along the insides of my folds and her nose bumped softly into my enflamed clit. I softly sighed and entangled my fingers around the bindings that held my arms in place.

She seemed determined to make me climax without ever penetrating me. She flattened her tongue and continued to lick along my wet channel, greedily drinking in all that I had to offer. I squirmed and struggled beneath her tight grip, intent on finding a quick release.

She looked up at me, our eyes meeting, and I almost lost it. God, I loved this girl.

"Lick my pussy, Hunter," I groaned. "Yes, baby," I urged, hoping my words would push her to more activity. "Fuck. Just like that." I gasped and moaned loudly as she continued her maddeningly gentle assault.

She sucked my swollen clit into her mouth and lightly nibbled on the bundle of sensitive nerves. When she flicked the bud back and forth with the tip her tongue, I couldn't tell if the bursts of light that flashed behind my pupils were from lightning outside or from my girlfriend's very talented tongue.

I thrust my hips up to garner more friction, grinding my naked pussy into her beautiful face. Hunter responded by pushing down hard on my pelvic bone and holding me still, licking my pussy into submission. I felt the explosion quickly creeping up. After all of her deliberate teasing, I knew it wouldn't take much more for me to crash over the edge.

I groaned in disappointment when she released her hold on my clit and moved instead to my inner thigh where my left leg connected to my tortured sex. Wordlessly, Hunter clamped her mouth onto the sensitive skin there and began sucking hard, alternately sinking her teeth into the flesh. My eyes flashed wide and my entire body shook and twitched from the new sensation.

Although Hunter had remained uncharacteristically quiet throughout our intimate exchange, I could now hear her soft growls. Her hold was unforgiving, unrelenting, as she branded the inside of my thigh with her mark. I wanted to grab onto her corn-silk soft hair and twist the strands around my fingers to encourage her, but the ties around my wrists held. With a final brutal bite, Hunter released her lock on my flesh and quickly returned her attentions to my aching sex. She sucked my inflamed clit back into her mouth and I bucked my hips.

I felt myself falling over the edge, closer and closer to my impending orgasm. I needed to grab onto the back of her head and pull her face impossibly closer, but for now it was my tortured fate to remain tied to my bed frame. Hunter licked and sucked at my tender nub again, now ready to give me the pleasure I desired. When I felt her fingers finally enter me, my body went rigid and I howled at my release, letting the orgasm that began as gentle waves lapping on a shoreline, escalade into a tidal wave from which I might never resurface.

I gasped, sucking in air in deep breaths while I rattled my wrists in their confinement. "That was…that was," I panted, finally finding my voice again. "Wow." Even without the use of my hands I could feel how hot and damp my skin had become in my exertions.

A silent smile slowly stretched across the expanse of Hunter's mouth as she stared up at me from between my still quivering thighs. Thick, bruising lips curled up playfully and deep, perfect dimples carved into her cheeks. She crawled up to eye-level with me, never breaking that wide smile. Briefly, I thought she might not be done with me, but then she rolled onto her back and stared up at the ceiling.

I jerked at the ties on my wrists again, but they seemed to hold me tighter than before. "Ready to untie me now?"

Her reply was immediate. "Not even close."

+++++

CHAPTER THIRTEEN

I was having lunch downtown with my mom at the little sandwich shop where I usually went to celebrate the end of another semester. The celebratory lunch was later than usual in the month and normally it was Nikole and Troian who sat across the table from me, but this was one more tradition I'd been forced to alter because of their move. It was mid-May, but it officially felt like summer even if I'd yet to see Hunter in a bikini. The sun was bright and hot today and the breeze seemed to perpetually smell like charcoal. It was practically as mouth-watering as the mental imagine of my girlfriend in a two-piece.

"Work still going well?" I asked my mom. We didn't see much of each other now that were weren't sharing a roof, but I was determined to maintain this relationship we'd been able to repair since her unexpected arrival.

My mom nodded and dabbed at her mouth with a napkin. "My hours were cut back because school's done for the summer, but they're still keeping me on. I'm thinking about getting a second part-time job just for the summer."

"Sounds like a plan," I approved.

I didn't want to derail her progress and good mood by asking her about her plans beyond the summer. How long did she see herself working for Circulation at the library? Had she thought about where she might live once Troian and Nikole's townhouse inevitably sold? Did she ever think about moving back to my hometown? All were questions that I desired answers to, but it wouldn't be fair of me to ask.

She was slowly, dollar by painstaking dollar, pulling herself out of debt. I was proud of her, but the words never came to my mouth. It seemed like an unnatural thing to say to a parent, even if said parent acted more like a child. Maybe that's where I got my irresponsible streak from.

"Do you and Hunter have big plans for the summer?" she asked. "Any fun...vacations?" She audibly faltered on the word. It was like ordering a beer in front of someone trying to get sober.

"No. No vacation plans," I said quickly. "But I am going to California at the end of the week to visit Troi and Nik."

"Just you?"

I nodded. "Hunter's got to work at the hospital. Since she just started, she can't really take a week off to go with me."

"Oh, that's right," my mom said, bobbing her head. "Her graduation was the other day, wasn't it?"

"Uh huh." I self-consciously looked down to my wrists. I wore a thick-banded watch on one arm and a leather bracelet on the other to hide the rope burn. Hunter hadn't untied me for a very long time that night.

My mom pointed a fork at me. "I hope you got her flowers."

"Nope," I said around a mouthful of salad. "Just a severed head."

"You are *such* a romantic." She rolled her eyes at me.

I snorted. That word in no way described me. "Speaking of romantic," I said, stabbing my salad, "Troi and Nik are getting married. That's actually why I'm going to see them."

"Oh, that's exciting." My mother practically clapped. "When are you and Hunter going to tie the knot?"

"*Mom!*" I nearly choked on my food. "We haven't even been dating a year."

"You're not getting any younger, Elle," she clucked in a very Mom-like way. "And even if you're gay, I'm still expecting grandbabies."

I rubbed at my forehead with my fist. "I thought Lauren getting pregnant would get you off my back about that."

"I'm expecting grandchildren from both of my daughters," she asserted. "Oh! I just had a brilliant idea – you and Hunter could get pregnant *at the same time*. You could experience the miracle of childbirth *together*." She looked particularly proud of herself.

I blinked. "That has got to be *the worst* idea I have ever heard, in the history of ideas. It's bad enough when we're both on our period at the same time."

"It's just a suggestion," my mom hummed.

"It's not happening," I said flatly.

"You're determined to break my heart." My mother was overly dramatic, but that was just part of personality. "I'm sure Hunter's parents are waiting for grandchildren, too. By the way, when do I get to meet them?"

"How about never?"

"Are you embarrassed of me?"

"No, Mom," I sighed and balled up my napkin. "I just...I don't really get along with Hunter's family."

"Then they must be idiots," she decided. "You're fantastic."

"Thanks, Mom."

I was sure that my disappearance on graduation day hadn't helped things with her family. I hadn't asked, but I was sure Hunter had probably made up some excuse on the spot to save face as to why I hadn't been there. Now having had more time to think about my decision to run away that afternoon, I was embarrassed and ashamed. No matter how annoyed I'd been because of Dean Merlot, Hunter deserved more from me. I should have brushed off my irritation and anger and salvaged the day.

I needed to do something to make it up to Hunter, but I didn't know what. I wasn't very good at romantic, grand gestures. Flowers were a generic, 'I'm sorry,' and I'd already done that once before when we'd nearly broken up over what other people thought — namely Hunter's mother, but also my own insecurities — about our age difference. In all of her lunacy, my mom was right about one thing though — Hunter needed a better present than just getting to tie me up.

+++++

The days leading up to my California adventure passed with no further drama. I was looking forward to the trip and I thought Hunter might have been, too. With no work and no deadlines to meet, I'd been spending my days shuffling around the house in my pajamas or visiting Nikole's greenhouse and playing in the dirt. I'd offered to visit Hunter at the hospital, but she'd asked me to wait on that. She'd just gotten the job and still needed to find her niche among the staff. She'd given me permission to surprise her with pre-packaged sandwiches once she'd taken on a more structured schedule.

I honestly didn't know how I was going to occupy myself all summer. Even though I didn't have to be on campus again until August because I had no summer courses to teach, I usually still had work to do. Typically I had a course syllabus to tweak or new assignments to design or a conference paper to research and write, but my second book proposal was stalled and Dean Merlot had rejected both new proposals for courses that would have kept me busy every day of summer break. I knew if I just took out the lesbian fiction from the syllabi the Dean would accept the courses, but I was annoyed and being stubborn. It set a dangerous precedent if I bent to the Dean's will. All of my interactions with the Dean, indirect and direct, had soured me from going above and beyond the university's expectations.

"Need a sous-chef?"

It was the night before my flight, and Hunter was making dinner at my house. She was spending the night and would drive me to the airport in the morning since I'd basically given my mom my car to use so she could get to and from work.

Hunter shook her head. "I've got this. You just relax."

Her grin was mischievous, sly, because she knew too well I had a problem just sitting and being taken care of.

"You're concentrating awfully hard," I noted, perking up on the kitchen stool upon which I sat.

"I don't want to lose a finger," she said, not looking up from the giant butcher knife as she sliced it through a red pepper. "I don't know if I trust you to sew it back on."

"And I'd hate for you to lose a single finger," I said without pretense.

I expected her to blush at the comment, but she stared at me, practically challenging me. I took that moment to push a small, lidded box across the kitchen counter.

Her eyebrow arched. "What's that?"

I smiled serenely. "Happy Graduation, Hunter."

"But you already gave me what I wanted." She set the knife down and wiped her hands on the front of her apron. It was one of mine — a gift from a former student — that had a nerdy statement about the Oxford Comma screen-printed on the front.

I made a noise. "More like you *took* it," I stated coyly. "I thought you needed something else to commemorate the day." I turned my hands over, palms to the sky. There were still faint marks on my inner wrists from the tight, tidy knots. "Something more than these fading bruises."

She still hesitated. "You know I don't like you spending money on me."

"I promise it wasn't expensive." I raised my right hand as if taking an oath. "Just humor me, okay?"

She bit her bottom lip and picked up the box. Removing the lid, she revealed the vintage locket and long silver chain inside. She carefully removed the necklace from the box. It was delicate, but she handled it like it might disintegrate in her hands.

I stood and walked around the counter to stand behind her. I took the chain from her hands and unfastened the latch. Her hand laid against the top of her chest as she waited for me to put it on her.

"It's beautiful, Elle," she nearly whispered.

It had taken me some time to settle on the locket and chain. I'd had the letter H engraved on one side and the letter E on the other.

She touched her fingers to the locket and fiddled with it against her breastplate. "Are there pictures inside?"

"No. I thought I'd leave that to you. But there is something else inside."

She slid a shortened nail between the front and back of the locket. It popped open with little effort. Inside was a thin piece of paper. She carefully plucked it from the hidden compartment.

"How we need another soul to cling to, another body to keep us warm. To rest and trust; to give your soul in confidence," she read aloud. "I need this, I need someone to pour myself into."

"It's from one of Sylvia Plath's journals," I explained when she'd finished reading. "You'd be surprised how long it took to find a romantic line of text by her."

She smiled. "If you don't expect anything from anyone, you're never disappointed."

I returned her smile, recognizing the line from *The Bell Jar*.

Hunter carefully refolded the tiny slip of paper and returned it to the locket. "This is really lovely, Ellio. Thank you. You really shouldn't have," she said crossly before the smile returned, "but thank you."

"I wanted to do something." I shook my head. "I *needed* to do something."

Dinner was forgotten for the moment. Her arms slipped around my waist and she stood up on her toes to press her lips against mine. She was so warm and so soft. My arms went around her and I pulled her closer.

"I wish you didn't have to go tomorrow," she breathed against my mouth.

"I'll cancel," I murmured back. "Troi and Nik can wait."

"I don't want to be that girl," she said, pulling back just enough that we no longer shared air. "The smothering girlfriend who needs to be tethered to you."

"You're not," I insisted. "We don't even live together," I pragmatically pointed out.

With some difficulty, she pulled away completely to return to preparing dinner. "My lease is up soon."

"I...is this a conversation you want to have right now?" It seemed to me the air had been sucked out of the room. I tried not to suffocate.

"Not tonight." She shook her head, hair falling around her shoulders. "But when you get back?" Her voice lilted with the question.

I settled back onto a kitchen stool. "When I get back," I echoed.

"How old is your neighbor?" Dinner had been eaten and now Hunter and I sat at the dining room table, finishing off a bottle of pinot noir.

"Which one?" I asked.

"The high school boy next door."

"Why? You want an introduction?" I tilted my wine glass to the side and swirled the liquid around inside. "I bet he needs a date for Prom still."

"That's funny," she said, not really sounding amused.

"I think he's a Junior in high school, so 16 or 17. Why?"

"He's smoking in his room. I can see him crouched by the window," she said, nodding toward the picture window in the dining room. "He's got the window and the screen propped open."

"What a rebel." I didn't know much about my neighbors on either side of me except that one was a chatty older woman with two small dogs and the other was a couple with two kids. The boy, Tyler, was the elder of the two siblings. I didn't see much of them except when I was shoveling snow in the winter or mowing grass in the summer.

"I wonder if Brian does that," Hunter murmured.

I had only met Hunter's younger brother once – the dinner at Hunter's family home that had gone horribly wrong – but he had seemed like a good kid. He and Hunter had the same yellow hair and intense blue eyes. He was quick to tease Hunter, which told me they'd been close growing up.

I really needed to make more of an effort to get to know her family. It was clear that her family had been tight before I had come into Hunter's world. I needed them to be close again for my girlfriend. She put on a brave front that it didn't affect her, but I could tell she wasn't being honest with herself or me about this. She missed her family and she wanted me to be a part of that. She needed that more than a sentence locked away in a necklace.

"How about a do-over?" I proposed.

She looked at me questioningly.

"We could do-over dinner with your family." I felt a sheepish grin form on my lips. "I know things didn't go as well as either of us wanted last Fall and then I chickened out at your graduation. I want to make it up to you."

She looked skeptical and I couldn't blame her. When it came to family, both of ours, I tended to run the other way.

"I don't want to get my hopes up," she said carefully.

"And I don't want to disappoint you again," I returned.

Those cornflower blue eyes watched me. Her eye contact never failed. "So don't."

+++++

I've always thought that airport terminals felt like an imagined space. Once you're beyond the security checkpoints, you could be anywhere in the world. I hated flying, but I found a lot of writing inspiration in airports – so many people coming and going to all corners of the earth. I often wished I possessed the spontaneity to show up at an airport with a small carry-on, and on a whim, travel to some place I'd never been.

Troian was holding a piece of white printer paper as a sign when I got off the plane. "Go Home, Bookworm" it read. The smirk on her face told me she was happy to see me though.

I dropped my wheeled bag and wrapped up my friend in a giant hug. I squeezed her tight and even lifted her off the ground a little.

"My ribs!" Troian squeaked.

I dropped her back to the ground and she readjusted her sunglasses, which my enthusiasm had nearly knocked off her face.

"Nice to see you, too," she snarked.

I should have felt embarrassed by the public display of emotion. I was usually far more tempered, especially in public, but this was the first time seeing my friend since she and Nikole had driven away for California months ago. It had been too long.

"How was your flight?" Troian asked routinely.

I slid my own sunglasses into place and picked up my discarded suitcase. "We didn't crash and my luggage made it here, so I've got no complaints."

"I'm proud of you for flying by yourself, Bookie. Did your seatmate mind you holding their hand for take-off? I hope she was hot."

She laughed, but I scowled. It wasn't far from the truth. I was a terrible flyer; I had a hard time relinquishing control. Very rarely did I fly on my own. Even when I traveled to academic conferences I found ways to have someone come with or I'd go to meetings close enough to drive to. I was the same way about driving, too. If I wasn't behind the wheel, I was convinced we were going to crash.

"No Nik?" I asked as we made our way from baggage claim to the covered parking lot. I dragged my wheeled suitcase behind me. I'd probably over-packed for the one-week visit. Thankfully Troian didn't comment on the size of my luggage.

"She has a meeting with a client."

"Landscaping?"

Troian nodded.

"That didn't take long."

"That's because my girl isn't satisfied sitting home, being one of the Housewives."

"Dude, sign me up for that life," I chuckled. "I'll be someone's trophy wife. I could sit at home all day and just write with no pressure to actually publish it if I don't want to."

"I've got a few execs I could introduce you to while you're out here. But they're all dudes," she noted. "How badly do you wanna be a trophy wife?"

"Gross." I wrinkled my nose. "Not *that* badly."

Troian walked up to a hot little sports car and unlocked it with her key fob.

"Not this again," I laughed. When I'd first met Troian, years ago, she'd been driving an impractical and flashy coupe that she'd bought with her first publishing paycheck. But after her first Midwestern winter of owning the car, she'd exchanged it for something more reasonable and with 4-wheeled drive.

"Hey, at least I have the weather for it now," she defended.

"That's true." I rubbed briskly at my bare arms. The hot mid-afternoon sun felt good on my skin. The woman who'd sat beside me on the plane must have been menopausal because she'd twisted the overhead air vents so that frigid air blasted down on her, but also on me, for the duration of the flight.

We climbed into Troian's toy car. The vehicle had no discernible backseat and the trunk was filled with subwoofers, so my luggage perched on my lap.

"How's life?" I asked as she pulled the vehicle out of hourly parking. We talked practically every day, but I felt like we had so much catching up to do.

"Just living the dream," she smiled.

"And the work? Still like it?"

Troian made an affirming noise and adjusted the rearview mirror. "It took me a while to figure out what kind of boss I wanted to be, but things are starting to feel routine – like this is what I'm supposed to be doing."

"That's really great, Troi."

I stared out the window and admired the city streetscape. Palm trees lined the median and we passed house after house with carefully manicured lawns.

"Are we doing any actual wedding planning while I'm here?" Troian and Nikole hadn't yet set a date because the engagement was barely a month old, so my being here was more for my own good than a practical wedding-planning trip. Still, I intended on being useful and throwing in my opinion where Troian didn't want it.

"Maybe just dresses. I got an appointment at some exclusive place, so we should probably check it out."

"Exclusive bridal gown shop? Oooh, you're so Hollywood," I teased.

"Shut it," Troian growled as we turned a particularly sharp corner. I grabbed the rollover bar to keep from falling out of the car. I was surprised my luggage stayed on my lap.

"How have you two divvied up the wedding day planning?" I asked, sticking to topics that wouldn't get me tossed from the vehicle.

"We have to get our own dress and pick out what we want our bridesmaids and grooms to wear. She's going to take care of the more technical stuff like wedding license and renting the space and the band and things like that since her work schedule is more flexible than mine," Troian listed. "And she's in charge of flowers, obviously."

"Obviously," I agreed.

"I'm hiring the photographer since I have those connections. And we're both doing the cake and meal picking together."

"Jesus," I muttered when we whipped around a corner, narrowly missing falling off a cliff on one side and being flattened by a semi-truck on the other.

Troian snorted. "You're such a backseat driver," she complained when the vehicle returned to all four tires.

I clutched my suitcase tighter to my chest like it was a life preserver. "Maybe if my life didn't flash before my eyes every time you drove."

Troian slapped her palm against the steering wheel. "Come on!" she yelled at the slow-moving vehicle in front of us. "Move over!"

"How does someone so small harbor so much road rage?" I openly wondered.

Troian hazarded a quick glance in my direction. "It's LA living," she explained.

"You're a natural," I said, gritting my teeth as we accelerated up a steep hill that would have been suicide if it had been located in the Midwest. "Where are you taking me?"

"My house. Unless you were planning on staying in a motel in the Valley and getting an STD?"

"Charming," I deadpanned.

"You think I'm exaggerating," she said, shaking her head, "but I'm not."

"Stop scaring the tourist." I refused to let go of the rollover bar.

"But it's *so* fun!" she smiled manically. The posted speed limits were merely suggestions at this point. We kept climbing. It was like a roller coaster incline; I didn't want to be around when we got to the top and had to come down.

"You haven't had many visitors, have you?" I focused on the horizon to swallow down my motion sickness.

"It is that obvious?"

After I'd aged a few years from fright, we finally made it to Troian's house.

"You asshole." I dropped my luggage in the doorway. "Why didn't you tell me you were such a big deal?"

I walked through the open-plan first floor to the back of the house. There was a floor-to-ceiling glass wall that could slide away completely to expose the dining area to the outside. Beyond the glass wall was a gorgeous patio with a sizeable infinity pool and an amazing view of the city below.

Troian took off her sunglasses and tossed them on a table near the front entrance. "I keep telling you, but you never listen."

"This place is *amazing*, Troi."

"Don't get too excited." Troian's easy smile slid onto her face. "This is the Studio's property. We're just staying here until we find something. Real estate is a bitch out here. You'd be surprised what a million dollars *won't* get you."

"So where's my room?"

Troian gave me a guilty smile. "Take your pick. There's like five guest rooms in this place."

"Let me amend my statement then – which guest room is the furthest from *your* room? I don't need to be overhearing anything, if you know what I mean."

Troian snorted. She grabbed the handle of my bag, intending on showing me to my room. "Jesus, Bookie," she said, feeling the luggage's weight. It probably weighed almost as much as her. "How long are you planning on staying?"

"Just the week."

"Uh huh."

Troian led me down a wide hallway that was bathed with natural light.

"Even your *hallways* have windows?" I gaped, following her.

"It's the Studio's," she reminded me over her shoulder.

She wheeled my bag into a sizeable bedroom. Like the hallway, there was plenty of natural light streaming in from large windows. The king-sized bed was more than enough for just me, and there was a cute sitting area in a bump-out enclave. The only thing missing was a walk-out to the back patio, but I assumed that was in the master bedroom.

"Nik should be home soon from her meeting," Troian said. She parked my luggage by the bed. "She's been marinating chicken all day; I thought we could grill on the back patio and hang out by the pool tonight."

"That sounds perfect." I shoved my hands in the back pockets of my jeans. "I'm just gonna freshen up and let Hunter know I made it here."

Troian gave me a knowing grin. "Whipped," she muttered under her breath as she left the room.

"I'm going to pretend I didn't hear that!" I called after her.

I pulled my laptop out of my school bag and set it on the bed. I clicked my video chat program open and called Hunter's laptop. I wasn't sure she'd answer. I'd told her approximately what time I anticipated arriving at Troi and Nikole's house, but had urged her not to sit by her laptop waiting for me. She answered the call on the third ring.

"Hey, beautiful," I greeted.

"Hey you," she returned. "I take it you made it to Troian and Nik's?"

I nodded. "Yup. You should see this place. It's almost as big as Troian's ego."

Hunter smirked, but didn't join my ribbing of my best friend.

"How's Sylvia?" I adjusted the top lid of my laptop so my built-in camera was better lined up.

Hunter's smiling face filled up my laptop screen. "She misses you."

"Liar," I scoffed. "She only cares if her food bowl gets filled when it's empty." My cat had that stereotypical aloof and independent cat personality. The only time she wanted to cuddle was when Hunter was on the couch with me, too.

"Oh, you'd be surprised. I caught her moping around today when I went to feed her. She definitely knows you're gone." Hunter humored me, but I knew the truth. If we ever broke up, my cat would probably want a divorce from me, too.

"How was work today?" I asked.

Hunter shrugged. "It was good. Played with some kids in the Children's Wing."

"You're cute."

"Bookworm!" I heard Troian yelling from another room. "Nik's back! Stop cybering and get your flat ass out here!"

"I should probably go hang out with my friends," I sighed.

Hunter smirked. "Yeah, we wouldn't want Troi thinking anything uncouth was happening under her roof."

"I would have video-chat sex in here just to annoy her."

She laughed musically. Hearing her laughter made me miss her and I hadn't even been gone a full day. This was going to be a long week.

"Go, go," she urged. "I don't want Troian thinking I'm a sex maniac. Can't be away from my girlfriend for more than a few hours without a craving."

"You're not?" I said, feigning surprise.

"I'm serious, Ellio. Go spend time with your friends. I'll talk to you later. Have fun, okay?"

"Okay," I said, properly chastened. She had a point. I was here to spend time with Nik and Troi, not hide out in their guest bedroom and video chat with my girlfriend.

"I wish you could have come."

"I know, babe. Me too. Have fun with Troi and Nik, okay? Tell them I say hi."

"Ok, I will. I love you."

"Love you, too."

I found both Nikole and Troian in the kitchen, standing around a large island counter. The kitchen, like the rest of the house, was gorgeous. Nikole had a craft beer in hand and Troian was predictably having water. They looked like they were starring in a celebrity lifestyle magazine feature.

"I hope you washed your hands," Troian said, making a disgusted face.

"For someone who talks a big game," I teased back as I entered the room, "you certainly can't back it up."

"That's because it's *you*, Bookie."

"So the thought of me having sex is repulsive?" I said, mocking offense.

Nikole waved her hands. "Before you two fall back into your old, married couple routine, someone here needs a hug."

"Looking good, Nik," I approved with a wink. Her naturally olive-toned skin was a shade darker than usual from exposure to the sun. "California life agrees with you." I greeted her with a tight hug, but since she was the same height as me, I couldn't lift her off her feet like I'd done to Troian.

Troian swatted my shoulder. "So you're just going to follow up cyber sex with your girlfriend by hitting on my woman?"

I laughed, but rubbed my arm. For such a tiny person, she packed a punch.

"Careful, Elle," Nikole warned with a playful grin. "She's gotten extra-jealous now that I've got a ring."

"Oh my God, that's right." I grabbed onto Nikole's left hand. I had minimal experience with engagement rings, but it was pretty and it sparkled and it was more than one diamond. I didn't doubt that Troian had hunted for ages to find the perfect ring. "Very nice," I approved. "No wonder you said Yes."

Troian made a disgruntled noise into her water glass.

"*And* this house is gorgeous, you guys." I walked over to the floor-to-ceiling windows and the multi-million dollar view. I could get used to this. "How long do you get to stay here?"

"My boss said we could stay as long as we want, but I don't want to abuse their hospitality," Troian said. "They have the house so they can host out-of-town talent, so it's not meant to be permanent."

"I can't wait to stop living out of my suitcases." Nikole leaned against the countertop. "I'm looking forward to us finally having our own space again."

I knew exactly how they felt. I was enjoying not having my mom staying with me anymore. I knew Hunter and I would soon be having a conversation about living together. I didn't know how to feel about that yet, so I pushed it from my mind. There was no sense stressing about co-habitation yet; I had a full week before I needed to think about that.

"We just need to find time to tour houses," Troian noted with a nod.

"Yeah, if I could ever tear this one away from her work," Nikole openly complained, "we might finally settle on a new place."

I looked back and forth between my two friends. Our conversation had become unexpectedly heavy over the course of a few flippant statements.

"Do you guys need to look at houses while I'm here?" I tried to appease. "I'm cool tagging along, or you could just leave me here so I can pretend like I'm rich."

Nikole pulled a number of alcohol bottles out of a lower shelf. "Oh, no, lady. No boring house hunting for you."

"But I love *House Hunters*," I protested.

"You're on vacation," Nikole said, "so you'd better start acting like it."

I eyeballed the various bottles she had magically produced. I picked up a bottle of flavored vodka. "And vacation equals alcohol?"

Nikole opened another cabinet and set two shot glasses on the quartz countertop. "I hope you packed your big girl pants."

"You should see the size of her luggage," Troian snickered. "I think that's all she packed."

+++++

CHAPTER FOURTEEN

It was early when Troian woke me up the next morning – too early. She pulled at the slatted blinds in the room I was staying. "Time to get up," she sang.

I flopped on my stomach and groaned into my pillow. A window was cracked open and I could hear the sounds of birds chirping and distant traffic. "Who plans a wedding this early in the morning?" I complained.

"Not wedding planning – work." Troian opened the second set of blinds and I hissed at the sun that flooded in.

"But I'm on vacation," I whined again. "It's summer." I couldn't tell if the disturbance in my stomach was hunger or hangover. At least the room wasn't spinning.

"Come on, Bookie." Troian bounced on her toes. "I want you to come to work with me. You gotta earn your keep."

"Can't I just dig around in the dirt with Nik?" If I had to get out of bed this early, gardening sounded more fun. Plus, I wouldn't have to shower.

"No, I want you to sit in on a table read with me."

"That sounds boring," I complained through a yawn.

"It usually is," she confirmed, "but today I'm firing someone."

"You get to fire people?" I smacked my dry lips. "Jealous." I'd probably need a gallon of water to get rid of this cottonmouth. I really shouldn't have switched from liquor to beer, and back to liquor last night. Troian didn't drink, but Nikole was a champion with an amazing poker face. Her smile got a little wider and her laugh a little throatier, but you couldn't really tell if she ever got drunk unless you knew those two tells.

Troian flopped down on the corner of the mattress. "Where's your shirt?"

I blinked a few times. "Huh?" I lifted the top sheet so I could better assess the situation.

Troian made a face. "Wow. You really *did* drink a lot last night."

"I blame your girlfriend," I grumbled, pulling the sheets over my head.

"You mean the hot chick in the kitchen who's making juice and humming like a Disney princess?"

"I loathe you both," came my muffled complaint. I thought about my undergraduate years when I could drink all I could handle, switch back and forth between alcohol genres, and wake up the next morning without feeling a thing. Now my hangovers tended to last multiple days. "When are we leaving?" I groaned.

Troian bounced to her feet. "About an hour, so get a move on."

I somehow managed to drag myself out of bed and into the bathroom. The bathroom was so high-tech, I was afraid if I pushed the wrong button it would launch a missile at Russia or re-configure an orbiting satellite. There was also a steam shower, but I didn't trust myself not to break anything, so I took one of those plebian showers instead.

I found a small hickey on the inside of my left arm and another low enough on my collarbone that as long as I didn't wear anything with a plunging neckline it could go undetected. As Hunter had been marking me the night before I'd left she'd said it was so I thought of her whenever I got into the shower. With our shared history, I didn't need any encouragement. It took effort to *not* think about her in the shower just so I could get through the daily ritual.

Forty-five minutes later I was crawling into Troian's toy car, sunglasses firmly in place, and clinging onto my seat as Troian zipped down the curvy decline of West Hollywood. The rollercoaster ride took about an hour before we rolled up to the gates of Pickfair Studio. The old production company was in the midst of a renaissance of sorts, largely focusing on web-based television programming that allowed for content that would make the FCC's hair turn white.

A security guard waved us through the gated entranceway without a second glance. Troian parked her fancy car outside of a mobile home that reminded me of my 4th grade classroom. We'd outgrown the elementary school and so the school district had purchased modular classrooms.

Troian unlocked the door to her trailer; her name was on a gold colored nameplate with the title of 'head writer' etched beneath it. Inside was an assortment of furniture that looked right out of the 1970s. She threw her messenger bag onto a desk and flopped down in a worn office chair.

"Make yourself at home," she told me. "I've got a few things to look over before we meet with the other writers."

I wandered around the trailer office with my hands shoved deep in my pockets. I didn't know why I felt nervous, but I did.

"Have you seen any of these movies before?" I asked. There was a series of framed movie posters on the wall. I barely recognized the titles and I considered myself pretty proficient with films. "Or are they just to impress the interns?"

Troian looked over her reading glasses. "They were here when I got the job. I haven't had time to redecorate."

There was a knock on the metal screen door and a girl wearing too much eyeliner poked her head inside. "Going for coffee," she announced.

Troian's nose was still buried in script edits. "Black for me, one sugar. Elle, what do you want?"

It took me a second to realize Troian was talking to me. It was rare she actually called me by my name. I usually got Bookie or Bookworm.

"Oh, um. Coffee would be great. Black, yeah," I stumbled out.

The girl's head was gone as fast as it had appeared.

"You get to fire people *and* you have coffee minions?"

Troian finally looked up from the thick stack of paper. "It's good to be me," she shrugged.

I flopped down in the chair across from Troian's desk. It occurred to me that this was the exact opposite of our usual work hangouts. Normally she was the one visiting me, and I was the one buried in edits. It was a bit surreal to be on this side of the desk.

"Who are you firing today?"

Troian sighed. "Ugh. Some Hollywood dickhead. He schmoozes too much and he hasn't been pulling his weight. I think he's over his head, to be honest, so he belittles the other writers so they don't see his insecurities."

"A high school Mean Girl."

"Yup," Troian agreed.

"I wish I could fire students sometimes," I said wistfully.

Troian made a clucking noise. "Nuh uh. No talking about work. You're on vacation, remember?"

"I know, I know," I sighed.

We left Troian's office to go to a nearby trailer that served as the writers' room. The space was dominated by a long, rectangular conference table surrounded by metal folding chairs. I dragged one of the chairs away from the table to sit along an adjacent wall. Troian had practically forced me to come to this meeting, but I didn't want to assume that meant I was invited to sit at the table with the writers.

Troian's new show had something to do with outer space and maybe time traveling and maybe even a little mythical creatures thrown in. She had once described it to me as *Saved by the Bell* in Outer Space. I had thought it sounded like a hot mess, but the Studio executives obviously thought otherwise. They'd interpreted the mixing of genres to be radically creative rather than derivative. But what did I know; I was just an English professor.

Troian wasn't the person who'd come up with the actual idea for the show, but she'd been tapped to lead the studio's staff of writers. The studio had green-lit the project and had ordered a 12-episode season. Shooting had yet to begun, however, and they might have even been working on casting still.

The walls of the trailer were blanketed with the headshots of attractive young people and sketches of scenes and set conceptions. Because the majority of the show would take place on spaceships and space stations I imagined they'd do the bulk of the shooting right at the studio. That would be nice for Troian because as head writer she would have to follow the shot locations to make necessary tweaks to dialogue and plot. I couldn't imagine her being separated from Nikole for an extended amount of time.

The writers bounced ideas back and forth and I sat in the

outskirts, trying to follow the storyline of whatever episode they were working on. From what I could observe, the lead character was a teenaged girl going through typical teenage drama, only in outer space. Her cohort of friends were both humans and aliens with her best friend being some purple, multi-tentacled creature. When I'd learned the bit about the alien-octopus best friend I'd tried to catch Troian's attention from across the room. I sincerely hoped I hadn't been the inspiration for that character.

"In your space utopian, are aliens kind of like second-class citizens?"

A dozen set of eyeballs focused on me.

I squirmed in my chair. I hadn't intended to speak. It had just happened.

"Yeah." One of the writers whose name I didn't know nodded. "It's like a caste system with humans at the top. We figure that End Game can be some kind of alien revolt for rights with the lead character leading the way because of her friendships with the aliens on the space station."

"What if it turns out the lead character isn't entirely human?"

The room grew quiet at my question.

Troian leaned forward in her chair and removed her reading glasses. "Say that again."

I cleared my throat. I was pretty sure I was blushing from all the attention. Everyone was suddenly focused on the weird woman sitting in the corner of the room. "Your lead character," I tried again. "What if she's actually part alien, but she – and the audience – don't find out for a few episodes?"

"But if her parents are both still alive, how do we account for the alien aspect?" another writer fired back at me.

"Her dad is actually her stepdad," I supplied. "But he and her mom married so early, he's the only dad she's ever known. Her parents both know she has alien DNA, but they didn't say anything to her because from the outside, she looks 100% human."

Another writer nodded, looking thoughtful as she chewed on the cap of her pen. "That might actually work. Her alien heritage could have been dormant all this time or at least just under the surface, maybe even giving her an edge over other kids."

With those suggestions, the room erupted into a flurry of conversations and brainstorming. I sat back, satisfied with my contribution. When I happened to glance in Troian's direction, I caught her staring back at me. I didn't know if she'd be mad at me for butting into the conversation. But she just regarded me with interest and looked at me as if she was seeing me for the first time.

+++++

At the end of the workday, Troian and I walked back to her parked car. She'd been quiet since the scriptwriting activity and it had me worried. She had been the one to make me come to the studio lot with her that day, but I was sure she hadn't intended for me to become an active participant in the brainstorming session.

I was worried I'd overstepped my boundaries. I was an English professor, not a television scriptwriter. What right did I have to open my big mouth during the meeting? I slid through the passenger-side door, a bundle of nerves. I could tell she was looking at me, but I pretended not to notice.

Troian was the one who broke the unsettling silence. "I want to hire you."

I barked out a laugh that was too loud for the interior of her car.

"I'm serious," she said, twisting in her seat to regard me. "You were really impressive today. Everybody sitting at that table thought so."

"I'm a teacher, Troi."

"*And* you're a writer."

"Yeah, but I don't write TV shows."

"Neither did I in the beginning," she reminded me. "I've read your stuff, Elle. You're really creative. Your book about people with super powers that aren't really super? That could be a show right there."

I worried my lower lip. "You weren't annoyed I chimed in out of turn?"

"Hell, no." She slapped the top of her steering wheel for emphasis. "Why do you think I dragged you to work with me today?"

"And you didn't think it was a dumb idea having the lead be part alien?"

"Dumb?" Troian shook her head and jerked the car into gear. It was a manual and the car protested as she found the right gear. "It's brilliant, Elle. As soon as you suggested that, my brain went crazy thinking about all the fun visual effects and scenarios we can put her through – it'll totally be a *Secret Life of Alex Mack* kind of thing with her trying to control her alien aspect and hide it from everyone."

"Come write for me," Troian urged. The car exited the gated studio lot. "It would be so much fun."

I still hesitated.

"Listen, if you suck I fire you, and you go back to teaching. It's not like if you stop teaching, you can never go back," she reasoned. "And aren't you due a sabbatical or something?"

The magic s-word. Another perk of being tenured. "I have to apply for one of those."

"Then apply," Troian said impatiently. "They won't say no."

I thought about those recently rejected course proposals. I hadn't thought those would be denied either. But who knew if Dean Merlot would allow me a break; she'd probably find a way to deny me a semester off because of my sexuality.

We didn't talk for the rest of the drive. Well, I was silent, just looking out at the southern California landscape and Troian yelled at the drivers who were going too slowly or who cut her off.

+++++

I called Hunter via Skype as soon as Troian and I got back to her house.

"How was your day? What did you do?" Hunter asked, blue eyes eager. Her visible earnestness made me miss her even more and wish she could have come along on this trip.

"Troian brought me to her studio. I got to sit in a brainstorming session with her team of writers."

"Oh, that sounds like it would have been a blast. I bet you were totally in your element."

"Yeah, it was fun," I agreed. I thought about Troian's offer. "Would you ever want to leave the Midwest?" I posed.

"Depends. Why do you ask?"

"Troian offered me a job," I revealed. "She wants me to be a writer for her show."

Hunter didn't look surprised. I guess I wasn't too surprised either. For as long as I'd known Troian, she'd been trying to get me to quit being a teacher and be a full-time writer like her.

"What did you tell her?" I couldn't read Hunter's emotions over the video chat.

"That I'm a teacher."

"You're a good teacher, too. I remember," she said with a wry smile. "But do you *want* to keep teaching, Ellio? I know how frustrated you were last semester."

I could always teach someplace else, but the job market was oversaturated. The professors who should have been retiring weren't because of the economy, yet graduate programs kept churning out new PhDs every year. I had friends from graduate school who still didn't have full-time work and here I was, already tenured. It made me feel whiny and ungrateful, or like I was making too big a deal out of Dean Merlot's interference.

I sighed and rubbed my hands roughly over my face. "I don't know anymore."

+++++

The next morning, Troian didn't wake me up by jumping on the bed, but she did tumble into my bedroom an hour earlier than I had planned on waking up.

"More work today?" I groaned into my pillow.

"Yup," Troian confirmed.

"Ok," I sighed, hefting myself up.

Troian hovered near the end of the bed. "Are you sure you're okay hanging out at the office again today?"

I didn't think I really had a choice. I was the one visiting, but I was also kind of interrupting her work schedule. From what I'd gathered from a few brief, tense conversations, Troian's spare time was precious and limited these days.

"Yeah, it's fine." I raked my fingers through my tangled hair. "But there *is* something I want to do with you while I'm out here."

"That sounds dangerous," Troian clucked. "Remember that I'm an engaged woman now."

I snorted. "Right. As if you could be any more committed to your future wife than you already were."

"What is it that you want to do?" Troian pressed.

I rolled out of bed. "Well first I want to shower."

"Yes, please."

"Is my hair crazy?" I asked through a yawn. I touched my hand to my hair. I'd been rolling around all night, unable to sleep. Thoughts about my immediate future career had preoccupied my brain.

"The craziest," she confirmed.

+++++

"I can't believe you made me stop for coffee."

I threw myself down on a vacant easy chair. "Not just coffee," I corrected her. "We're going to have a coffee *date*."

I wiggled in my chair, trying to break it in like the beat up hand-me-downs at Del Sol.

"What are you doing?" She glanced around the coffee shop as if I was causing a scene and she worried people were watching us.

"Getting comfortable, duh."

Troian sat down in a chair of her own, only more cautiously than my dramatic sit down. "You're really weird, Bookworm."

I sat up more rigidly. "Hey, I don't know the next time we'll have this opportunity," I pointed out. "You decided to leave me for California and Fame."

"You could come too you know. The offer's been made."

"I'd never fit in around here," I flippantly dismissed. "I'm a Midwest girl all the way."

The coffee shop was a sea of laptops and cell phones, people taking advantage of the free Internet or working on the next great American novel – although in southern California they were probably working on a screenplay. Everyone was too pretty, both the men and women, for this to be a real place.

"Do you actually like it here?" I flagged down a barista who brought us two coffees.

Troian picked at the material of her easy chair. "Well, it's no Del Sol, but it's less than half an hour from my house, so I can't be picky. Everything takes so fucking long to get to. I miss the days of stumbling out of bed to meet up with you."

I stopped being critical long enough to smile at my best friend. "But look at all this eye-candy," I observed. "If I lived out here, I'd get in trouble." As if to prove a point, I let my gaze follow a woman in a skirt so short it should have been illegal.

"Eh, even a horn-ball like you would get desensitized to all the pretty faces. It's like working at a strip club; eventually you stop noticing the meat market." She shook out her raw sugar packet before tipping it into her black coffee. "But on the plus side, not as many people flirt with my girlfriend out here."

"Your *fiancée*," I corrected her.

"Right." She chuckled and shook her head. "That still sounds so weird."

I dipped a stir-stick into my coffee. "Were you serious yesterday about giving me a job?"

Troian's face looked eager at my question. "Are you thinking about it?"

"Maybe. I don't know." I made a frustrated noise. "It would be a really big change from my life right now."

"That's certainly true."

"What would I do? I'd be a real writer, right?" I stated with caution. "You wouldn't make me get you coffee?"

"Don't be ridiculous; I already have someone who does that." She paused, and I could tell she was mulling the idea over. I knew she'd enjoy hazing me too much. "But seriously, you'd be doing the same thing you did yesterday, only you'd actually get paid for your ideas. I don't know how much you're making right now, but I can guarantee you'd make more at the Studio."

I stared into the top of my coffee cup. More money would be nice, but that wasn't my concern. Uprooting my life was.

"What about job stability?" I posed. I had tenure at my university, which was supposed to be the ultimate in job security. But with Dean Merlot's new regime, who knew if she'd actually honor tenure in the future.

"That's a bit of a gamble," Troian admitted. "The Studio green-lit this project, but if we don't get ratings, they won't keep ordering new episodes. *I* don't have to worry as much because they gave me a Talent Contract. So even if the show gets canceled, I still have a job."

"But all the other writers would be out on their cans." I frowned. "So I could potentially give up my life to come out here, only to fail in a few months time."

"Welcome to Hollywood," she nodded.

"How does Nik like living here?" I asked.

"She puts on a brave face, but I think she hates it," Troian said glumly.

"Because she's not getting hit on?" I ventured. I didn't like the somberness that had reached Troian's face.

"No. I was so busy the first month trying to get into a routine at the Studio that I kind of neglected her. I think that's why she went back to landscaping so quickly."

I sensed we'd broached a sensitive subject. I couldn't recall Nikole and Troian ever having a rough patch in their relationship, but moving across the country as they'd done could certainly cause tension.

"Hey. Plastic Barbie-type near the bathroom," I said, nodding toward a blonde woman who sat by herself. "Top, Bottom, or Switch?"

+++++

Nikole was home from work by the time we returned from the coffee shop. She must have just returned, however, as she was still in her landscaping uniform and had dirt smudges on her cheeks. She waved at us when came in while she filled up a glass with water from the refrigerator.

"You two are back early," she observed. "Short day at the Studio?"

Troian tossed her keys on a table in the foyer. "We didn't make it," she admitted. "Elle distracted me with coffee instead."

Nikole grinned. "I'm impressed." She tipped her water glass in my direction. "I owe you one, Professor Graft. Even I haven't been able to distract her from going to the office with offers of much more than overpriced coffee."

"Damn you, Bookie," Troian grumbled out of the side of her mouth.

"What?" My eyes widened on their own accord.

"Do you see that?" she said, gesturing at Nikole. "I could be ravishing my fiancée on the kitchen countertops right now if you weren't here."

Nikole's smile was as brilliant as ever. She hopped up to sit on one of the counters and swung her bare legs back and forth. "Oh, I'm sure Elle wouldn't mind," she winked.

I turned on my heel to escape down the hallway that led to the guestroom. Nikole's laughter followed me as I ran away and shut the bedroom door behind me.

+++++

"You're on early," Hunter observed.

I hadn't really expected her to answer the video-chat call. Her hours at the hospital were all over the place, but I thought I'd give it a try in case she was home and in earshot of her laptop.

"I'm avoiding Nik and Troi; they're trying to suck me into a threesome."

Hunter frowned and looked uncomfortable.

"I'm kidding," I reassured her. "Neither one is my type."

She gave me a small smile, but it didn't reach her eyes. "That's nice to know."

"Are you okay?"

Even though we were early into the conversation, I sensed that something was a little off. She kept looking away from the screen, unwilling to look at me straight on. Coming from a girl with unfaltering eye contact, it made me feel strange.

Hunter worried her lip. "I have to tell you something, and I don't know how you're going to react. And it would probably be better if I told you in person, not like this," she said, waving her hands animatedly, "but I wanted to tell you right away because honesty and transparency is the foundation of a healthy relationship."

I wanted to laugh because she had worked herself up so much that it was almost comical. But instead of chuckling, I immediately anticipated the worst. I didn't know if I could handle more disappointment and frustration. These past few months had not been kind. My only constant had been my relationship with Hunter.

I took a deep, cleansing breath. "What is it?"

Hunter worked the muscles in her throat. "Loryssa kind of, um, prepositioned me last night."

"Prepositioned you?" My stomach sank at the words.

"I don't want you to get mad." Hunter bit her lip again.

"I can't make that promise."

Hunter looked away from her laptop as if she needed to check if anyone might overhear. It didn't take me long to realize that person would be Loryssa.

"She climbed into my bed last night." The words coming out of her mouth were getting worse and worse. "I'm pretty sure she'd been drinking."

"And?" My voice sounded strangled even to my own ears.

Hunter looked away from the computer again. I heard muffled voices in the background.

"Hold on," she told me.

She rose from her bed, all elegance and long limbs, and left the direct view of the built-in webcam. I heard her steps on the creaky wooden floor and the sound of her bedroom door opening. The voices became clearer, one male and one female, but I still couldn't make out the words.

I started to nervously sweat as I waited, helpless and thousands of miles away. God, why was this taking so long? Why couldn't she just rip the band-aid off and tell me she'd had sex with her fashion model roommate who was closer to her age and had more in common with, and that they were soul mates, and she was going to keep my cat as well as my heart?

Hunter returned into view and settled back onto the bed. The voices had become quieter, and I guessed she'd closed her bedroom door again. I tried not to appear too eager or anxious for her to continue her story.

"Sorry about that. Eric, Loryssa's boyfriend, just came over."

My mental panic continued. Loryssa was probably telling her boyfriend about her wild night with my girlfriend at the same time that my girlfriend was going to tell me about her night with Loryssa. Synchronized heartbreaking. A new Olympic sport.

"They had a fight or something last night," she explained. "I think that's why she ended up in my bed."

I threw my hands in the air, unable to restrain my emotions. "Just say it, Hunter."

"Say what?"

"That you cheated on me."

"What?" Hunter's jaw dropped. "I didn't cheat on you, Elle."

"You didn't?" I was experiencing too many emotions in too short of a time.

"Of course not. Loryssa hopped in my bed and I turned her down. Nothing happened."

"Really?"

"*Really*," Hunter confirmed. "And she's totally embarrassed about it. She's been apologizing all morning."

"You turned down sex with a runway model." I said the words out loud and they sounded just as preposterous to my ears as they had inside my head.

"Yes. Nothing happened." Hunter's face and her tone were serious. "I wouldn't do that to you."

I let myself relax a little bit, but not entirely. "And that's it? That's what you were nervous to tell me?"

She nodded. "I just know it's been kind of a weird start to our relationship already, and then add to that Loryssa being one of your students, too..." She trailed off.

"Be honest, were you the least bit tempted?" Why was I such a masochist? Couldn't I just let this be?

"She's hot. Anybody with eyes can see that," Hunter shrugged. "But she's not you."

This was the epicenter of my self-doubt and insecurities. I wanted to cut my trip short and fly back immediately. I hated our physical distance, that I was on the opposite side of the country and couldn't hold and kiss her. I would probably continue to feel unsettled until I could see her in person.

Hunter's generous mouth flopped into a troubled frown. "You're not going to, like, beat her up or anything, right?"

It was a fair question. I was pretty famously a jealous person. Plus, it wasn't like the threat was gone. Loryssa still lived there with her. What was to stop her from crawling into Hunter's bed the next time she got drunk or fought with her boyfriend? What was to stop Hunter from giving in the next time?

I had so many unanswered questions, but the gory details of Loryssa's failed proposition would only aggravate the gnawing jealousy in my gut. I was naturally territorial, but I had to believe that Hunter wouldn't betray my trust. She could have chosen to keep this from me, but she'd been forthright.

I cleared my throat. "Your roommate is safe." *While I'm still in California*, I mentally added.

Her lip twitched, curling up on one side. "She'll be relieved to know that."

+++++

CHAPTER FIFTEEN

I sat by the infinity pool that overlooked some undistinguishable southern California geography. The sun was warm on my face and it was remarkably quiet outside. There were no birds chirping, just the occasional roar of a leaf blower filtering from a neighbor's yard.

I had once warned my ex-girlfriend Cady when we'd first started dating that if she wanted to be with someone who had banker hours that she should date a banker, not me. There would always be student papers to grade when the teaching day was done, or student emails to respond to, or research of my own to complete. But not today. I had no papers to grade, no lectures to prepare, no research or writing of my own to complete. I felt like a regular person with a regular work schedule.

It was the kind of morning that made me miss my girlfriend. I imagined her splashing around in the pool, unwilling to sit idle for too long. She always had to be moving, even on what should be a lazy weekend. I imagined her laughter in the background. I thought about calling her, but after our intense conversation the previous night, I didn't want to seem like I didn't trust her and was checking up on her.

The sliding door opened and Troian appeared, bleary-eyed and blinking into the sun. Her glossy black hair stuck out this way and that, and she was barefoot on the patio in her sleep shorts and t-shirt.

"Wow." I couldn't help laughing at her disheveled state. "Good morning, sunshine." I set my e-reader down and took a sip from my orange juice. "Rough night?" My own night had been emotionally exhausting, but I'd somehow managed to turn off my busy brain long enough to fall asleep.

Troian ran her fingers roughly through her wild hair and padded across the backyard to sit down at a vacant patio chair across from me. "That woman is going to be the death of me." She rubbed gingerly at the hinges of her lower jaw. "I think I dislocated my jaw."

I nearly spit out my orange juice. "Let me stop you right there."

"Good." She sighed and leaned forward so her forehead rested against the glass table. "I need a powerbar or gatorade or something."

"No wonder you stay so tiny without ever working out," I ruefully stated.

She lifted up her head just a little. "Oh, I work out," she assured me. "You just won't find my exercise regime in any fitness magazine."

"No, just the porn ones," I quipped.

Troian's head dropped back to the table. "I think I strained a muscle in my right bicep, too."

"You need to sign an insurance waiver before having sex with your girlfriend." I didn't feel sorry for her, not one little bit. She was having acrobatic sex with her partner while mine was deflecting the advances of a runway model. I bit my tongue. I couldn't tell Troian about that yet. I was too much in my head about it still. I needed to work it out for myself before I could tell her. I knew Troian would have an opinion. She had an opinion about everything.

"So what's the plan for today?" I asked instead.

Troian grunted. "An ice bath."

"And then?"

She heaved her head up like it was a great chore. "And then I've got an appointment at a bridal shop, but I don't think I'll go."

"Why not?"

"I hate shopping for clothes," Troian said, making a face.

I wasn't a big fan of clothes shopping either, and I really didn't possess an ounce of interest in trying on bridesmaids dresses or watching Troian try on bridal gowns, but I supposed this was the kind of chore that went with Best Woman territory.

"Are you going to wear a dress to your wedding?"

"Of course I am — what else would I wear?"

I shrugged. "I think you'd look cute in suspenders and a bow-tie."

Troian wrinkled her nose. "I don't want to look *cute* on my wedding day. People think I'm 12 years old already."

"Do you know what style of dress Nik is going for?"

"What – no suit and tie for my fiancée?" Troian challenged.

I arched an eyebrow. I was sure Nikole could pull off a tailored suit, but she was definitely a wedding dress kind of bride.

"No. She wants it to be a surprise."

"I hope you two don't end up with the same dress. How embarrassing would that be?" I snorted. "If you thought Prom was bad…"

Troian cracked a smile for the first time that morning, and I felt lighter, glad to have her in my life. While I couldn't entirely dismiss the unsettling thoughts that lingered from my conversation with Hunter the previous night, spending the day with my best friend certainly helped.

+++++

The bridal shop Troian took me to was a cute boutique, not one of those franchises you find in strip malls. We'd been buzzed in from the outside after providing Troian's name. I hadn't been a part of too many bridal parties, so I was a bit of a novice when it came to dress shopping and everything else that went into planning a wedding.

I pushed around some dresses on a rack, all of them too expensive and too small for me. I was a reliable size 10, an 8 on a good day. Southern California seemed to have a shortage in sizes. From looking at just one dress's price-tag once inside the shop I'd also surmised that I was out of my league. I'd hardly paid that much for my used car. I wondered if they did layaway.

"How'd you find this place?" I felt like I should whisper. We seemed to be the only people in the shop.

"One of the interns at work." Troian still had on her aviator glasses, which made her look like she was nursing a hangover, mid-week; she'd only overindulged on sex though. "She said everyone who's anyone comes here. I even had to name drop one of the studio execs to get us this appointment."

If this was such a fancy place I would have expected to be greeted at the door with flutes of champagne and staff catering to our every whim. I couldn't spot a single sales associate, let alone anyone giving us celebrity treatment.

"Sure your intern wasn't punking you?"

"I'm starting to wonder." Troian pulled a dress from a rack and held it up to her torso. She made a face and returned it to the dress rack. "Speaking of work, have you thought more about my job offer?"

"I couldn't do that to Hunter," I said determinedly.

"Do what? Become wildly successful? Get invited to fancy Hollywood parties? Win pretty statues for your writing? Wow," Troian snorted, "what a deal breaker."

"That's not what I mean," I said, rolling my eyes at her antics. I'd thought about Troian's offer again last night after ending my video call with Hunter. "I can't do long distance relationships, and I wouldn't let Hunter move out here." I also couldn't trust that Hunter's roommate wouldn't jump into her bed a second time; and maybe the next time Hunter wouldn't show such restraint. I kept those thoughts to myself. I still wasn't ready to tell Troian about what had happened.

"Nik moved out here for *my* job," Troian pointed out. "We made it work."

"You two don't count," I grumbled. "Your favorite pastime is adoring each other."

"That's because we're awesome," Troian sniffed, turning her attention back to a rack of white dresses.

Troian was a bit of an anomaly to me. I could seriously imagine her lounging in a field of overgrown weeds, staring at the clouds as they changed shapes in the wind, reflecting on the awesomeness of her girlfriend.

A woman who looked to be in her mid-40s approached us. I had been focusing on Troian so I hadn't noticed from where she'd suddenly appeared. "Troian Smith?"

Troian abandoned her fruitless search. She removed her sunglasses, but they got caught in her long hair. "Yeah," she said, carefully untangling herself, "that's me."

"Welcome." The woman spread her hands at her sides. "We're so glad you've chosen us to help make your special day even more special."

"Uh, thanks." Troian turned to introduce me. "This is my friend,

Elle."

I gave the woman a small, cheerful wave. "Hi. I'm the Best Woman."

I spotted a ghost of a smile on the woman's lips, but it was soon gone. "What can I help you ladies find today?"

"Well, I'm getting married," Troian said. She jerked her thumb in the direction of the dress rack she'd just been perusing. "So I guess I need a dress, probably one of these white ones."

"And I'll need something, too," I chimed in. "But probably not in white. There's going to be enough chicks standing at the altar without me confusing the other guests."

The sales woman smiled mildly. "Did you have a particular designer in mind?"

"Not really," Troian admitted. "I'm not into labels."

"Okay, well have you thought about a silhouette?"

Troian's eyes perceptively widened, giving her a slight deer-in-headlights look. "No."

The woman turned to me. "How about you? Any style or color palate in mind? What about fabric?"

I jerked my thumb in Troian's direction. "Whatever she wants me to wear. She's the bride. Well, *one* of them," I corrected myself.

I imagined we weren't exactly the kind of customers this woman was used to dealing with; I'd never looked through a bridal magazine in my life and I had a hard time believing Troian had either.

As if sensing Troian's impending panic, the woman nodded curtly. "Let me set you up with dressing rooms and I can start to bring you some options."

By the time we were assigned fitting rooms and had tried on half a dozen dresses, I'd about had my quota of wedding prep. Maybe Troian should have asked one of her twenty cousins to be her Best Woman. The only good thing to happen that morning was the complimentary champagne that had finally found its way to us in the dressing rooms. I'd volunteered to drink Troian's share of the bubbly.

I squeezed into the next dress the sales associate had brought me – a violently pink A-frame dress that I'd probably have to stop eating carbohydrates for. The sales woman had told me not to pay attention to the color when she'd handed me the dress, but I couldn't help feeling like a bottle of Pepto-Bismol.

I heard Troian quietly swear in the fitting room next to mine.

The dressing rooms didn't have actual doors, just fabric partitions. I knocked as best as I could on Troian's dressing space. "How's it going in there?"

Troian yanked the curtain open. She was still in all her clothes and looked like she hadn't even attempted to try on a dress yet. "I don't know what I'm looking for," she sighed dramatically. "I played with Lego's as a little kid, not Barbie and her Dream House."

"Then why go to all the trouble of a wedding?" I pragmatically asked. "If you want to get married, but without all this hassle, just bring Nik to a Justice of the Peace."

Troian shook her head. "I'm only getting married once. I want to do it right. Besides, it's for Nik."

I nodded. That was really all she needed to say. I knew she'd walk across hot coals if she thought it would make Nikole happy. The same went for Nik though; she was just as crazy about Troian, only she was more subtle about her affections.

"Do you have regrets?" I asked.

"About what?"

"About not sleeping with more people or dating someone other than Nik," I clarified.

Troian was a gold star in every way possible. She'd never had sex with a man, she'd only ever seriously dated one person – Nikole – and Nikole had been her only sexual partner. It was sweet, but a little unnatural to me for whom monogamy was often a chore.

"No. No regrets."

"You're not just saying that because you're getting married?"

She laughed. "I lucked out, ya know? And why would I look elsewhere when what I've got is so perfect?" Her brow creased. "But you're not asking about me. You're thinking about you and Hunter."

I was always thinking about Hunter, waiting for the other shoe to drop or something. If I wasn't fretting about the nearly decade age difference, my worries circled around the simple fact that I was the first women with whom she'd ever had a relationship.

I felt guilty too often that because she was committed to me, she was missing out on life experiences. When I'd first Come Out, I'd hopped from one mattress to the next, often eschewing the mattress altogether.

"Remember my Glamazon student from the coffee shop?"

Troian's face crunched as she tried to recall to whom I was referring, but then her eyes widened in recognition. "Oh yeah. What about her?"

"She's Hunter's new roommate."

"*Her?* No way. When did that happen?"

"A few months ago."

"Why am I just hearing about this?"

"Because it wasn't a big deal at the time," I reasoned. "I basically avoided Hunter's apartment last semester because of it."

"But now it's a big deal?" Troian correctly guessed.

I hesitated momentarily. I still wasn't sure I was ready to tell Troian because I still hadn't wrapped my head around what had happened. Plus, when you say something out loud, it just makes it more real. I took a deep breath. "She-she apparently hopped into bed with Hunter last night."

"Hunter told you this?"

I nodded. "She said she promptly kicked her out."

"And you believe her?"

"Do I have a choice?" I threw back.

"The Elle I used to know would have gotten out while she was ahead," Troian remarked.

I stared straight ahead at an overflowing rack of taffeta bridesmaid gowns. It wasn't a lie.

"Is the Glamazon gonna keep living with her?" Troian pressed.

"Sounds like it."

"And you're gonna let that happen?"

"I can't just pack the girl's bags and toss her to the curb," I scowled.

"If someone snuck into Nik's bed, that someone would be losing body parts."

"I can't do that."

"Why not? She's not your student anymore, right? I see no reason why you can't kick a little ass."

"Hunter wouldn't like it."

Troian raised a skeptical eyebrow. "Sure it wouldn't get her wet?"

Some women nearby must have overheard Troian because they looked at us in horror and hustled out of the fitting area.

"Troi…" I said warningly. No matter how long we'd been friends, I couldn't get accustomed to the explicit-nature of her conversations. I certainly wasn't a prude, but Troian could be so *earthy* sometimes in her word choice that even after all these years of being friends it still made me uneasy.

Troian gave me a cheeky grin, but she held her hands up in surrender.

"I'm half-tempted to tell Hunter to go ahead and have sex with Loryssa," I admitted. My stomach twisted as the words fell out of my mouth.

Troian stared at me, mouth slightly agape. "Don't you *dare*, Elle Richard Graft."

"Why would you think my middle name is Richard?" I blinked.

"Because you're being a dick!" Troian practically yelled. "Why would you do that to Hunter?"

"What? Give her a free pass to sleep with a gorgeous woman?" I rolled my eyes. "Geez, that *is* awfully cruel of me."

"It is!" Troian's voice was shrill. I could sense more eyes on us; we probably shouldn't be having this conversation about infidelity in the middle of a bridal gown shop. "What kind of head games are you trying to play with that poor girl? She chose *you*, Elle. You have no right to belittle that."

"*Belittle?*" I spat the word back. "I'm not belittling anything. I just don't want her to have any What Ifs."

"She turned down the Glamazon for a reason," Troian pointed out. "Hell if I know why," she snorted, "because you're clearly not that great of a girlfriend."

I scowled, but I couldn't deny what she was saying wasn't true. "I just don't want to be the reason she doesn't get to experience other things, other people."

"You've had multiple partners. How'd that turn out for you?" Troian challenged. "Can you honestly tell me that any of them were worth the heartache, or that if you had to do it all over again, you'd date them all again?"

"If I hadn't dated them all, I wouldn't be where I am today," I stubbornly pointed out. "If you change the past, you change your present and your future."

"Thanks for the lesson in time-traveling, Professor," Troian rolled her eyes. "What's your number, anyway?"

"God, don't ask me that," I groaned, throwing my head back. "There was a revolving door in my college dorm room."

"You seriously don't know how many people you've had sex with?" she openly gaped.

I shrugged and pretended to check myself out in the full-length mirror to avoid her judging eyes. "12? 15?" I conservatively guessed. "I just haven't taken the time to count."

"Well all I'm saying is that, unlike you, maybe Hunter doesn't need to go kissing a bunch of chicks to figure out what she wants. And if you love her, you don't put in that situation."

"Of course I love her," I snapped, biting back my anger. We were making a scene for sure, but I didn't want it to escalade. "That's why I'm being the bigger person and wanting her to have more experiences."

Troian shook her head so hard, I thought I heard it rattle. "It sounds to me like you're scared. You're scared of Hunter finding someone else and breaking your heart. You want to throw this other girl at her before she can hurt you first."

"What if we're all wrong for each other, Troi?" The words caught in my throat. "What if I'm just her transitional period from straight to gay, and she leaves me for someone her own age?"

"Then you two weren't meant to be," Troian said simply. "But you can't keep sabotaging yourself, Bookie."

"It's the only way I know how to have relationships," I admitted bitterly. "Screw things up before they can hurt me first."

"Well, stop it."

"Easier said than done. Old habits and all that," I sighed. I wiped at my eyes, feeling on the verge of weeping in a bridal shop of all places.

"When are you going to get it through that thick skull of yours that you're a Keeper, Elle Richard Graft?" Troian said. "You're smart, kind, generous, complicated, and you're currently rocking that bridesmaid dress, even if it's the color of vomit. Hunter doesn't have to look any further because she's already found her perfection in you."

I felt a smile at the corners of my mouth. "Perfection, eh?"

Troian snorted. "Don't be getting a big head about it. I'm just feeling extra sentimental because I get to marry the woman of my dreams."

I gave my best friend a hug. "Thanks, Troi. Sometimes the words that come out of that big mouth are actually nice."

"You love me, Bookie." She slugged me lightly on the arm. "You wouldn't want it any other way."

+++++

CHAPTER SIXTEEN

I rocked back and forth from my heels to my toes on the front stoop of Hunter's apartment complex. My California trip was supposed to last until the following afternoon, but I'd cut it a day short. I'd done all the shopping with Troian that needed to get done – and honestly the trip had been more about me needing to see my best friends than about actual wedding preparations.

When I'd told Troian that I needed to leave, she knew why. And since there was no real reason for me to stay the entire week, I'd called the airline to book an earlier flight. There was a penalty fee to pay, but it would be worth it to see Hunter a day sooner.

I buzzed the front entrance. I'd wanted to surprise her, but the extra security at the front door was determined to ruin everything. It was late. I had no idea if anyone would still be awake. I had been traveling all day because of two layovers and part of me just wanted to sleep in my own bed and bribe Sylvia to cuddle with me. But a bigger part needed to see my girlfriend's face and hear her voice and hold her in my arms.

As I waited for either Loryssa or Hunter to answer the door – although I really wasn't in the mood to confront Loryssa that night – one of Hunter's neighbors came home. I recognized the elderly man from the few times I'd retrieved Hunter's mail for her from the lobby.

The man, a slight figure probably in his 70s or 80s, held the heavy door open for me. "You coming in?" he said with an impatient huff.

I smiled and ducked my head to follow him inside. After a

genuine thank you, I bounded up the three flights to Hunter's apartment. The pungent scent of Indian food perfumed the air. My stomach reminded me that I'd missed dinner in my haste to return.

I knocked loudly, but not impatiently. Footsteps groaned on the other side of the door, and I uttered a silent prayer that it wasn't Loryssa. The chain was removed and the deadbolt was unlocked. The door swung open and Hunter stood in the threshold, barefoot and beautiful. I wondered if I had interrupted her nightly ritual. She was dressed for bed in a tank top and cotton pajama pants, and her face looked freshly washed and makeup free, but her hair hadn't made it up into a ponytail or bun yet. Instead it fell softly in layers, framing her heart-shaped face. She looked like an angel.

"Ellio!" she exclaimed, looking surprised. "I thought you weren't getting back until tomorrow. Did you have to take a taxi from the airport? You should have called. I would have picked you up." The words tumbled from her perfect mouth.

"I missed you," I offered up sheepishly. I had thought my spontaneity romantic at first, but now that I stood in front of her, I realized she might think I had ulterior motives for coming back early. I hoped she didn't think I'd cut my trip short because I didn't trust her.

I was about to say as much, but she lunged forward. Her hands slid behind my neck and her fingers curled around the waves at the base of my neck. Her mouth found mine, hard and eager like it had been years instead of days since we'd last seen each other.

I brought my hands up to cup her face and slide my fingers through her silken hair. Her candy tongue sought entrance, which I gladly granted. She tasted like a mixture of sugar and mint.

My hands left her face to feel beneath the soft cotton of her tank top. I slid up the flat plane of her stomach to cup her bra-less breasts. Her shirt bunched as my hands glided higher and I dropped my head to kiss the soft skin in the crook of her neck.

With my mouth working against her sensitive neck, she was momentarily frozen. I took the opportunity to walk us into the apartment and I shut the door behind me with the help of my foot, unwilling to let her go. I only stopped walking her backwards until her back hit against a wall in the foyer.

I inhaled deeply between alternating wet kisses against her neck and sharply nipping at the tender flesh. She smelled so good. I hefted the equal weight of her breasts and pinched each nipple between the pad of my thumbs and the side of my index fingers. Her nipples responded immediately and she arched her back off the wall, thrusting herself more solidly against my hands.

I tugged free the knot at her waist, loosening the pants in which she slept. I was met with no resistance and no underwear either. I unabashedly groaned into her mouth as my hand met her sex, warm and soft. I resisted the urge to immediately plunge inside of her and instead brushed along the outline of her swollen sex with just the tips of my fingers. My fingertips danced over the small nub of her clit. Her body involuntarily jerked when I flicked over the sensitive bundle of nerves.

I thought I heard a door open and then promptly shut, but it was hard to tell over the breathy gasps directed in my ear.

"Is she home?" I didn't have to say her name. Hunter knew to whom I was referring.

Hunter gasped into my ear when my thigh pressed hard against her core. "Uh huh. But don't you dare stop," she groaned. Her hands gripped the front of my shirt. "Let her hear."

I dropped to my knees while keeping her pinned to the hallway wall. I nuzzled my nose into the soft flesh of her belly, and she squirmed when my canines grazed over the vulnerable flesh. She submitted to my touch, not hesitating or stopping me or trying to regain control as if she recognized that I needed this more than she did.

I looked up at my beautiful girl. Her arms were elevated, raised above her head and flat against the wall. Her eyes were scrunched closed and her pink mouth was slightly open, panting and waiting for my next move. In the back of my brain, something Loryssa had said to me once tickled at my memories: *"Go mark your territory, Professor."*

I tugged her sleep pants down over her hips and they free fell to pool around her ankles. I grabbed her taunt thighs and pulled her to me. I licked the length of her, ending at her clit. She tasted so good. My fingers sought her entrance, and I pressed two into her, bottoming out. She gasped loudly and her eyes flew open at the intrusion. There was nothing gentle about this. I wanted her. Now.

I wrapped my left arm around her lithe waist even though I knew she had no intention of going anywhere until I had completed my task. She was so warm and wet and soft around my fingers, I could have cried. Instead, I suckled at her clit, causing her hips and thighs to twitch and jump.

She dropped a hand to cradle the back of my head and hold me in place. Her hips moved against me, setting a rhythm as I worked my fingers, coated with her arousal, in and out of her.

Her moans were loud and I grunted against her. "Fuck, fuck, fuck," she chanted in time with each punishing thrust. The lewd sounds of skin slapping against skin rang in my ears.

"Do you want to continue this in the bedroom or stay right here?" I asked, looking up at her.

Her eyes narrowed perceptively. "I told you not to stop," she practically growled. She took a more firm grip on the back of my head, and I closed my eyes, allowing her to resume the frantic pace.

I was gasping for air by the time she did let me stop. We laid on the floor, still in the front foyer, surrounded by shoes. My jaw and my right bicep ached and the hardwood floor dug into my tailbone. I stared at the white ceiling above me as my lungs continued to struggle.

"That ceiling plaster is cracked," I breathed out. I turned my head to look at Hunter and watched the rapid rise and fall of her chest.

"I think it's water damage from the attic," she said. Her voice sounded rough; I'd never heard her scream like that before. "I told the super about it months ago, but he's a lazy dick."

"That's the worst kind." I sat up momentarily and grabbed the loop rug from the entranceway to make us a pillow. It was moderately more comfortable than before with a rolled up mat cushioning our heads, but I wasn't about to suggest we go back to her bedroom. There was something comforting and intimate and raw about being out in the open like this.

"My lease is up soon."

I sucked in a deep breath. "I promised we'd talk about that when I got back, didn't I?"

She pulled her hair out of the way and rolled onto her side. I didn't know how the floor wasn't painfully digging into her hipbones. "You did," she confirmed.

"I guess this is as good a time as ever," I said. I drummed my fingers against my stomach. "When exactly do you have to make a decision about the apartment? When's your lease officially over?"

"Two weeks."

"*Two weeks?*" I echoed. "Why didn't you say something earlier?"

Her eyelashes fluttered. "This is going to sound ridiculous," she muttered, "but I didn't want it to be my idea."

"Moving in with me?"

She nodded, looking bashful.

I reached out for her. "God, I'm sorry, Hunt." I interlaced our fingers and brought our conjoined hands to rest on my breastplate. "I know we talked about it at the beginning of the semester, but then I got so busy between my mom showing up and Dean Merlot being a bitch and Troi and Nik leaving."

"I know," she sighed. She rubbed at her face with her free hand. "And it was really irresponsible of me to let it go for this long. I'm never like this. I never wait until the last minute to make plans, especially for something important like *where I'm going to live.*"

I made a noise in the back of my throat and continued to stare up at the ceiling. Two weeks.

"You wouldn't have to worry about Loryssa anymore," Hunter said in a careful, soft voice.

I turned to look at her. She was biting down on her lower lip and staring at the ceiling as well.

"I trust you, you know. I didn't show up like this to check up on you."

Her blue eyes regarded me. "You really changed your flight and cut your visit short with your best friends *just* because you missed me? I don't believe that."

"Fine." I hid my face behind my hands. "I might have wanted to stake my claim, too." I peeked through my fingers to gauge her reaction.

She rolled her eyes, but she looked amused rather than annoyed.

"Two weeks."

"It's not an ultimatum," she was quick to elucidate. "And I'm not going to be homeless if you don't want to move in together; I can very easily continue living here. All I have to do is sign a new contract. I don't want us to rush into anything," she cautioned.

"That wouldn't be us though," I said, thinking out loud. "The not rushing things part," I clarified. "Because if you think about it, we kind of jumped into this relationship head first and have been doing stuff like that ever since. And it's worked out pretty well so far, don't you think?"

Her lips curled at their edges. "So are you saying you want to move in together, Ellio?" Her words were cautious, but hopeful.

Butterflies attacked my stomach when I thought about waking up to her every morning. Good butterflies. "Yeah. I am."

+++++

I slept better that night than I had in recent memory. Having made a decision about my future seemed to put my mind to rest. I had experienced so many restless nights over the past few months, that I'd nearly forgotten what it was like to have an entire evening of uninterrupted sleep. I woke up early the next morning with a refreshed outlook, but a growling stomach; I hadn't eaten anything since I'd left California, unless you counted my girlfriend.

Hunter slept soundly on her back beside me. One long limb was thrown across her eyes and her mouth was slightly open. I wondered if she ever had problems sleeping. I smiled at the sight and pressed my lips to her forearm before I slid out of bed to forage for breakfast.

I padded to the kitchen, wincing under each creaky footstep. I wanted to let Hunter sleep in, but I also didn't feel like seeing Loryssa until after I'd had a shower and a cup of coffee. I opened and closed cabinet doors and drawers as silently as I could to avoid waking up anyone in the apartment. Midway through my bowl of cereal, however, I had a visitor.

"Good morning, Professor Graft."

"Loryssa," I greeted back. I dropped my spoon into my half-eaten bowl of cereal and self-consciously wiped my hands on my pajama bottoms. It was more than a little awkward seeing her. I was no longer her professor, so it didn't bother me that we were both in pajamas. But hovering between us was the fact that she'd crawled into my girlfriend's bed with less than honorable intent. Moreover, there was no way she hadn't heard Hunter and me the previous night in the hallway and then again in Hunter's bedroom, unless she wore noise-cancelling headphones to sleep.

"You can call me Elle, you know," I told her. "I'm not your teacher anymore; I'm just your roommate's girlfriend."

"Right." She made a pained face. "About that. About the other night..." she trailed off.

This was where I was supposed to interrupt her and insist it was no big deal she'd tried to seduce my girlfriend – water under the bridge and all that. A bigger person would take pity on this girl. I wasn't the bigger person though. I didn't mind seeing her eyes dart everywhere except to me, witnessing her squirm uncomfortably.

"Eric and I had a fight, and I had too much to drink, and I guess I got lonely or something," she confessed.

She kept pausing and gesturing helplessly, waiting for me to stop her, no doubt, but I wasn't going to make this easy for her. Maybe that made me petty, but I didn't really care. Actions had consequences and I wanted her to know that what she'd done wasn't okay.

"I'm not a home-wrecker, and I respect you and Hunter's relationship," she said, "so I wanted to apologize and assure you that it'll never happen again."

I leaned back in my chair finally, relaxing my body language. Loryssa continued to fidget in her place as she waited for my response.

"I'm happy to hear that." I didn't really know what else to say. I wasn't versed in the protocol for confronting someone who'd tried to get into your girlfriend's pants. I supposed there was always hair-pulling, but that seemed a little beneath me.

"So...we're good?" Loryssa's voice lilted hopefully.

I nodded and shoveled more cereal into my mouth.

She seemed to have grown taller, lighter, from our conversation. "That's a relief. Hunter's a great roommate and this is a great apartment."

I made an agreeing noise around my raisin bran. I didn't bother telling her that Hunter would be moving in with me in two weeks. I didn't want her to think that she'd been the cause of that mutual decision. I trusted Hunter implicitly; this was just the right move forward for our relationship.

"Okay," Loryssa chirped. She bounced on her toes. "I've got a photo shoot today, so I should probably take a shower. See you later!"

I watched the girl skip down the hallway and disappear behind the bathroom door. Loryssa was admittedly beautiful. It was the kind of beauty that made you do a double take. But a beautiful woman like Loryssa could stand in front of me in her pajamas, and I wasn't tempted the way Hunter had had me obsessing when she'd been my student. I wasn't just into Hunter because of her beauty. She wasn't your typical co-ed. She was mature beyond her years; she was an old soul who somehow, at the age of 21, had her life on track. Now I just needed to do the same.

+++++

"I'm going to apply for a sabbatical."

Hunter's eyes jerked away from the mirror in her bedroom where she'd been getting ready for the day. "I don't know what that means. Should I be excited or worried?"

I sat down on her bed, tucking my legs beneath me. "Probably both," I admitted. I took a deep breath. "If Dean Merlot will give me at least a semester off, I want to use that time to explore my options beyond teaching."

Hunter turned to me with a serious face. She set her makeup bag down on top of her dresser bureau. "You're going to take that TV job in California with Troian, aren't you?"

I patted the space beside me on the bed. Hunter abandoned her morning routine to sit next to me. I took her hands in mine and kissed her knuckles.

"For as long as I can remember, I've wanted to be a writer. But somewhere along the way I lost sight of that because of teaching. I always had a plan. I always knew what that next step was going to be. After college, that meant grad school, after that, getting a job."

"And then getting tenure," Hunter supplied.

I nodded. "And now, now there's not an extra step that's already been decided for me. I'm at a point where I actually get to make a *choice* about my career. Nothing has been predetermined." I paused to wet my lips. "I figure that I can work for Troian for a few months and see if I like it or not – if I think there's a future for me there. And if not, my job at the university will still be waiting for me."

Hunter sucked her lower lip into her mouth. Her voice came out very small. "So what does that mean for our plan to live together?"

"If the Dean denies my sabbatical, nothing changes," I said. "Your lease ends here and you move into my house."

"And if she doesn't say no? If you get your sabbatical?"

I dropped my eyes to the pattern on her duvet. "Then...you still move into my house."

"But you go to California without me," Hunter continued for me.

I finally looked up. Her mouth was set in a hard line.

"Is that why you agreed so easily to let me live with you?" she accused. "Because you weren't planning on living there anymore?"

I held up my hands. "No, baby. Nothing like that."

"Don't infantilize me," she snapped.

"I'm sorry."

Those grey-blue eyes flashed with defiance. "Why can't I come to California with you?" she demanded.

"Because it might not be a permanent move," I reasoned. "You've worked so hard to get on the rotation in pediatrics. If I find out Hollywood isn't for me, you would have given that up for nothing."

"Not for nothing," she protested. "To be with you. You need to let me make decisions about my life on my own."

"I'd fly you over whenever you had a break from work," I promised.

"You were gone less than a week and my hot roommate jumped into bed with me," she pointed out.

"You'll be living at my house, so I won't have her to worry about," I countered, not taking the bait. "Besides, someone needs to watch over Sylvia and you're the only one she likes."

Her eyes narrowed. "Am I your girlfriend or a cat sitter, Elle?"

My mouth opened and closed. "I didn't mean it like that."

"Unless you don't want me there?" Her eyebrows arched.

"Of course I want you there." That was the most ridiculous accusation I'd ever heard. "I miss you every day even when you're just at the hospital."

"Then why would you want to do a long-distance relationship?"

"Your schedule is four on, three off. You could come to California on your off days."

"And spend half my time off in airports?" she huffed. "No thanks."

"I can't let you drop everything," I continued to protest, even though I felt my resistance slipping. "All your friends and family are here."

"But *you* would be in California," she pointed out. "And it's not like I wouldn't know anyone out there – I'd have Nik and Troian. And if I couldn't find a nursing job right away, I could always do landscaping for Nikole. I did that before," she reminded me.

I bit my lower lip. "It sounds like you've given thought to this."

A half-smile curled onto her mouth. "Well when you were in California and you asked me if I'd ever leave the Midwest, I kind of anticipated this might happen."

"So if I go talk to Dean Merlot on Monday about a sabbatical, you won't be mad?"

"Ellio, it's your life. I can't be mad at you for wanting to explore your options." She smirked. "Your *career* options, that is."

"This conversation could be totally moot, you know? I don't exactly have the best track record with that woman. Chances are she'll say no."

"But you'll never know until you try."

I felt the tell-tale prick of tears sting the corners of my eyes. I jumped up from the bed; I didn't want to cry in front of her. She looked startled by my abrupt movement. "Uh, you want to go out for breakfast or something?" I sniffled, giving myself away.

She didn't comment on the emotions currently spilling out of my eyes and I loved her just a little bit more for that.

+++++

It was a warm, sunny morning; one of my favorite kinds of days with just enough of a breeze to assure it wouldn't get too hot by noon. Hunter and I left her apartment to do some lazy shopping at the downtown farmer's market. The main street shut down for pedestrians every Saturday in the summer from sun up to about noon or whenever the local farmers ran out of produce. We didn't bring a grocery list, but it was fun to wander from booth to booth, drinking coffee and nibbling on chocolate croissants we'd bought at an adjacent bakery.

We walked, hands loosely clasped but together, joined arms slightly swinging, inspecting each booth. Most were local vegetable farmers, but a few sold things like raw honey, natural soaps, or even cheese. My favorite was the fresh-cut flower stands. I myself didn't care for flowers, but I loved the way Hunter's face lit up when I bought her a bouquet.

She looked amazing, as always, wearing a tank top and torn denim jeans that hung low on her hips. The tops of her rounded shoulders were tinted pink from early summer sunshine.

I was inspecting a mountain of sugar snap peas and thinking about stir-fry for dinner when I heard the panic in Hunter's voice.

"My mom is here."

I resisted the urge to dive behind one of the booths and hide. "Where?"

Hunter pointed as unobtrusively as possible. "By the booth with the stone-milled flour."

Ellen Dyson, Hunter's mother, was a statuesque woman. Her honey blonde hair was pulled back in a tight ponytail, reflecting the sunlight. Her face was half-hidden behind oversized Jackie O sunglasses. The collar of her sleeveless button-down was popped, making her look even more suburban than usual. At any rate, she looked too polished and prim for the farmers' market.

I self-consciously touched my messy bun. I hadn't bothered showering knowing that when we got back we'd probably nap or do yard work at my house. The flower garden Hunter had helped me plant when we'd first started dating was in full bloom and starting to get overrun with weeds. Nikole would shame me if I didn't do something about it soon.

"What is she doing here?" Hunter hissed. "She hates farmers' markets – says they're for hippies and Communists."

"Maybe she's become a fan of Marx and Engels," I unhelpfully suggested.

Hunter's hand tightened around mine. "Do I go over and say hi? Or do I pretend like I didn't notice her?"

"Come on," I said, feeling strangely empowered. I tugged Hunter in the direction of where her mother stood.

"Mrs. Dyson?" I called out, catching her attention.

"Hunter?" she said when she saw me and her daughter. Her grey-blue eyes, the same shade of color as her daughter's, caught mine. "And…"

"Elle," I quickly supplied, not giving her the opportunity to admit she'd forgotten my name.

I was actually relieved for the opportunity to confront her out in public like this. If my suspicions were correct, Ellen Dyson wasn't the type of woman to cause a scene in front of strangers. She'd at least pretend to be civil rather than draw unwanted attention to us.

"What are you doing here?" Hunter asked.

Her mother lifted a canvas grocery bag. "Shopping."

"I thought you didn't like farmers' markets," Hunter said, almost accusingly.

"Well, everyone's allowed to change their opinions, right?" Her eyes lingered on me purposefully.

"Would you and your family like to have dinner at my house?" I blurted out. From beside me I heard Hunter's sharp intake of air.

Hunter's mother, however, did not appear taken aback by my question. She took her time, thinking my invitation over. I tried not to fidget as I waited.

"I think that would be lovely," she finally agreed.

"Maybe later this week if you're available. How about Wednesday?" I could match her polite veneer with my own.

She nodded. "I'll have to check with my husband, but I think that would work."

"Fantastic. I'll have Hunter email you the details."

I could feel Hunter's eyes on me when her mother walked away to continue shopping for quinoa or kale or whatever suburban housewives eat. *Oh lord.* I had to figure out something to make.

Hunter continued to silently stare at me. "What?" I asked, feeling self-conscious.

She slowly shook her head. "I can't believe that just happened. You totally just invited my family to dinner like it was no big deal."

I honestly couldn't believe I'd done it either. Maybe my conversation with Loryssa that morning had empowered me. I looped my arm through Hunter's. "Think of it as a brand-new Elle."

"I didn't think there was anything wrong with the old Elle," Hunter countered.

"That's because you're too nice, love. I'm far from perfect, especially when it comes to relationships." I searched her eyes and touched my fingers to her cheek. "But I really want to try harder for you. I want to be the girlfriend you deserve."

+++++

CHAPTER SEVENTEEN

I sat anxiously in the outer office of Dean Merlot. The reception area was stiflingly quiet with only the measured chimes of a grandfather clock and the erratic typing of Dean Merlot's administrative assistant spoiling the complete silence. I tried unsuccessfully to get comfortable in a straight-backed antique chair. It was a Monday and even though classes weren't in session because of the summer season, most staff and some faculty still kept business hours. Dean Merlot wasn't the exception.

"She'll see you now," the Dean's administrative assistant said, not bothering to look away from her computer screen. I wondered if she was playing Candy Crush.

I stood from my chair and ran my sweaty palms over my dress pants. It was too warm for the outfit, but I hadn't wanted to show up to this meeting looking unprofessional. As I felt the beads of sweat accumulating in the small of my back, I second-guessed my wardrobe choice.

I sucked in a deep breath and pushed open the heavy, cumbersome door to the Dean's office. It was like opening the door to a tomb that hadn't been opened in thousands of years.

Dean Merlot sat behind an expensive-looking wooden desk. "Elle!" she greeted, actually looking pleased to see me. Her kindness was disorienting, but I was reminded of the charming personality she'd displayed at the end-of-the-year party, so I tried not to dwell on it.

"What brings you to my neck of the woods?" she said, standing from her chair. "What does that even mean, 'Neck of the Woods'?"

I dislodged the frog from my throat. "Uhm, 'neck' means a narrow strip of land, like someone's plot," I informed her. "So if it's 'your neck,' it's your settlement or house."

Dean Merlot grinned charmingly. "I guess that's why you're the English teacher and I'm just the Dean."

I cleared my throat again. Damn frogs.

"Come on in," she said, ushering me into her inner office.

I didn't think I'd ever been in Dean Krauss's office when he'd inhabited the space, so I didn't know what changes the new Dean had made, if any. Dean Merlot's office was sizeable and formal. It was much roomier than my office and its windows offered a view of the campus green instead of the parking lot. The furniture matched, unlike the hand-me-downs in my office that I'd had to scavenge from around campus. Her degrees were framed and hung on the wall that overlooked her desk. Apparently she wasn't the type to worry that decorating her office might be bad luck.

"Something to drink?" she offered. "Coffee? Tea?" Her generous smile grew mischievous. "Something stronger?"

"No, I'm fine," I dismissed. "This shouldn't take long." I sat down without being offered first.

Instead of returning to her office chair, she perched on the corner of her desk. I tried to ignore the way her pencil skirt inched up her legs when she sat down, showing off two femininely muscled thighs beneath a dark nylon.

She wasn't much older than myself, if at all, and our few brief interactions had left me perplexed about her agenda. There was something about Jessica Merlot that reminded me of Ruby, and it unsettled me. She was charming to my face, but from the safety of her office she'd done nothing but seemingly sabotage my career happiness as well as the happiness of quite a few of my colleagues.

I ran my palms over the tops of my thighs. "I'd like to ask you about getting a sabbatical."

Dean Merlot's lips pursed in thought. "You didn't get one before you were up for tenure?"

I shook my head. "I was supposed to get one; it's in my contract. But Bob needed me to stay on to cover the classes of some senior faculty who were taking a leave of absence."

"That was charitable of you," she observed. "Normally junior faculty require that sabbatical to finish getting a book contract before their tenure review. That's why we put it in your contract."

"Yeah, it was pretty stressful meeting my tenure benchmarks without the typical course reduction," I admitted, "but I wanted to help out."

The Dean stood from her perch on the corner of her desk. "Well I don't see any reason why we can't accommodate you with a sabbatical now," she said as she maneuvered around the desk to sit down in her office chair.

Her encouraging words helped me relax. "I'm glad to hear that because I'd like a sabbatical for next Fall."

"Next Fall?" she echoed. "As in the semester that's going to start in a few months?"

I nodded. "I know it's short notice, but an opportunity has presented itself." I left it at that; she didn't need to know that I wanted to try my hand at writing television scripts and that ultimately I might abandon teaching and this university altogether.

Dean Merlot frowned. "I couldn't possibly grant you a sabbatical with this short of notice. You're scheduled for three classes in the Fall if I'm not mistaken."

"Which could very easily be taken over by an adjunct for cheap." I had anticipated these excuses.

The Dean frowned more deeply.

"I was supposed to get a sabbatical the semester before I was up for tenure. It never happened. The University owes me." I stared purposefully. "*You* owe me this, Dean Merlot."

"It's Jessica, remember?" she lightly corrected and looked away. I could tell she was uncomfortable.

We had never spoken about how she'd rejected both of my course proposals. In hindsight it was probably a good thing she hadn't been in her office when Bob had broken the bad news. I might not have behaved very professionally. I still felt betrayed, but at least now with some distance from the unexpected rejection I could maintain my composure.

"I'll look into it," she stated carefully. She played with the double-strand of pearls around her neck. They probably cost more than what they'd pay an adjunct to take over my classes. "But I can't make any promises," she warned.

"When will you know?" I pressed. I didn't want to be strung

along the entire summer not knowing when or if I might have to move to California.

"I'll let you know by the end of the week."

It wasn't the answer I had wanted when I'd set up this meeting, but it wasn't an outright refusal, so there was still hope. I recognized that it was short-notice on my part, but they did contractually owe me the semester-long break. If I wasn't granted a sabbatical this Fall, then perhaps I'd get one in Spring and Troian would still need another writer.

I stood from my chair. "Thank you for seeing me and considering my request," I said cordially.

Dean Merlot nodded, looking absent-minded. I moved to leave, but stopped at her office door when she said my name.

"Elle."

"Yes?"

"I'm-I'm sorry we keep butting heads like this," she stumbled on her apology. Her words expressed her remorse, but her face reflected it even more so. "I envy you, you know? Not everyone can be so brave." Her youthful features looked nearly pained by what she wasn't revealing.

I nodded once, feeling a world of confusion.

+++++

"She's gay. The Dean is gay," I proclaimed. "And that's why she's been picking on me."

I'd texted Troian a message of S.O.S. and both she and Nikole had come on Skype to talk. I could tell it was another gorgeous, sunny day in California as the sun streamed in through their kitchen windows, making my friends practically glow on my laptop screen.

"How do you know?" Troian pressed. "Did she Come Out to you?"

"Or *come on* to you?" Nikole chuckled.

"No, neither one," I clarified to Nikole's amused grin. "But she practically Outed herself saying weird things like how she was 'envious of how brave I was.' Who talks like that?"

"The gays," Troian agreed.

"It makes sense — getting the most backlash from someone who should be your biggest ally," Nikole observed with a sage nod. "She must really be locked up tight in that closet."

I sighed miserably. "So what do I do about it?"

"Is there anything you *can* do?" Nikole asked.

I sighed deeply. "Nothing comes to mind except waiting. Waiting to see if she grants me the sabbatical."

"If she rejects you, I'm calling the ACLU or the HRC or something else that uses an acronym," Troian declared.

I tried to be more levelheaded. "I've just got to be patient," I reasoned with myself. "She said she'd let me know by the end of the week."

"I bet she'd decide a lot faster if you gave her a lap dance," Troian snickered.

I flashed my friend a warning glare.

She held up her hands. "Hey, I didn't say *you* had to give her a lap dance."

I shook my head, but laughed. For being the most dedicated girlfriend I'd ever met, Troian always thought lap dances made everything better.

"I want my friend in California with me," Troian pouted.

"I know, I know," I sighed.

Nikole rolled her eyes. "Get a room, you guys."

"Have you talked to Hunter about moving?" Troian asked. "Or are you being a bad girlfriend again?"

I didn't know if the two questions were mutually exclusive. "I talked to her about it Saturday morning," I confirmed.

"Is she excited for the move?" Nikole asked.

I opened my mouth to respond – to tell them to temper their enthusiasm because I might not even get the sabbatical and that I was overly hesitant to have Hunter stall her career for a gamble – but my cell phone rang.

My friend and colleague, Emily's, face filled up the screen. I was tempted to let it go to voicemail so I could continue this conversation, but I couldn't recall Emily ever calling me at home; something had to be up.

"I should take this call, guys," I said. "I'll talk to you later."

I answered the phone after ending my Skype session, feeling all kinds of trepidation. I wondered if Emily had heard about my request for a Fall semester sabbatical already and was calling to yell at me for waiting until the very last minute. I was sure it was going to put the English department in a tough position.

I answered the phone just before it went to voicemail. "Hello?"

Emily didn't waste any time with niceties. "I can't believe you got married and I didn't even get an invite."

"I did what?!" I sputtered back. I hadn't been expecting that at all.

"You got married."

"I did?"

"You didn't?"

"I definitely did not," I assured her. "Hunter and I haven't been together even a year."

"Oh." Emily paused. "I didn't even think about that. Well, maybe I did, but I thought maybe lesbians worked at a different speed than the rest of the world."

"What did you hear exactly?" I pressed.

I heard Emily's intake of air. "There weren't a lot of details, just that you went to California and you got married."

"I was *in* California a few days ago, but it wasn't to get married. My friend *Troian* is getting married, but I was just there to visit."

I could practically hear Emily shaking her head. "Wow. How do these rumors get started?"

I had a pretty good idea, but I kept it to myself. The only people who knew I'd gone to California were Troian and Nikole, Hunter, and my mom. I could imagine my mom had probably made some innocent comment at the library about me, California, and a wedding, and it had gotten twisted into me going to California to get married.

"I should have known it wasn't true," Emily chuckled, "but the last time I heard a whopper about you, it actually turned out to be true."

"Fuck," I uncharacteristically swore. *Fuck, fuckity, fuck.*

"What?"

"If Dean Merlot hears I got married, she's going to think I did it just to piss her off; like I'm rubbing her nose in my gayness."

"Oh gross, Elle. Please don't rub anything on Dean Merlot."

"I can't believe this is happening. I just asked her for a sabbatical." I pressed my palm against my forehead. "I literally just left her office."

"Sabbatical? It's about time, lady; you deserve a break."

I hadn't told Emily yet, or really anyone besides Hunter, Troian, and Nikole about my proposed Fall sabbatical. "It was more like I *demanded* a sabbatical. I basically barged into her office and told her to give me next semester off."

Emily whistled. "*Next* semester? Girl, you've got balls."

"Do I call her office and head off the rumor mill?" I worried out loud.

"I imagine she's already heard the news," Emily offered. "You're kind of a fount for juicy gossip."

I rubbed at my forehead. My timing for these kinds of things seemed to be disastrous. The semester before my tenure review meeting, the campus had been abuzz about my relationship with Hunter, a former student. And now, just as I was trying to get a semester break from my homophobic, closeted boss, rumors about me getting married were floating around the skeleton crew still left on campus.

"If you keep hearing the rumor, will you do me a favor and protect my honor?" I made a mental note to tell my mom to never talk about me ever again on campus.

Emily laughed. "It would be my pleasure, m'lady."

"Thanks for the heads up *again*, Em." She'd been the one who'd let me know when news was spreading that I was dating a student. It had been immeasurably valuable knowing to anticipate being questioned about my relationship with Hunter during my tenure review. I couldn't even begin to wonder how I would have reacted had I been blindsided with that question.

After another thank you and the promise to get together soon for coffee, I hung up with Emily. As if in a trance, I set my phone down and made the trek upstairs to the master bathroom. I hadn't taken a bath in a very long time. I had nothing against baths, but like taking naps, I generally didn't have time for them. Showers were more efficient, but I needed to force myself to take a moment to myself so I could just breathe.

I filled the oversized tub with steaming, hot water and poured a generous dollop of bubble bath into the tub. I was still in my outfit from my earlier meeting with Dean Merlot. I carefully shed the dress pants and crisp Oxford shirt and set them on the double vanity so they wouldn't get wet.

I didn't set up any music in the bathroom; there was no sound except for the gentle hum of the bathroom exhaust fan and the lapping of water against the inside of the tub whenever I moved around.

I slowed my breathing and tried to empty my mind. It was easier said than done, however. I'd felt so confident over the weekend. Invincible, even. I'd even been so bold as to invite Hunter's family over for dinner. But now, just days later, my confidence was shaken again. Two steps forward, one step back.

I heard some noises outside the closed bathroom door. I knew I was alone in the house; my mom was cataloguing books or something at the university library, and Hunter was at the hospital. I heard Sylvia romping around. She was a big cat and it sounded like a bowling ball falling to the ground when she hopped from one piece of furniture to the next.

She wasn't the most affectionate cat, but she became whiny and needy when a barrier like a closed door was in front of her. There was a two or three-inch gap beneath the bathroom door and the floor from the previous owners who'd covered the hardwood floors in the master bedroom with ugly carpeting. I could see Sylvia's pink nose and white chin poking beneath the gap at the bottom of the door, and she howled as if in pain.

I just needed to be alone for a while – alone with my own thoughts. I submerged my head under the water.

CHAPTER EIGHTEEN

I once thought I'd experienced the epitome of nervousness. It had been my tenure review meeting – a conversation with the collected faculty to determine the future of my employment with the university. But in hindsight, it paled in comparison to the butterflies I currently felt. Hunter's family was coming over in a short while to have dinner at my house.

I looked over the open floor plan of my kitchen and living room. I rarely ever ate in the dining room, which was its own separate room, filled with formal dishes I never used. I had breakfast at the kitchen island, and most nights dinner was on the coffee table in the living room. My family hadn't done the everyone eats dinner at the same time thing, but I knew that's what Hunter's parents would be expecting. Maybe someday I could invite them over to eat pizza in front of the TV, but that wasn't today.

Hunter let herself in through the front door. Her arms were filled with canvas grocery bags. She dropped them on the kitchen countertop with a great sigh, blowing the hair that had escaped from her ponytail out of her face. "I thought I was going to have to arm wrestle a little old lady for the last steak."

I squeezed her right bicep. "Well I'm glad it didn't come to that. We would have been one filet short."

"Hey!" she complained. She spun around and my hands went to her waist. Having her close made me momentarily forget my nerves.

The oven timer went off and I left her briefly to check on the apple pie. If dinner went well, her family would stick around for dessert. If it didn't go well, we could console ourselves by splitting the pie. It was a win-win.

I pulled the pie from the oven and the warm, homey, cinnamon scent intensified.

"God, that smells good," Hunter approved. "Forget dinner; we should just eat pie."

I shook my head and set the pie plate on top of the range. "This will be our reward for behaving during dinner."

She arched an eyebrow. "Worried you'll misbehave without an incentive?"

I shrugged, not sure how to answer. I wanted everything to be perfect for her. I felt wound up, strung tight. If I screwed this up, who knew if I'd have another chance to make things right.

"I'm going to hop in the shower quick," Hunter said. "Want to come?" Her words were hot against my neck. She didn't talk much, but when she did, her word-choice tended to make my knees buckle. Or maybe that was from her canines scraping across my neck.

I audibly swallowed. "I've got to get the charcoal started."

She pursed her lips into a well-practiced pout. "If you got a gas grill, you'd save us time."

"Yeah, but nothing beats the taste of charcoal."

"Okay." She skipped off and pulled her top off so she was just in a flimsy bra and shorts. Her torso was just starting to tan. "Your loss."

"Don't I know it," I grumbled as I turned back to scrubbing the dirt from the baked potato skins.

I nearly jumped when the doorbell sounded. I know my heart at least leapt into my throat. If that was Hunter's family at my front door, they were early – nearly an hour early. Hunter was still in the shower, and I still had so much prep-work to do for dinner.

I wiped my damp hands on the front of my apron that I wore in case I spilled all over myself. I wasn't usually so Jean Cleaver-esque, but I had nearly had a panic attack deciding on an outfit, and I didn't want to have to change clothes. In the end I'd gone for skinny jeans, ballet flats and an off-the-shoulder three-quarter length top that was casual, but not sloppy, and youthful without being age inappropriate.

Clothes were important to me. I used to teach only in fancy, feminine outfits to closet my sexuality and to create some professional difference between my students and myself. Now I was far more comfortable in my skin, at least in my interactions with students, but today my outfit similarly was a little like Dumbo's magic feather. If I looked the part of the young, feminine girlfriend, I hoped I could make a better impression on Hunter's family. It was wishful thinking that clothes alone would help the situation, but at this point I'd take whatever I could get.

I peeked briefly out one of the side windows to make sure it was actually Hunter's family at the door. I really didn't need any surprises tonight. When I saw Hunter's mom, dad, and brother standing on my front porch, I began to panic. I hadn't even started the charcoal yet. If Hunter's family insisted on being early to dinner like this all the time, I might have to get that gas grill.

I took a deep breath and pushed a smile on my face. "Welcome!" I greeted as I swung the door open.

"Elle, you have a lovely home," Hunter's mother routinely complimented. "The neighborhood is charming." I searched her face for signs of emotion, but she wore her practiced politeness like a mask.

The scent of her light perfume trailed behind her as she stepped inside. She was dressed more formally than we'd seen her at the farmers' market in a sleeveless shell, light cardigan, Capri pants, and wedge heels. She pressed a bottle of red wine into my hands and I was momentarily frozen. Hunter's family didn't drink alcohol, so I hadn't expected the kind gesture.

Hunter's father followed his wife inside. He looked like he'd come straight from work in his button-up shirt, tie, and flat-front dress pants. Only Brian, the last one inside, looked reasonably dressed in cargo shorts and a t-shirt. He wore a tattered baseball cap that I was sure drove his mother crazy.

"Brian, take that thing off," she scolded, confirming my observations. "We're inside."

Brian obediently tugged the hat off. He ran his hand over the top of his hair, but his hair was short enough that the hat hadn't done any damage.

I cleared my throat. "Can, I, uh, offer anyone something to drink?" I spun the wine bottle in my hands to inspect the label. It looked far pricier than the brands I was used to.

I could see Ellen Dyson's gaze traveling the expanse of the first floor, taking in the living room and kitchen. Out of view were the formal dining room, the guest bedroom and bathroom, and my office. I didn't imagine giving them the full house tour, but I'd scrubbed and tidied every corner of the house just in case.

My mom had wanted to meet Hunter's family, but thankfully she'd agreed with me that it would probably be too much for one night. I'd make nice with Hunter's family first, and if all went well, then maybe my mom would get to meet them at a later date.

"Where's Hunter?" her mother asked. She craned her neck this way and that as if she thought I was hiding her daughter.

"She's in the shower. She should be down soon," I reassured them, but also assured myself as well.

I looked up at the ceiling when I heard the distinct sound of thunder rumble above. "Is it supposed to rain?" I said out loud without meaning to.

"The weather report said a fifty percent change of rain this evening," Hunter's father contributed.

Of course there'd be a storm cloud hovering over my house.

"Let me go check on Hunter," I blurted out.

I bounded up the stairs, two at a time. Hunter was just walking out of the master bathroom when I came in. Her hair was wrapped in a towel, but she'd forgone the second towel for her body. I stopped abruptly in the doorway to enjoy the view. She grinned, wide and lazy. She knew exactly what she was doing to me.

"Your family is here," I announced.

Hunter let out a shriek and ran back into the bathroom, slamming the door behind her. I laughed, despite my desire to puke.

"Give me five minutes," she hollered through the closed door.

"I think it's going to rain." I pressed my palm flat against the door that separated us. Maybe I could just hide up here until she finished getting ready.

"Okay," came Hunter's response.

It was turning into a humid evening and as the thunder continued to rumble above us, a warm wind whipped through the open windows in the bedroom. There was a small overhang on my back porch to protect me and the grill if it started to rain, but if the wind continued, the charcoal would struggle to heat the food evenly or heat it at all. I mentally catalogued the contents of my fridge and pantry because I had a sinking suspicion that steak and potatoes wasn't going to work.

"I guess I'll go downstairs," I said dejectedly.

"Okay," she said again.

I turned, sighing heavily. I thought I heard Hunter chuckle, but I couldn't be sure because of the closed bathroom door.

I descended the stairs heavily as if marching to my firing squad. I hoped Hunter's promise of five minutes didn't turn into half an hour. Her mom, dad, and brother, Brian, stood around the kitchen island looking equally uncomfortable. I mentally shook myself, forced a broad smile to my lips, and marched towards my death.

Hunter was true to her word and was downstairs just a few minutes later. Her hair was still wet and her cheeks flushed from the shower. I was sure she'd wanted to look perfect for dinner with her family, but she knew better than to let me sit downstairs making awkward small talk; I'd ruin things before she even got downstairs.

I thought she looked more than perfect though in skinny jeans and a scoop-necked top that showed off the fine bones of her clavicle. I grinned, realizing she wore the necklace I had gotten her for graduation. As I watched her approach, however, and my eyes drifted to her exposed collarbone, I thought maybe a better choice for tonight would have been a burlap sack. Although, if she managed to make shapeless scrubs look sexy, I was probably in trouble regardless of what she wore.

She was barefoot, which didn't help those ill-timed thoughts. Something about her freshly showered and barefoot on my hardwood floors never failed to excite me. It was like a Pavlov's Dog response. She padded over to me after briefly greeting her family who continued to hover around the kitchen island and pick at a vegetable tray I had set out. She stood up on her tiptoes even though we were basically the same height and placed a chaste kiss on my cheek.

"Change of plans?" she murmured for only my ears.

I nodded and turned over an oversized meatball in the saucepan.

I'd abandoned the steak and potatoes plan for spaghetti and homemade meatballs. The charcoal would have taken forever to get ready, and by the time the grill was set up, who knows what the weather would have been like. Plus, all that extra prep-time would mean awkward conversation with Hunter's family while we waited with empty stomachs. I could make the meatballs quickly, all while fulfilling my hostess responsibilities. I had salad supplies in the fridge that I could dump into an oversized wooden serving bowl and a loaf of frozen garlic bread in the freezer that I could throw in the oven.

"Need any help?" she asked, returning to the ground.

I took a sip of red wine. It was from the bottle Hunter's family had brought with them. They didn't drink, but I needed just this little bit of courage. "There's things for salad in the fridge if you want to tackle that," I said. "Otherwise, just play nice with your family."

A smile crept onto the corners of her generous mouth. "I'm always nice," she rasped.

Dinner conversation wasn't easy, but I hadn't expected it to be. Hunter's mother was still frosty and reluctant to warm up to me, but it was a vast improvement over the hostile reception we'd received at the first family dinner. Hunter's father and Brian were different though; they both possessed a boyish charm that put me at ease. I had never enjoyed small talk; I would rather eat in uncomfortable silence than participate in forced conversation. But for Hunter, I would do it.

Hunter's mother cut daintily through the *el dente* noodles. I'd thought for sure that she would have been a fork and spoon kind of spaghetti eater. "How has your work been, Elle?"

I sat to attention and self-consciously wiped at my mouth with the napkin from my lap. "To be honest, it was a challenging semester."

"Bad students?" Hunter's father guessed.

I shook my head. "The administration, actually. I've got a new boss and we don't ever seem to get along." I didn't go into more detail about how my sexuality was at the epicenter of those problems.

"Sounds like a real ball buster," Hunter's dad grinned.

Elle Dyson made a disapproving noise in the back of her throat.

"If I go to your school for college, will you give me an A in English?" Brian posed with a boyish grin.

"I don't *give* students grades," I gently corrected him. "Students *earn* them."

"What grade did Hunter *earn* in your class?" Brian asked, grinning as wide as ever.

I glanced once in Hunter's direction. "I actually don't remember." I did remember though. I remembered because it had been such a painstaking process as I added up the final grade.

Hunter cleared her throat. "I got a B+."

"No A?" Hunter's father frowned.

"No A," Hunter echoed with a casual shrug.

I caught a glimpse of Hunter's mother's face in my peripheral vision. She looked very invested in our conversation.

"You must be a hard grader," her dad said as he swirled more spaghetti around on his fork. "Our Hunter is very smart."

"She just said students don't get grades, Dad," Hunter said, sounding exasperated. "And I didn't earn the A."

"Well why not?" he wanted to know.

"I was...I got distracted in that class," she mumbled in a low voice that didn't really want to be heard.

"What would you..." Her father's words fell off. "Oh." Recognition colored his face.

I bit back my laughter. I should have been embarrassed along with Hunter, but I enjoyed the quiet discomfort that had her squirming in her chair.

Hunter's arm was around my waist as we waved goodbye to her family as we stood on the front porch.

"I think that went well," she observed as her parents and brother climbed into an SUV parked in front of my house.

"It could have been worse," I confirmed.

By the time I had brought out the apple pie, ice cream, and coffee, the thick tension of the shared meal had abated substantially. I could see it in their expressions and in their body language. Hunter's family sat more relaxed, even her mother, as I passed out slices of the still warm pie.

"I'm kind of proud of them," Hunter said with a wistful look, "especially my mom."

"What about me?" I pouted. "I played nice all night."

"I'm proud of you too, Ellio." Hunter tugged me inside and out of the night. The wind had yet to calm down and random gusts sprayed mist in my face like I was on a boat on a choppy day at sea.

"So is this going to be a standing date kind of thing?" I worried out loud. "Like we have dinner with your family once a week?"

She smirked. "Maybe we shouldn't press our luck."

I locked the front door and turned out the porch light. "I never want you to have to choose between me or your family."

"I know you'd never put me in that position," she said, nodding. "But just so you know, I'd choose you. I'd always choose you."

My arms went around her waist and I pulled her to me, our hips smashing together. We didn't go to sleep for a long time after that.

+++++

CHAPTER NINETEEN

I was spending a lot more time at Hunter's apartment once the school year came to an end. Since she wouldn't have the apartment for much longer, I wanted us to enjoy this place that had been her home for the past three years for as long as we had access to it. And, I also wanted to nonverbally remind Loryssa that even though I was no longer her professor there were still boundaries to be maintained – mainly that my girlfriend was off-limits.

Hunter was on her laptop, downloading new music while I was on my laptop, catching up on emails. She'd just gotten home from an early shift at the hospital, while I'd spent the morning writing at Del Sol and weeding my flower garden. I deleted a number of mass emails from academic publishers wanting me to adopt their latest textbook in my courses and responded to a few student inquiries, but the email I was hoping for had yet to appear in my Inbox. I shut the lid of my laptop with a dramatic sigh.

"Still no word from the Dean?" Hunter asked, correctly interpreting the source of my disappointment.

I nodded. "Yup."

It had been over a week since I'd asked for a sabbatical. Dean Merlot had said I would find out by the end of that week, but when her deadline had come and gone, I'd assumed her decision was no.

Hunter shut her own laptop and gave me a quick peck on the lips. "How about this for a plan?" she proposed. "I'll go grab you a beer and me something that's not-a-beer and we can spend the rest of the day binging on movies. I'll even give you first pick."

"How about you get yourself a beer, too?" I grinned at my girlfriend.

She wrinkled her nose adorably. "How about no." She hopped up from the bed and skipped out of the room.

"I'm going to convert you one of these days, Hunter Dyson!" I called after her.

I continued to lay on Hunter's bed for a moment longer, wallowing in my self-pity for just another minute. I couldn't reasonably be upset with Dean Merlot for denying me a Fall sabbatical. It had been short notice even if finding an adjunct or two to take over my classes would have been easy and inexpensive. But I was more annoyed that she hadn't at least emailed me to say so; and if I couldn't get a sabbatical for Fall, she should at least have granted me one for Spring semester.

I shook my head as if to rouse myself out of this self-depreciating funk and refocused my attentions to pick out a movie. Hunter's DVD collection was modest compared to my own. I was a bit of a movie junkie; I loved getting lost in cinematic storytelling. I scanned the list of the titles feeling uninspired until the spine of a familiar DVD case stuck out at me.

"Find anything good?" Hunter asked upon re-entering the room. As promised, she had a bottle of craft beer for me and something non-beer for herself. Her face was scrubbed clean and her hair was pulled back in a high ponytail with any loose tendrils held back with an elastic headband. She looked completely edible in her tank top and short sleep shorts. Her legs seemed to go on forever and I imagined them wrapped around me. Normally I would have abandoned the movie idea for more physically demanding activities, but the DVD I held in my hand was distracting me.

"Is this my copy?" I asked. Tom Hanks and Meg Ryan grinned at us from the cover of the DVD case.

Hunter looked pleased. "No, I picked one up. I figured you should have a copy of it at my apartment, too. You know, kind of an In Case of Emergency situation."

I swallowed hard at the lump in my throat.

"Baby, are you *crying?*" Hunter's face crumpled with concern.

I hastily wiped at my eyes. "What? No. Maybe." My voice cracked. "I don't know."

Hunter had only really seen me cry two times until this semester from hell. Once, when I couldn't find the remote quick enough during one of those ASPCA commercials – because I'm human, after all, and the only other time was when I'd finished my tenure committee meeting, convinced that I'd bombed it.

Hunter shut her bedroom door and lowered her voice. "What's wrong?" She set our drinks down at her desk and came to sit next to me on the bed.

I wiped at my eyes again, sloughing away the warm tears. "Everything has just been falling apart. But not you. Not us. You're so wonderful and I love you and I can't imagine not being with you."

She smiled warmly. "I don't understand these tears, Ellio." She rested her hand on my forearm. "Are they happy tears?"

"No, not really," I admitted. "I just feel like everything is so up in the air with my job. Part of me wants to keep teaching because it's familiar and it's the safe choice, but another part of me wants to go to California. But Dean Merlot won't let me know what's going on with my sabbatical, and I'm just so frustrated."

"Why don't you go see her, face-to-face?"

My chin trembled. "Because I'm scared. What if she says yes?"

Hunter's eyes seemed to widen. "You're worried she'll award you the sabbatical?"

I nodded somberly. "I've been thinking about it a lot lately." I sucked in a deep breath. "I don't know if I can take the job."

"Why not?"

I worried my bottom lip. "I-I trust you. Unfailingly," I emphasized. "I just...I don't trust anyone else."

Hunter's head drooped. "Oh. *That.*"

"I'm sorry," I sighed, hanging my head a little. "It just still feels so fresh, you know? And every time I think about that girl and what she did, I get angry all over again." I hazarded a glance in the direction of Hunter's closed bedroom door.

Their apartment lease would be up soon, but Hunter hadn't talked about what Loryssa would be doing – if she was going to continue living in the apartment or not after Hunter was gone. Hunter didn't talk about Loryssa often. It wasn't a noticeable change from before, but I'm sure she was mindful not to bring up the topic of her roommate around me for obvious reasons.

"You're allowed to be angry," Hunter conceded. "Just don't punish me or push me away, okay? I didn't do anything wrong."

"I know. I'm sorry," I breathed out another apology. "I'm doing my best to stop dwelling on it." I laughed without amusement. "God, I can't believe I ever suggested to Troi that you should just sleep with Loryssa and get it over with."

Hunter's eyebrows disappeared into her hairline. "My intensely possessive girlfriend wants me to have sex with someone else?"

"No, of course I don't want that," I scowled.

"Then why would you ever consider..."

"Because how do you know you really want to be with me when you have nothing to compare our relationship to?"

Hunter looked at me as if I'd grown a third eyeball. "Are you suggesting that I go out and experience horrible dates and relationships to justify what I know is already great?"

I rested my head in my hands. It suddenly felt too heavy, too filled with self-doubt. "I just don't want to hold you back from life experiences."

"The idea that I have to fail a million times to validate being with you is ridiculous," Hunter scoffed beside me.

"Well maybe not a *million* dates," I grumbled, casting my eyes to the ground.

"If I'm always hunting for better, I risk losing the best person there is for me. Being with you isn't settling, Ellio." I felt her hand on my knee. "Hey."

I looked up at the prompt.

"I'm trusting my instincts."

I sighed, feeling lighter at her words. "How do you always know the exact words to say?"

"I had a really great English professor, once upon a time," Hunter smiled back.

I picked up the forgotten DVD case. "Are you still okay to watch this? Or do you want to do something else?"

Hunter laughed. "I don't know. Are *you*?" she countered. "Are you going to transform into a quivering pile of a girlfriend?"

I smiled sheepishly. "I make no promises. Nora Ephron just gets me."

Hunter gave me a coy smile. "I'll try to curb my jealousy."

We crawled under the blankets and I slid the DVD into my laptop and pressed play.

"Comfy?" Hunter asked. She reached across my body and retrieved our drinks.

I nodded and snuggled deeper beside her. The opening credits, graphics, and the familiar song at the start of the movie flooded me with a warm, happy feeling. But those feelings were short-lived.

A pop-up box flashed on the screen, indicating I'd received a message to my school email. I wanted to ignore it and enjoy the movie and this moment with my girlfriend, but I couldn't.

I sat up and pressed the spacebar to pause the movie.

"What's wrong?"

My throat was constricted. I'd seen in that brief pop-up who the email was from, and I knew what it meant. Dean Merlot had made her decision regarding my sabbatical.

"I can't open it," I choked out. "I'm too nervous."

Hunter sat up next to me, suddenly alert. "That email. You think it's about your sabbatical?"

I nodded.

"Do you want me to read it for you?" Hunter offered. She didn't tease me for being ridiculous. She knew the importance of this email.

"Would you?" My voice wavered, but I was too distracted by anxiety to be embarrassed about it.

A ghost of a smile played on Hunter's lips. She took the laptop from me and set in on her own lap, positioning it so I could no longer see the screen. "Here goes nothing," she murmured.

I closed my eyes and held my breath. This decision could change everything.

"'Dear Professor Graft.' She's awfully formal, isn't she?" Hunter grinned, but I was too strung-out to return the smile.

"'Dear Professor Graft,'" she began again. "'I have taken your request for a sabbatical under advisement. As we discussed in our meeting, your desire for a sabbatical this Fall is rather short notice as well as a challenge to replace an excellent educator such as yourself.' Wow," Hunter paused again. "She's really buttering you up. Are you sure she hates your guts?"

I looked at Hunter with a pained expression. I couldn't handle the distractions and tangential questions.

Hunter raised her hands. "Sorry. I'll just read."

"Thank you."

Hunter's eyes scanned the computer screen briefly, looking for the spot where she'd last read. "'In light of recent circumstances,'" she resumed, "'I find it would be of mutual benefit to grant you this request.'"

Hunter paused. The goofy grin slipped off her face. "'I hope you find this time off intellectually rewarding. I look forward to welcoming you back on campus to resume your teaching and service responsibilities in the Spring at the completion of your sabbatical. Congratulations. Sincerely, Jessica Merlot.'"

I pushed my hair away from my face and released a long breath. I didn't know if I should laugh or cry. Maybe both. It felt like the first victory I'd had in a very long time – probably the first since getting tenure.

"What did she mean 'in light of recent circumstances?'" Hunter asked. Her face was scrunched up as she re-read the email.

"Who knows." I shook my head. "Maybe she's worried I'm going to Out her, so she's getting me off campus before I can ruin her career."

"Your Dean is gay?"

I shrugged. "I think so, but it's just a guess. Either that or she heard that you and I got married."

An eyebrow arched. "We did?"

"Just another campus rumor," I dismissed.

Hunter shut the lid on my laptop. She was noticeably quiet. We hadn't talked about what would happen if I did get the sabbatical since our original discussion where I'd all but forbade her from coming to California with me. I wondered if maybe she had hoped I wouldn't get this semester break because it meant me leaving for four months.

It wasn't that I didn't want her there with me; I missed her every moment we weren't together even when she was just at work or I was on campus. But having her come to California would put too much pressure on our still-new relationship. I could practically anticipate fights about the sacrifices she'd have made, like leaving her family and stalling her career. I didn't want to have that shadow looming over us when we hadn't even celebrated a year of being together.

But I knew it was her decision ultimately, and not something I could command her to do either way. If she decided to come to

California, I'd trust her instincts that we were doing the right thing.

Her silence rattled me, but finally, she spoke: "You got what you wanted, Elle. So what are you going to do?"

I got momentarily lost in those pale blue eyes that now regarded me with a wounded ferocity.

"I don't know." My words were barely a scratchy whisper. I felt the tears well up in my eyes for the second time that afternoon. "Going to California feels a little bit like giving up. Like, being a professor got too hard, and I just gave up." My head dropped.

She captured my chin between her thumb and forefinger and lifted until my eyes met hers. "Maybe it is giving up," she confirmed. "Or maybe it's being brave – imagining that you could have a career beyond teaching college. Oh, I know you feel like a big fat failure right now." A peculiar smile settled on her lips. "But you're not."

Despite my dour mood, I couldn't help my own smile. "Did you just paraphrase my favorite movie?"

"Nora Ephron's a smart lady, Ellio; you should listen to her advice." Her grin rivaled my own. "But just know, either way, I'm going to support your decision."

I couldn't ask for anything more.

+++++

EPILOGUE

Hunter wiped her dusty hands on the front of her denim shorts. "Well, it's about a year late, but we finally got that U-Haul."

"I know," I laughed. "We're the worst lesbians ever."

"Is there something I'm missing?" my mom chimed in, looking between mine and Hunter's secret smiles.

We'd rented a moving truck for the day to move Hunter's belongings from her former apartment into my house. She was moving in, but I was moving out. Bravery isn't the absence of fear. It's taking action despite that fear. And so, I did what I believed to be the brave thing. I accepted Troian's offer to work for her in California.

I'd been awarded, albeit grudgingly, a sabbatical from Dean Merlot. I was contractually due a full-year break, but because of the short notice, the best she'd been able to finagle was a semester off. It actually was the perfect amount of time for me to test the television-writing waters. In four months time I'd be able to tell for certain if this was what I should do, or if I should return to teaching. It was to be a trial period; if I liked Hollywood enough and everything that went with it, I would stay. And if it turned out to not be what I had expected, or I found myself missing teaching too much, I'd come back to the Midwest.

The Studio was going to find me temporary housing, nothing as fancy as Troian's digs, but nice enough that I wouldn't have to share with the cockroaches. It was to be fully furnished, so the only thing I needed to bring with me were clothes and other immediate essentials.

On that list of essentials included Hunter, but because I didn't know where I would be in a few months' time, I couldn't in good conscience let her give up her work at the hospital. Yes, California had hospitals. But if it turned out I was just going to move back, I didn't want to mess up everything she had worked to achieve.

Thinking about the strain that the move had put on Troian and Nikole's relationship had kept me up at night. Hunter and I still hadn't been together a full year, and my friends had been partners for over ten. I couldn't imagine the kind of pressure it would place on our relationship if I expected Hunter to give up on a job she'd only recently secured that she'd worked so hard to get.

But Hunter wasn't concerned about her career; she worried about the strain of a long-distance relationship. Neither option was ideal, and we knew it. After a few more heated arguments, I'd finally conceded that the decision wasn't mine to make. She'd fought long and hard about coming to California with me, but in the end her pragmatism won out. She was going on the cross-country road trip with me, but was then catching a flight back home. We would see each other as often as our schedules and savings accounts allowed.

I was going to miss her so fucking terribly. But this was something I had to do. Just like I'd pursued Hunter instead of letting her become a 'What If,' I had to go after this writing opportunity or I'd forever wonder how things might have turned out otherwise.

To be honest, with me now leaving having Hunter live at my house had become a point of contention for us. Before I'd heard back from the Dean, the plan had been to move in together. But now, Hunter hesitated, not wanting to live in my house all by herself. I didn't want her to think of herself as a house-sitter, looking after Sylvia for me, but practically I did need someone to look over both my house and my cat, and it made sense for her to be the one to do it. Plus, it got her out of her apartment and I wouldn't have to worry about Loryssa tiptoeing into her bed at night, either.

My phone buzzed with a text message from Troian: "Are you here yet?"

She had been nothing but a bundle of energy – even more so than usual – since I'd told her the news. She'd emailed me a list of all the things she wanted to do once I arrived in Los Angeles. I wondered if we'd ever have time to actually write a television show.

"See you in a few days," I wrote back.

Today the sky was clear and cloudless, and the weather forecast was agreeable for the next few days as well. I took it as a good omen. Hunter and I were leaving first thing in the morning; I wanted to cross at least a few state lines before we stopped for the night. If we shared the driving responsibilities we could be in Los Angeles in just under 30 hours, but I was in no hurry to reach our final destination.

I probably could have squeezed everything I needed to bring with me into a couple of suitcases and flown, but I was excited about a road trip with my girl. It would also give us more time to talk about the future. We had been avoiding that conversation, but now the moment was upon us. She'd make the cross-country trip with me and unless one of us had a change of heart, she'd be on the first flight back.

My mom wiped at her forehead. "Almost done," she panted. "In the homestretch now." The back of the moving truck had only a few more boxes of Hunter's things.

"Vivian, you didn't have to help," Hunter insisted. She rested her hands on her hips. "No one likes helping other people move. And it's just a few things; Elle and I could have done this ourselves."

"Nonsense," my mom chastised, perking up immediately and grabbing for another box. "It's a parent's duty to help their daughters move."

I caught Hunter's eye and she gave me what seemed to me a sad smile. She'd told her parents that she was moving in with me, but they hadn't been as ecstatic about the news as my own mother had. Honestly, I think my mom was just excited because in her mind that meant we were one step closer to getting married and having babies. I tried to console Hunter about it – my mom had had a lot more time to wrap her head around me being gay. The news was still pretty fresh for Hunter's parents. They'd be more supportive with time, I had reassured her.

"You also know you didn't have to quit your job at the university just because of me," I added.

After I'd told my mom that I was taking a semester sabbatical, she had promptly quit her job with the college. I didn't know if she was just biding her time at the university library until she had an excuse to quit. Her new plan was to move back to my hometown so she could be closer to my sister and help her raise the baby who would be arriving soon.

My mom rested the moving box on her hip. "No, I could never work someplace that didn't support my daughter and her partner 100%," she said, shaking her head adamantly. "Besides, it's time I go home and be a grandma."

I pulled another box out of the back of the moving truck. The word 'Sweaters' was scrawled on the outside in Hunter's careful hand. I could still smell the scent of the black permanent marker.

I followed my mom inside the house. The front door swung wide open, and I stuck my leg out when I saw Sylvia creeping towards a great escape. With boxes in our arms, there was little either my mom or I could do.

"Get back," I sternly ordered.

Sylvia hopped over my leg and scampered outside.

"Damn it," I cursed.

I heard Hunter's voice call to me from outside. "Don't worry; I've got her!"

"Asshole cat," I mumbled.

"Where is this one going?" my mom asked, nodding to the box in her arms.

"What does it say on the box?"

She struggled a bit to read its contents while still holding the box aloft. It was almost too large for her short arms. "Kitchen stuff," she read aloud.

"I think you have your answer," I grunted.

"Your girlfriend is very organized," my mom observed.

I chuckled, but said nothing more.

I hefted my box up the stairs to the master bedroom. All of my clothes were already out of the closet and wardrobe drawers for my own move and to make room for Hunter's things. I wasn't planning on bringing much with me to California besides my laptop, a few books, and my clothes. And even then, most of my winter wardrobe was staying behind. I really just wanted to pack Hunter into a box and start the trip already.

I set the box on the ground and kneeled down beside it. I wiped at my forehead with the back of my arm; it was hot outside, but even hotter upstairs. I pulled open a bottom drawer and started to unpack the box, carefully refolding each of Hunter's sweaters. I knew she'd appreciate the gesture rather than me dumping the contents of the box into the drawer and moving on.

I paused when I saw a familiar blue fabric poking out from beneath the remaining sweaters in the box. I reached in and pulled out Hunter's blue, puffy winter jacket, spoiling the carefully folded sweaters that had sat on top of it.

I was immediately distracted from my task; Hunter's delicate scent covered the jacket. I blinked once and my eyes felt wet. I brought the jacket to my nose and inhaled, not caring if anyone walked in on me. A rough sob caught in my throat, and I pressed the jacket to my mouth to smother the sound.

I heard footsteps up the stairs and Hunter appeared in the doorway. Her cheeks were red and her brow glistened from the heat of the day and the exertion of moving across town.

"Everything's out of the truck; do you want to come with me to bring it back? I've still got loads of boxes to unpack, but that can wait until later."

She seemed not to notice my distress or else I'd done a good job of covering it. I nodded. "Yeah."

She reached out a hand to me and pulled me up from the ground. I let the inertia of the action carry me and our hips knocked together. She smiled, warm as the day. I stroked my thumb along her jaw line and pushed a stubborn lock of hair that had escaped her ponytail behind her ear.

I swallowed back another sob. She was so beautiful, so good. Was I destroying perfection because of my need for more?

She led the way down the stairs, and I refused to let go of her hand as we walked outside and into the hot afternoon sun. I was going to hold on for as long as she'd let me.

ABOUT THE AUTHOR

Eliza Lentzski is the author of lesbian fiction, romance, and erotica novels including *Apophis: A Love Story for the End of the World*, *Winter Jacket*, *Second Chances*, *Date Night*, *Diary of a Human*, *Love, Lust, & Other Mistakes*, and the forthcoming *All That's Gold* (Fall 2014). Although a historian by day, Eliza is passionate about fiction. She calls the Midwest her home along with her partner and their cat and turtle.

Follow her on Twitter, @ElizaLentzski, and Like her on Facebook (http://www.facebook.com/elizalentzski) for updates and exclusive previews of future original releases.

Made in the USA
San Bernardino, CA
21 June 2016